Rollercoaster

Other books by Barbara Crossley

Candyfloss Coast

Rollercoaster

Barbara
Crossley

Published by VIRAGO PRESS Limited, July 1994
42–43 Gloucester Crescent, London NW1 7PD

A CIP catalogue record for this book is available
from the British Library

Printed in Great Britain by Mackays of Chatham plc

One

Bonfire Night, sharp stars and a wilful wind that pierced my padded jacket, gusting one way then the other, keen as a knife. I scrambled over the dunes by the light of the moon, crunching the salt crust in my loaned cowboy boots. My daughter might be too old to drag along to bonfires, but she did have her compensations, such as feet the same size as mine.

Anna Knight, I accused myself, will you ever grow up? Long after Shelley had out-grown fireworks, I still lusted after whiz-bangs and roman candles. Try keeping me indoors on Bonfire Night; the scent of gunpower in the air, and I'd spontaneously combust.

Tonight Marianne Knatchbull had lit my blue touchpaper – she had organised this beach bonfire in aid of her pet charity, Journey of a Lifetime – and I was doing her a service by coming along. Or so I argued to anyone who bothered to ask.

The bonfire, as yet unlit, stood silhouetted on the sand above the tideline, a black mass. Figures milled around it, flashing torchbeams, and a shiver prickled the back of my neck. Shivers like that can catch you unawares ... I was suddenly arrested by thoughts of the man at the heart of this annual pyromania. What had I against Guy Fawkes that I revelled in his symbolic burning? There was something savage in this ritual, as if we danced with glee around a dummy on a gibbet. Was this how the scene had looked the night of Guy Fawkes' execution four centuries ago? A funeral pyre, waiting to devour the human flesh at its heart?

I pulled my red scarf tight and headed beachwards.

Hundreds of people were streaming the same way in chattering, laughing groups, their breath steaming in the cold, and many hundreds more would follow in our wake. Children shouted in anticipation as two men ignited the pile with flaming torches. Close up it looked less ominous – a tower of detritus, a monument to woodwormed chairs, broken bedsteads, splintered doors.

'Burn your bygones,' the posters had urged. 'Bring all your old household items to build our bonfires and send them up in smoke for a good cause. All proceeds will go to Journey of a Lifetime, the charity that sends terminally ill children on trips of their hearts' desire.'

Charity collectors threaded through the crowds, thrusting their boxes under parents' noses, refusing to budge until cash was exchanged for a Journey of a Lifetime sunshine badge. I paid my dues and watched the fire-lighters retreating as flames licked the outer layers.

I scanned the crowd for Marianne Knatchbull, and spied her behind a stall, selling paper cups brimming with spicy punch. She looked as ebullient as ever, reminding me of a doughty colonel's wife from the old Empire days, ready to cope with siege or pestilence, jollying the troops along with tea and buns.

'Anna! Greetings and blessings upon you,' she beamed, her face plump and glowing in the light of the barbecue. 'We are honoured. Does this mean I'll get my little event in the paper?'

That was Marianne all over – she had worked like a demon to make this the biggest bonfire in town, and to make sure everyone knew about it – not least my boss on the

Northport News, who had assured her of coverage if only to get her trumpeting laugh off the newsdesk phone. But still she never took such publicity for granted.

Naturally I had volunteered for the job – far removed from my usual round of crime, industrial and political news – for not only was I passionately fond of bonfires, I had an affection for Marianne and her enthusiasms. She was a well-off, middle-aged and middle-class housewife who could have filled in her time on the bridge party circuit, but instead poured her energy into charitable causes. She had made herself a figurehead for Journey of a Lifetime, which had caught our readership's imagination quite extraordinarily.

Marianne certainly knew how to rally an army: legions of buttoned-up revellers were tramping over the dunes towards the growing throng. It was a Friday night, the end of a school and working week, and everyone was primed for the event.

Bribery was one secret of Marianne's success – she had promised not only fireworks, but her own special recipe, Knock-out Punch, and a gargantuan barbecue – a roasted ox was now being sliced and priced to add its contribution to charity funds.

My photographer was late; I bought punch and quaffed it while I waited. It was surprisingly good. I have to confess here that among my manifold weaknesses is a taste for Kentucky bourbon – neat in winter, over ice in summer – and I was sure I could detect the sweet oak-barrel of America's finest mingled with the warming wine. I buried my nose in the paper cup, sniffing up the aroma.

'Music, maestro please!' commanded Marianne, and a youth in charge of a vanful of equipment obeyed, blasting out the Rolling Stones to instant effect. 'I Can't Get No Satisfaction' seemed to find an echo in many parents' hearts that night – not least mine – and, limbs loosened by the punch, we found ourselves jigging away, to the derision of offspring. I didn't care; the music was intoxicating, the bonfire was gathering force, potatoes were baking and, bliss upon bliss, Marianne was signalling to start the fireworks. Rockets boomed, Catherine wheels span, the sky lit up with showers of red, silver and gold, children's eyes opened as wide as their mouths, and I danced to the rhythms of my youth, warmed inside and out.

As the Stones made way for synthesised disco-pop I came away, breathless, to confront a delighted photographer, Jon Spry, a newish recruit to the paper. He was in his early twenties, tall, wiry and somewhat vain about his hair, a Renaissance splendour of dark twining curls.

'Magnificent,' he clapped. 'Anna, the queen of the bylines loosens her stays and actually bops.'

'Careful, Jon, or I'll ram your teething ring down your Pampers.'

'Hey, hey, peace and love, sister,' he parodied, giving the peace sign. 'Anyway, rave on, Anna, bopping's obviously good for the figure – I'm all in favour of fit older women – I used to get off on my mum's Jane Fonda tapes.'

To avoid a thump, he veered towards the queue for the punchbowl, a giant dustbin. A tall, well-dressed, slender woman in her mid-thirties was leaning over it, trying to fill enough cups to keep up with demand.

'Marianne,' she frowned, holding a hurricane lamp to peer into the bin, 'I think we're going to run out soon.'

Marianne, who was taking the money, replied: 'Not to worry my dear, I can top it up. I've plenty of wine in the Range-Rover'

Seeing me she called: 'Anna, would you be a brick and help Liza for a minute while I fetch fresh stock? You've met Liza Boyd-Adams before? Sterling girl, don't know what we'd do without her.'

Liza shook her sleek bob of auburn hair with a gesture of self-deprecation as she handed me the cups and took over at the cash-box. I knew her only vaguely as some high-flier of an accountant whose firm held fund raising events for Journey of a Lifetime. There was no time for pleasantries, the queue was growing.

I was reaching the dregs when Marianne returned with her wine case. As she uncorked and poured I stood back, my attention taken by the labels on the bottles: a Château Lafite-Rothschild was followed by an equally impressive Gevrey-Chambertin. Marianne's punchbowl lapped with grand, prestigious vintages normally treated with holy reverence. I stared, incredulous, as she glugged the bottles into the bin, and Liza's jaw dropped as she looked at the empties.

'Marianne,' I ventured. 'Are you sure you've got the right bottles here? I mean – surely you've made a mistake.'

'No, no, my sweet, no mistake,' she declared. 'I chose them specially for tonight – why drink the rest when we can have the best?'

She began to fill more paper cups with her extravagant brew, and it suddenly hit me that she was under strain. Marianne, comfortably off, well-upholstered in Aran and Barbour, had taken on a desperate look. She was smiling as ever, but the smile was clamped on to a tightened jaw. She was putting on a show. Why?

I looked round for her husband, Barnaby. He was invariably on hand for these affairs, dispensing drinks and *bonhomie*. He should have been easy to spot, for he was a man who patently enjoyed his job as regional director of an upmarket grocery chain. Fine food and drink were his passion – and as a result he had never lost the heavy bulk of his rugby-playing youth. If these were the contents of their capacious cellars at Highfield House, where was Barnaby?

I asked Marianne whether her husband was away at the moment.

'Away,' she said, airily, 'yes, you could say that. Barnaby is away.'

Her voice broke into a quavering note and she began to stir the pot ferociously. What was going on?

'Thanks for standing in, Anna,' she beamed, regaining her composure and thrusting two full cups in my hands.

'Have these on me. Enjoy, enjoy the fruits of my twenty-six years of marriage to Barnaby – drink up to give me pleasure.'

A newspaper story flashed across my memory – a wronged wife who delivered her husband's best vintages to village doorsteps like bottles of milk – was this Marianne's revenge for a similar hurt? I searched her face, but more punch-seekers engulfed her. Beside me, Jon took a deep draught and exuded a satisfied sigh.

'You're not supposed to drink it like Ribena,' I admonished him. 'That stuff's liquid velvet. Appreciate the scent of the delicate spice notes and savour the oaky underlayers.'

'Rot,' he said, deservedly, then smiled: 'I'd rather appreciate your delicate scents and oaky underlayers.'

Indulge me – a woman reaching her prime tends to appreciate these small compliments.

'What d'you want in the pic?' asked Jon as we moved close to the bonfire. 'I do a very pretty kiddie and sparkler ensemble – popular with grandmas – or something a bit more colourful? A roman candle, or Marianne Knatchbull astride a rocket when her husband finds out what she's done with his *appellation contrôlée*? Ouch – that fire's hot.'

'Better not go too near – I'd hate you to scorch your lustrous locks.'

'Anna, I never thought you cared.' I waited for the sly smile of sarcasm, but no, he coiled a stray ringlet round his finger and gazed moodily into the flames. What was this – an infatuation, sitting up and begging at me like a puppy-dog? Ah, the sweet dalliance of youth. And should I dally back? I never could resist puppy-dogs.

'You know,' he turned to me, 'there's something missing . . .' His voice trailed off.

'Missing?' I prompted with an indulgent smile. 'In your life? Jonathan, I—'

'In my life?' he exploded into laughter. 'Anna, if I needed an agony aunt I wouldn't bother you with my problems, I'd bash them out on a squash court and finish them off with a mate over six pints of beer.'

I shrank, all five foot nine inches, to the level of a shoelace. A worn, frayed – old – shoelace. When a gal's made a fool of herself there's only one thing to do – ignore it: 'Missing from what?'

'The bonfire.'

I must have looked blank.

'Remember, remember the fifth of November, gunpowder, treason and plot?' he repeated the old saw patiently. 'The reason we go through this whole pantomime every year – the poor sod caught among the gunpowder barrels trying to blow Parliament to a Catholic kingdom come?'

'Guy Fawkes. You're right – there's no guy on the bonfire.' I looked round, scanning the crowd for Marianne. 'I'm sure there must be one. Marianne's so organised, she wouldn't forget the guy, surely.'

Indeed she hadn't. She was pushing her way towards us even now, a monstrous effigy in her arms, almost dwarfing her.

'Gangway, gangway! Make way for Guy Fawkes! Watch him burn, people, watch the traitor frazzle.'

Marianne's face, which I could just see behind her guy's shoulder, was strangely contorted. This was not just excitement at the night's events, it was anger, and more than that, bitterness.

'Anna,' she appealed as she saw me in her path. 'Help me throw him on the fire.'

I grabbed one of the guy's arms and was astonished at what I held. It was the sleeve of an expensive suit, and underneath it I could see more layers of suits, not worn or old-fashioned, but new – and large, tailor-made for Barnaby Knatchbull's bulk. Beneath them was a cashmere sweater that I'd seen Barnaby wear recently at a drinks party, and beneath that a fine lawn shirt, topped off with an array of silk ties that she had tightened round the guy's neck like so many nooses.

The body was heavy and stiff, she must have used a tailor's dummy, and nailed on top of it was a pumpkin head, eyes, nose and mouth hollowed out with the gashes of a knife. The trousers were slashed around the fly, and I could see they were stuffed with the bottom halves of each suit that graced the torso above.

I looked at Marianne with alarm, but she was unheeding – all she could see were the greedy flames in front of her, all she wanted was to toss this grotesque mannequin into the inferno.

'On the count of three, Anna, heave-ho! One, two – THREE!'

She moved with such command and energy that I had to comply, and on the count of three Guy Fawkes met his fate dressed in the contents of Barnaby Knatchbull's sumptuous wardrobe.

'Burn, Barnaby! Burn!' she shouted, unable to control her feelings any longer.

'Marianne,' I implored. 'Marianne, calm down, please.'

'Calm down!' she crowed. 'My husband's run off with his bit of totty and you say calm down!'

'His bit of – ?'

'Some career-woman bint who's just been made Master of Wine. Twenty-six years of marriage, and he's finally shown what he thinks of me. Coward!' she howled at the burning dummy. 'Why couldn't you've made a clean breast of it years ago? Because you were too comfy, weren't you? You liked the house and the convenient wifey to bolster you up while your mistress bedded you down. Barnaby's a glutton, you see, and career women don't cook, do they? Except the occasional seductive dinner. Microwave madam – that's what she is!'

I tried gently to pull her away, 'Marianne – come and get a drink.' She turned on me, all bloodshot eyes and blazing face: 'To think he must've used the children all this time as excuses to her – "Can't leave home, my darling, oh no, can't leave the children." Well now he's got no more excuses. The children have gone, there's only jolly old expendable wifey, tossed away like an empty bottle from that precious cellarful of *premiers crus* he chose with her. All drained, Barnaby – all your liquid assets mixed up in a dustbin and poured down people's throats—'

If she could only cry, I thought, if she could only collapse into her grief then she'd stop this manic baying. I tried to put an arm round her, but she swivelled away: 'I don't need pity Anna, all I need is to see that monster burn, burn!'

The guy, however, was refusing to co-operate. Too closely packed to be immolated, it stubbornly smouldered, belching smoke. This seemed to infuriate Marianne even more: 'It's not burning enough! Let me through.'

She ran away from me, wellingtons lolloping, towards the barbecue and the crowd parted as if she were a rogue elephant. Then back she came, hauling an open vat of cooking oil used to baste the ox, and before anyone could stop her she hurled the whole container on to the bonfire.

Immediately it blasted into flame, an explosion of light followed by spitting fireballs. Then the whole structure of the bonfire began to topple, flaming wood slid sideways and showers of sparks blew towards the crowd. Pandemonium followed as parents pulled screaming children away. Jon grabbed my arm: 'For God's sake Anna, move! This is too dangerous.'

But I couldn't leave Marianne, for I half-feared she was going to throw herself after the vat of oil. She stood rigid, silent and tense, as though readying herself for the leap.

I put up my arm to shield our faces from the heat and shouted her name, but she seemed deaf, in a trance. An irate voice, a man's voice, cut through to her: 'It's veering towards the engine house, Mrs Knatchbull. We'll have to call the fire brigade to damp it down. That old engine's worth a fortune.'

He was talking about a miniature railway that ran

along the seafront, with an antique engine that was lovingly tended by its owner and housed in a wooden shed for the winter. Sparks were indeed raining on the engine shed. Marianne saw it and shuddered. She was not so far gone as to dismiss a threat to someone else's property, not when it was her fault. She turned to the anxious man: 'Oh, goodness, yes, please Mr Blaby, get the fire brigade – forgive me – oh gracious, Anna, I'm sorry – I –'

'Marianne, just come away from the fire.'

She did as I urged, and a worried Liza came running towards us.

'What happened?' she asked. 'Is the bonfire – Marianne – are you all right?'

Hurried explanations were followed by a stiff bourbon for Marianne before the fire-engine arrived. Lights flashing, siren blazing, it trundled down a slipway as near the beach as it dared. With practised speed the hose was reeled out and the firefighters flooded the runaway flames.

'Oh, what a shame,' Marianne murmured, watching the crowds ebb away. 'I've spoiled people's fun – or have I? Perhaps they enjoyed watching the old frump go bonkers. I'm glad I did it though, Anna – you've no idea how I've been bottling this up – I had to explode somehow. And what a release it was! I felt liberated, in free-flight. Barnaby and his fancy woman can rot in hell now for all I care.' She gasped in surprise at herself, and then let go a tremendous, whooping laugh.

It was infectious, I laughed with her until we both had tears in our eyes. Liza still looked anxious, and suddenly broke through our guffaws, 'Look, I'm sorry Marianne, I'm going to have to leave you. Babysitter problems, I have to get back. Can you cope?'

Marianne's mirth subsided, and she nodded, still smiling: 'Oh, of course, Liza, don' t worry. I think I can cope with anything now.'

Liza disappeared, and Marianne wiped a smudge from my face with a handkerchief: 'Bless you, my dear, I'm so glad you were here. And you will make sure every word of this gets in the paper, won't you?'

'I will, yes, if that's what you want – but are you sure?'

'Undoubtedly. I want Barnaby's dirty linen washed in public, thank you very much. He needn't think he can hide it away to fester discreetly. Then I'll feel clean at last, Anna, clear of his sordid deceptions.'

I was about to help her tidy up when a fireman clambering over the dying embers let out a shout, sharp as an axe. His colleagues hurried over, and they all circled round him, probing something in the charred wreckage.

Jon had dashed up, but he quickly turned away, photographs forgotten, his camera hanging loosely round his neck, shock leaching his lips white.

'What on earth's happened? Excuse me Marianne.' I ran forward.

Other stragglers also moved closer, drawn by curiosity. The firemen moved to repel us, but they might as well have tried to stop the tide. As the circle parted we saw, outlined in a torchbeam, a half-burned body, wreathed in smoke.

Its flesh was black, its face blistered, but its teeth – bared in the moonlight – were undoubtedly human. I heard Jon's hoarse voice at my side. 'She's bloody killed him, Anna.'

It had been my thought too – Marianne's final revenge on the faithless Barnaby. I looked round to find her. She was standing alone, and people were giving her a cold, stunned stare.

'What's happened?' she appealed helplessly. 'What have I done?'

As she came forward I put my arm through hers. God knows, she would need all the support she could get. The body's shroud had evidently been a carpet; its semi-burnt remains were still wound round the legs.

'What's all the fuss for – an old rug?' asked Marianne

– then with a sudden intake of breath she saw what lay inside.

Someone murmured the name, 'Barnaby,' and she must have known what everyone was thinking.

'No! No!' she cried, but could not articulate any more. She looked at me in stark agony, and I held her head as she sobbed against my shoulder. A man's voice, confident, commanding, approached from behind us: 'Has anyone seen Marianne Knatchbull? Is she still here?'

Marianne looked up, hope and fear criss-crossing her crumpled face.

'Barny? – Barnaby?'

He strode over, a powerful man in a weighty great-coat: 'Good Lord, Marianne, what a mess this is. I'm sorry I've got bad news for you. The house has been burgled. I went home to pick up some – well, it doesn't matter – and it looks like a bomb's hit it. I called the police. Clothes all over the place, suits gone, and my wine cellar – oh, I could've wept. The filthy beggars must've switched off the security alarm somehow.'

'No, Barnaby, they didn't.'

'What d'you mean? Oh, for God's sake, Marianne, don't tell me you forgot! This is important – the insurance.'

I stood back as Marianne told him the galling truth.

The explosion of rage was as mighty as the bonfire's blast. Quivering with disbelief, he demanded she show him the remnants of his suits.

'It's impossible, Barnaby, look they're cordoning off the site. I told you, they've found a body in the ashes. Why do you never listen to me?'

'I can't believe you've done this, Marianne. I thought we were being civilised about matters, but this is nothing short of barbaric – my wine treated like swash, suits in tatters.'

And while he blustered about, we all pondered what he had ignored: whose was the body in the bonfire?

Two

It was the teeth, grinning in the wan moonlight, that bothered me. Washed clean by the firemen's hose, they gleamed out of the charcoal like a cheery mask. I was taking notes, hurriedly grabbing whoever would talk. The police tried to fend me off, but as long as I kept in the background they tolerated my presence. I busied myself getting the reactions of Marianne and her helpers, nabbing the fireman who first spotted the body, gleaning every scrap of information I could. But each time I looked up, passing from one witness to another, the corpse seemed to grin in mirthless mockery on its bed of ashes.

'Cover it up, for pity's sake,' growled the newly arrived Detective Chief Inspector Alex Anderson, a grizzled Scot looking forward to retirement. 'Can't you see we've got an audience?'

He was torn between an instinct to shove the gawpers away and the need to keep possible informants closely corralled. It was a weary disappointment to him when he found none of us would readily confess to having put the body there, or to knowing who put it there, or indeed to having the faintest notion about the body at all.

Having probed us, he instructed a young subordinate

to probe the cadaver. I moved further round the beach, hovering under cover of darkness, until I could see what was going on in the torchlight behind the screens.

'Nice set of gnashers,' I heard the young detective comment as he crouched by the skull. 'Doesn't look as though it was a tramp, not with dental work like this.'

He pushed a pen between the jaws which gave a sickening click: 'Look at that, white fillings – you don't get them on the NHS, I had one last time – cost a bomb. He's a mouthful of 'em.'

The detective examined further, delicately inserting latex-gloved fingers between layers of clothes, into the remains of pockets. 'Sweet Fanny Adams,' he said brightly, standing up empty-handed. 'Not even a rubber Johnny or a boiled sweet.'

Chief Inspector Anderson sighed. So the grinning corpse would give him no assistance. No wallet, no credit cards, no identification whatsoever – only charred clothes and the old industrial carpet that had been its winding sheet. He looked down at the body sourly, muttering, 'Some help you are.'

The detective said in an injured tone: 'I did mention the teeth, sir.'

'Ah yes,' mused the chief inspector, 'the teeth,' and seemed to perk up.

Eventually teeth, bones, carpet and all were bundled into a black body bag, zipped up and sent off to a lab for examination.

Other police officers had taken our names and phone numbers, and Marianne and a few of her stalwarts were left to pick up the pieces of their abandoned party. I was surprised to see Barnaby among the helpers, filling a bin-bag with litter, looking unusually subdued.

Jon saw the focus of my gaze: 'Someone told him we thought he was the stiff, just to shut him up. It took his mind off the suits, I can tell you.'

HORROR OF BODY
IN BONFIRE
by Anna Knight

POLICE today launched a murder inquiry after the body of a mystery man was found in the embers of a charity bonfire.

The gruesome discovery was made when the fire brigade was called to douse the flames of a beach bonfire in aid of Journey of a Lifetime, the charity that sends terminally ill children on dream trips.

Hundreds of people were enjoying a firework display and barbecue last night on Northport's East Beach, but happiness turned to horror when organiser Marianne Knatchbull threw the guy into the flames and the fire blew out of control.

'I thought the fire was dying down, so I threw cooking oil after the guy,' said Mrs Knatchbull. 'It was stupid, I realise now. The flames exploded, the bonfire collapsed and I was horrified when I saw the wind was blowing sparks towards the miniature railway. We called the fire brigade, who soon got it under control, and that was when they found the body, right at the base of the fire.

'I'm devastated. I don't know who could have done such a thing. The problem is that we appealed for people to bring all their old furniture and so on for the fire. They've been piling it on for days, perfect strangers, I've no idea who could have put it there.'

The body was first spotted by Leading Fireman Jim Thompson: 'I took it to be a roll of old carpet till I tried to move it and it felt heavy,' he said. 'I saw an arm but I just thought it was part of Guy Fawkes. It wasn't till I saw the teeth I realised I had a body. It was a good job we were called out – otherwise it would have been burnt to ashes and the police would have nothing to go on.'

Detective Chief Inspector Alex Anderson said today that the cause of death appeared to be a single stab wound to the heart, applied through the left side with a long, wide-bladed knife.

He appealed for any information to help identify the mystery man.

'He was a white male, aged between 30 and 50, five feet eleven inches tall, of medium build. He was not particularly muscular, so he could have had a sedentary occupation.

'Thanks to the carpet which wrapped his body, his clothes were not totally destroyed. He was wearing grey trousers from Next, a striped shirt, a black sweater and a woollen jacket, probably grey. His shoe size was nine.

'We believe he was dead when he was laid in the bonfire, but he died no more than forty-eight hours before his body was discovered. Whoever carried out the killing is likely to have bloodstained clothing.

'Someone, somewhere could be shielding a dangerous individual. We would like to speak to everyone who put material on that bonfire, particularly between 3 and 5 November. If anyone saw anything suspicious in the vicinity of the bonfire, or if they suspect someone they know might have been involved, please contact us.'

Forensic tests are being carried out on the clothing, and dental records are being checked.

That story appeared on the Saturday. By Monday the corpse still had no name and Chief Inspector Anderson was getting increasingly short-tempered. The phone rang on my desk as I was about to go for lunch. 'Anna? It's Rosie Monteith.'

'Rosie ... how's the PR business treating you? Anxious to get back to the cut and thrust of real journalism yet?'

'I am anxious, Anna, but not to get back to the *Northport News*. I think my boats were well and truly burnt when I told Ellis Clancy what to do with his night jobs, don't you?'

I laughed. Petite, black-haired Rosie had become the

object of our news editor's desires shortly after her arrival, but a quickfire affair soon frizzled out when she discovered Clancy's one true love was his own reflection. She told him so, and was subsequently victimised with night duties week after week.

'So what can I do for you, Rosie?'

'It's this story of yours, Anna, in Saturday's paper, about the mystery body.'

'Yes, I was there when they found it. Not recommended for sensitive souls – the face was burnt black.'

'Oh . . . that bad.' Her voice became faint.

'Rosie? You sound upset. I'm sorry, take no notice of me, I'm just a hardened old hack.'

'It's just . . . I think it might be my boss.'

'Oh God, no . . . at Mad Mad World?'

'No one's seen him for four days. We didn't think anything of it because he always spends the first Thursday of every month in London, talking to investors, and he often stays the extra day and makes a weekend of it. This morning he was due back for an appointment with his accountant – he was going straight there – and it wasn't until the accountant rang, wondering where he was, that we began to get worried. There was no reply from his home, the answering machine wasn't even switched on. We sent someone round, the house was empty, but his car was in the drive. Then I saw your story. He fits the description.'

'Surely his family would have reported him missing?'

'He lives alone, he's divorced. We checked with the people he was supposed to see in London, and apparently he rang up cancelling his appointments early on Thursday, pleading illness, but he didn't tell anyone here. No one saw him over the weekend. I'm fond of him, Anna . . .'

'Oh, Rosie.'

'I seem to make a habit of it, don't I? Bedding the boss. Not that it's done me any good . . . you'd think I'd learn. Anyway, this wasn't a full-blown rollercoaster of a romance – more a quick whirl on the waltzers – dizzy, thrilling and short. I think we were both secretly glad it was over – work, rest and play can be too much of a good thing. But he wasn't like Ellis Clancy; he didn't use work to get at me, in fact he seemed to trust me more.'

'You were still on good terms, then?'

'Yes, very . . . look I can't stand this, talking about him in the past tense. It may not be him at all.'

'That's right – the details they gave must fit half the men in Northport. I should get in touch with Chief Inspector Anderson if I were you.'

'Ah yes, the grumpy Scot. I remember him.'

'He's even more grumpy now – he doesn't want to retire with an unsolved murder on his books. Look, they're floundering until they get an identity. At least you could help eliminate one possibility.'

'I hope so.'

With Rosie's assistance a certain dentist was called out of his surgery that afternoon, and by 4 p.m. he realised he had lost one of his best customers.

The dentist's charts matched the corpse's teeth, in fact, he knew them well. He had drilled and filled them for the past six months in a course of expensive private treatment, polishing the smile of Llewellyn Madden, commonly known as Llew, managing director of the Mad Mad World amusement park, who would smile no more.

I headed for the cuttings library for background to my story.

The files told me he was forty-one, grandson of the founder of the amusement park, long since dead. His father, Maurice Madden, was still the company chairman, though he was in his mid-seventies and appeared to have handed over the running of the park to Llew.

Reading between the lines, Llew seemed to have had a bust-up with his father when he was a young man, and left to launch his own amusement park on the south coast, near Brighton. The prodigal had been welcomed back, however, eighteen months ago, and had taken over the reins of Maddens' Mad Mad World when his father's health began to fail.

The park was a Northport institution – the destination of inland trippers as they had poured off the trains in decades gone by for their two-week escape from mills and factories.

As I reeled back the microfilm from the 1950s I could tell this was its heyday, and since the 1970s its popularity had begun to wane. The rides were ageing and old-fashioned, whereas modern trippers craved new delights, preferably computer-controlled and spectacular. Llew had evidently come back to bring fresh life and inspiration. Instead he had met violent death and immolation.

Who on earth could want to kill a man in such a harmless profession, a man whose job was to bring fun to the lives of others? I needed Rosie's help to unearth possible answers.

Someone shouted from the newsroom: 'Phone for you, Anna – shall I put it through to you in there?'

'Yes, please,' I replied, hoping Rosie had picked up my telepathic appeal and come on with the goods. 'Who is it?'

'Marianne Knatchbull.'

'Oh.' I cast a desperate look at the ceiling as I remembered my unfulfilled promise.

'Hello, Marianne. Look I'm sorry about having to leave out all the stuff on you and Barnaby in Saturday's paper.'

'Actually, my dear, that was rather a relief. That's why I'm ringing – I had to let you know – Barnaby's come back.'

'You mean he's left his – ?'

'His hussy, yes. I told you, Barnaby's army marches on its stomach, not its nether parts. I don't expect Miss Microwave appreciated that. You see, I know my husband, and one thing he cannot abide is a scene. My Guy Fawkes in bespoke tailoring certainly created that. I think he realised, apart from missing his dinners, I'm not a soft sofa to be sat on. I've as much spirit as Johnnie Walker, my father always said – more than a match for Madame Sip'n'Spit and her wine tastings. He's come home, tail drooping, bouquet held high, full of small kindnesses he hasn't paid me in years.'

'I'm very glad for you, Marianne, I hope things will work out for both of you now.'

'Thank you, my dear, I'll live to fight another day. Bless you for being so charming to a silly old chump.'

'Not silly at all. Anyway, don't mention it.'

'I'm only sorry my mad gesture probably cost Journey of a Lifetime some cash – people beat a hasty retreat as soon as the fire got out of hand, and then the body didn't help matters. Oh, how can I say such a thing? That poor chap didn't ask to be buried in my precious bonfire. Have they found out who he was?'

'Yes, Llew Madden, boss of Mad Mad World.'

'Gracious! I wonder why? It's more of a sad, sad world these days, I fear.'

I said goodbye to Marianne, inwardly thanking her for suggesting a phrase for my intro. It was around 6pm by then, probably too late to catch anyone if I drove round to the fun park. I rang Rosie's office, thinking she might be working late, but the answering machine was on. I tried the police, but they refused to reveal any leads – if they had any.

After ringing round various of Llew's business colleagues, I had a crop of tributes, but no inkling of any murky dealings, no glimmer of a reason for his death. Llew's father was ex-directory.

With a heavy sigh I began typing, and an inane chant began to rattle through my brain: 'Who killed Llew, what did he do, find me a clue, why kill Llew?'

In the end it frustrated me so much I tried Rosie again. This time someone answered, only to tell me she'd gone home. Damage limitation is part of a public relations manager's job, but I guessed the murder of her boss and former lover was damage that exceeded Rosie's limitations. I asked if there was anyone else who'd talk to the press. An abrupt 'No.'

I asked if I could call her at home. This brought a blast from the phone: 'Don't you people have any feelings? You won't find her there. She's gone to her mother's, and no, I don't know where that is. Goodbye.'

So she'd let the media go hang and gone home to mum. I couldn't blame her, Rosie had the kind of mother to supply comfort, warmth and large malt whiskies at a time like this. I had never achieved this acme of motherhood, a fact of which Shelley reminded me whenever she felt like a good whine, which seemed more and more frequent lately. Comfort, warmth and large malt whiskies were rare enough for me, I reflected, never mind providing surplus supplies for unhappy offspring.

Shelley was coming round that night for a meal and it was already getting late. I really had to get this story finished before the supermarket closed. Anyway, I argued mentally, as I tapped away, she had earned more money than me, she shouldn't need my consolations. But there was the rub – the emphasis on *had*. Her career as a comedian had boomed young and fizzled fast. Leaving school at sixteen, she had shot to the heights of a pier show of her own, cabaret plaudits and a TV tryout. Then she faltered, missed a couple of engagements, took a break, and the clapping stopped. It came home to her that she was a fad: last year's darling, forgotten among this year's pets, too old to be a novelty, too inexperienced to adapt. Her glitter faded, material staled, contracts dried up, and her flashy apartment was on the market at a knock down price.

Poor Shelley, burnt out at twenty, and when she turned up on my doorstep that night seeking solace she found a cold flat (boiler on the blink), a cook-chill dinner (I missed the supermarket) and an empty wine rack (ditto).

Still, the qualities of motherhood also encompass

holding back on 'I told you so' when a child has ignored parental misgivings, and I gave Shelley the indulgence of wallowing in self-pity while I lent an unjudgmental ear. 'Told you so' could come later, when I no longer wanted her cowboy boots.

Three

'**C**rap!'

I looked up: this early-morning expletive from Ellis Clancy's newsdesk was common, but it was not normally aimed at me. He was staring into his screen, my story for that night's paper scrolling up before his eyes.

'What's the matter, Ellis?' I responded.

'You should know what's the matter, or if you don't you can get out of my newsroom and go fanny around in features.'

'There's nothing more to get on Llew Madden. I worked my arse off last night' – Ellis's crudities provoked responses in kind – 'I rang everybody from his cleaner to his maiden aunt. They all say the same. He was a hard-working, upstanding pillar of the community who never even had a parking ticket.'

'Oh yeah, and the sun shines out of my armpits. Get a grip, Anna, you could've lifted this straight from the breakfast news – any old waffler can do a cuttings job. Someone hated Llew Madden enough to stick a knife through his heart and dump him on a bonfire, and the best you can do is recycle old newsprint.'

'It's all anyone else'll have, Ellis, you know I was down at the park first thing this morning with the rest of the pack – local radio, the *North West Sentinel*, freelances. We all got the bum's rush.'

'I don't want what everyone else, has, Anna, I want a new line.'

'I got a new line – from the police.'

'Oh yeah. I'm sorry, I forgot the good old chief inspector and his excuse for a statement: "There were no bloodstains or signs of fighting at Mr Madden's house, and both his cars appear untouched, but I am appealing for anyone who saw anything suspicious in the vicinity of the house last week, particularly Thursday, 4 November, to come forward. We're examining all possibilities and keeping an open mind." Well I must say, Anna, you and Anderson deserve each other – neither of you has a frigging clue what's behind all this.'

'Do you?'

'No – but I can spin a yarn out of invisible thread when I have to. The punters want colour, they want entertainment. Your stuff's about as colourful as the black and white minstrels. Take it back and get weaving, sharpish – I want it by first deadline.'

Ellis, self-styled Boy Wonder of provincial journalism, was not worth an argument. Young, edgy and on the make, he charged through life with the sound and fury of a balloon let go before the air was tied in. He would not listen, and so I hastily rewrote the story, adding the spicy mixture of fact and fabrication that he craved, carefully larding it with words like 'understood, could, possibly', to slip past the libel laws without making Ellis any more apoplectic: 'Police are understood to be probing Mr Madden's business contacts for any sign of a motive for his killing. Mr Madden, the lonely-heart divorcee who came back to rescue his family business, had a great deal at stake in ensuring its success: he had ambitious plans for expansion and modernisation, but finance on such a scale is hard to find. He could have got embroiled with shady characters to get Mad Mad World back on its feet.

'The police are also interviewing his staff, past and present. Possibly an ex-employee with a grudge against his boss could hold a clue – maybe a score was settled in a fight that went too far.'

Followed by more such gruesome guesswork.

Ellis hardly cracked a smile:'OK, at least we've got the bones of a story – now get back down to Mad Mad World and don't take "no comment" for an answer. Let's see if you can find me a fresh piece of flesh in time for the final edition.'

I drove straight to Mad Mad World, a large site at the eastern end of the seafront, crammed with rides and hemmed in by hotels. The winter was a closed season for the park – the ferris wheel stood clamped, the wall of death idle, and the rollercoaster stripped down, ready for repairs and repainting. Usually workmen would be here, preparing for the next season, but today it must have been silent in honour of Llew. It was an eerie place to be on a cold November morning, with huge concrete clowns beckoning to no one, their laughter frozen in the air.

Into this silence my heels clicked announcing my approach to the administrative building, decked out to look like a giant yellow submarine. My fellow hacks who had hung round in frustration earlier that morning had gone, other stories to cover, other deadlines to meet.

A microphone cleared its throat and squawked: 'If you're looking for Miss Monteith, I'm afraid she's not here.'

I looked round – I hadn't even pressed the entry-phone buzzer on the door – and saw a camera's eye scrutinising me from a corner.

'No,' I replied to the faceless female speaker. 'I know Rosie's away. I'm from the *Northport News* – Anna Knight. I–'

'We know why you're here, we've had just about

enough of your kind here this morning. We're sorry, but we've no comment.' Squawk!

I was about to protest that local readers deserved more than this when I heard a male voice in the background: 'It's all right, Jennifer, I'll deal with this.' Louder: 'Ms Knight, would you like to come up please?'

The door lock was electronically released and I took a lift to the upper reaches of the submarine.

A large, bearded, warm-looking man was awaiting my arrival. My hopes sank – large, bearded, warm-looking men are usually too nice to peddle dirt, and let's face it, that's what I was here for.

However, I gleamed a smile as he gave me a strong handshake: 'Hi, I'm Matthew Whittaker, personnel manager. I hope you'll accept me as Rosie's substitute on this occasion. I think we owe the local press a little more consideration than those out-of-town stringers who've been bothering us.'

His accent was American – Californian at a guess – but softened, as though he had lived in England for some time. He looked to be in his thirties and was seriously heavy, built like an American footballer past his prime. He wore a loose but sober suit and a merry tie, crimson with big white spots, a positive cock-a-snook of a tie. I followed his broad back along a corridor, past a tear-stained receptionist and through a secretaries' room where crumpled Kleenex betrayed communal grief.

As soon as we were settled in Matthew Whittaker's office, coffee was called for and supplied, and I pulled out my notebook. 'I'd like to know if Mr Madden had any enemies, Mr Whittaker.'

He rubbed his large hands and said: 'Obviously he did or he wouldn't be in the morgue.'

'All right, any enemies that you know of.'

'No, none that I knew of. We don't tend to make enemies here, we're a friendly ship, in a fun business.'

'Indeed, but even fun businesses have to sack people

occasionally – was there no one who might have felt ill-used?'

'None.' He looked mildly affronted. 'As personnel manager I pride myself on letting people go in as sensitive a manner as possible. Even miscreants. They could cause trouble if I didn't.'

'All right, what about Mr Madden's associates? Were there any arguments that you knew of, was there anyone Mr Madden might have upset in his business dealings?'

He gave me a steady gaze of appraisal before answering: 'Of course I was not privy to all his activities, but I've worked in several leisure parks both here and in the States, and we just don't tend to get involved with those kinda people. What are you thinking – Mafia links, drug barons?' He laughed. 'Can you imagine those macho hoodlums laundering their cash through the Alice in Wonderland kiddie ride?'

'Come on, you know Mr Madden had bigger ideas for the future – he'd have to get the money from somewhere.'

'Sure, but Llew played a clean hand for it. Look, Llew was always on the side of the angels, he was a well-liked, hard-working man who wanted nothing more than to lead Mad Mad World back to success in the world of amusement parks. That's why I'm here. I could see he was a man of vision, I wanted to be in on the rebirth of one of Britain's best-known attractions. It's very sad that Northport's been robbed of his talent and expertise.'

I had to stop this flow of treacle: 'I didn't come here for tributes, Mr Whittaker, I've already got those in plenty. Someone may not have agreed with your estimation of his worth. Someone who wanted him dead. If that's so, don't you owe it to him to ask why?'

He shrugged his well-padded shoulders and leaned back with a grin of appreciation: 'Call me Matt, even if you think I'm a regular little Pollyanna, huh? Too good to be true. Well I'll tell you something, Anna, you're damn right. Look, I'll take my tongue out of my cheek and level with you, I can see you're nobody's fool. Put away the notebook, I don't want to be quoted speaking ill of the dear-departed, but here's the truth: Llew Madden was a loser.'

'A loser? What d'you mean?'

'Well, the reason he came back here was because his amusement park in the south collapsed under mountains of debt – his family rescued him from that particular mire – he lost everything.'

'He could have learnt from that mistake.'

'It made him paranoid about failure, he worried too much about the opposition. No one ever won in business by constantly watching over his shoulder, you've got to keep your eye on the ball. I told him that.'

'And why are you telling me?'

'Oh, because I'll probably be out of a job pretty soon. Now Llew's gone, his father's too sick to carry on. The only Madden left is Llew's brother, and he's a pilot. I can't see him wanting to take over. What do you think?'

'Someone could buy it.'

'Yeah, and flatten it. We're on prime building land here.'

'Why did you stay with Llew Madden if you thought so badly of him?'

'I didn't, I liked him, believe it or not. He may have been a loser but I've worked for enough winners to know they can be ruthless, egotistical and right royal pains in the butt. Llew had charm, he'd been on the ropes and it made him realise his shortcomings, plus he did have the good sense to appoint a few good people to make up for them. Together we were making it work. That's what's so darn tragic about all this.'

I sighed, 'Why should someone want to kill him.?'

'Don't you think I've been asking myself the same question?'

And Ellis would be asking it too: 'I need more than this,' I said, rather too sharply. 'I need specifics, I need names of people he might have upset, companies he regarded as competition.'

'Huh.' Matthew Whittaker's eyebrows raised. 'You're insatiable – I bare my soul before you and nary a word of gratitude. You're a hard taskmistress, Anna Knight.'

I smiled despite myself: 'I'm sorry, I am grateful – Matt.'

'Grateful enough to have dinner with me?'

'Is that a personal invitation or a professional one?'

'Mmmm . . . let's say both. A filet mignon for two might jog my memory a little more.'

I realised as I left his office that I didn't have much to feed Ellis's relentless appetite for that day's paper, but at least dinner with Matthew Whittaker might give me a start for tomorrow. OK, I know, when a story's in the air I'm anybody's – offer me a tasty bait and I'll snaffle it, hook and all – but you must admit filet mignon was tastier than most.

As I made my way back to the promenade, where I'd parked my cherished but rusty black Metro, my attention was caught by a passing Peugeot saloon with a woman driver, her black hair coiled up in a red ribbon.

'Rosie? Rosie!' I waved.

She saw me and drew up. The enviable car was a perk of the job, but she looked distinctly unhappy as she got out, breath steaming in the bitter air. 'Anna, what's got into you – why are you making up stories about Llew?'

I saw she had a copy of that night's paper crumpled up on the back seat. 'I'm casting round in the dark, Rosie, there are no new leads – that's why I'm here. I don't like it any more than you do.'

'Llew's been murdered, Anna – that's bad enough without you people concocting all sorts of lurid reasons why.'

'Come on, Rosie, you were one of us a short while ago, you know what Ellis is like. Give him plain vodka and he wants a Pimms – fruit, cherries, sparkler and all.'

'It's your byline, Anna, your cocktail—'

'Of lies, you were going to say? Be fair, Rosie, it's not lies, it's speculation. I'm sorry, I shouldn't have tried to hide behind Ellis. But what else could I do when there are no hard facts to go on? He's my boss, heaven help me, he gets what he wants.'

'Yes, well, Llew was my boss, and he didn't get what he wanted.'

'Meaning?'

A seagull came screaming out of the air, landing heavy and expectant near our feet, scavenging for crusts. Rosie flinched from it, looking fragile and tense: 'I'm going for a walk,' she said, locking her car. 'I need to clear my head.'

'I'll come with you,' I offered. 'It might help if you tried to get all this out of your system.'

She said nothing, setting off towards the beach. It was overcast, but the tide was out, and we dropped down barnacled steps to the empty sands. It started spitting with rain, and Rosie unfurled a large green umbrella which overshadowed her tiny frame and yanked at her arm in the wind.

'I will tell you what I know,' she said abruptly, 'on condition you stop these guessing games. They upset Llew's family, they upset me.'

'All right – can I use it in print?'

'Not with my name anywhere near it.'

'You've learnt the PR get-out line pretty quickly.'

She stopped, her voice trembling: 'Anna, we're not playing Trivial Pursuit here. Llew's been murdered. Someone might have killed him because of what he knew. I don't want to be next.'

'I'm sorry. Please, go on.'

She took tight hold of both her wayward umbrella and her emotions, forcing herself to expel words as we walked on: 'Mad Mad World was on a slippery slope by the time Llew came back.'

'Losing money, you mean?'

'Not quite, but Llew had just lost a lot of his own money, and he could see the family fortunes going the same way if he didn't do something. He had the next generation of the Madden dynasty to think of, and he was damned if he'd let the old heritage slide.'

'He has children?'

'A daughter, about twelve. She lives with his ex-wife, but he doted on her. Llew drew up a revival plan, and he was really positive about the park's prospects; he was also persuasive enough to enthuse some new investors, and he brought younger staff into key posts to inject a bit of dynamism.'

'Like you and Matthew Whittaker?'

'Exactly. Together we were turning the big old submarine round. But then I noticed some cracks in Llew's armour – he was working too hard, worrying too much. By the time he and I got together, he was very wound up, and I discovered it was all because of Futures, you know – ?'

'I know it – that big new fun-park between here and Liverpool. Miles of space, acres of advertising. In fact I think I've met someone who works there – Liza Boyd-Adams – friend of Marianne's. Isn't she their head accountant or something?'

'Financial director, I believe they call it, and she has a hell of a lot more finance to direct than us. For Llew, Futures was everything we weren't – young, innovative, room for expansion, bottomless cash. He was convinced Futures would kill Mad Mad World's business unless he did something dramatic. Oh, he kept his head, and on the face of it he was still confident, no one but me realised how rattled he was. Quietly he worked away, and came up with an idea to save the park.'

'Which was?'

'A TV tie-in. He was perfecting the plans for months. What he envisaged was a TV studio tour, you know, a bit like Universal Studios in America – all excitement and special effects?'

'On this site? Surely there's not enough room?'

'He reckoned we could do it if we built upwards.'

'Someone said that about castles in the sky.'

Rosie flinched and I bit my lip. Callous, cynical old hack – yes, I know the words – I've whipped myself with them often enough.

She put her head down and battled on: 'We'd have room if we demolished the older rides that aren't paying their way. They're only there for sentimental old Maurice. Llew knew he'd have to hurt his father by pulling them down, and he didn't find that easy. Anyway, he managed to get a TV company interested. They've done a lot of location work in Northport, they've even used Mad Mad World as a backdrop many times. They could see the attraction of putting a studio tour here, where the action is, right on the seafront where millions of people come for holidays each year – a ready-made audience if you like. Llew was really excited. All these negotiations were top secret, to shield them from his rivals, but he was so full of them he had to confide in someone.'

'And your head happened to be handy on the pillow?'

That hurt look again. I really must quit this game. As if in retribution I found myself sinking in a belt of squelchy sand. Misery rose as my shoes soaked up salt water, and my padded jacket slowly saturated in the thin mist of rain. As Rosie strained to help me out I nearly missed her whisper: 'Then it all fell apart.'

Misery forgotten, I regained firm sand: 'What? You mean the studio plan or you and Llew?'

'Both. The TV company was on the point of signing the contract when it pulled out. No explanation, no apology. Llew kept up a brave face, but underneath he was devastated – there was nothing I could do to console him. I felt useless.'

Her mind with Llew, she lost concentration on her umbrella. It blew inside out and gusted away. I ran to the rescue.

As I returned it to her grasp I said, 'You couldn't be useless, Rosie,' and I smoothed a lock of hair back behind her ear. She smiled weakly. That's better, Anna, she needs stroking.

'I couldn't seem to help him,' she insisted as we walked on. 'Then it got worse. He found out that Futures had muscled in, and the TV company was switching the whole project to them. He was absolutely furious. He was thrashing around for someone to blame, and he lighted on me.'

'Why, Rosie?'

'Because he thought I'd tittle-tattled everything he'd told me. He even accused me of being a Futures spy, infiltrating his bed to steal his secrets.'

'Ridiculous!'

'I know that, but he was obsessed with Futures. It took a monstrous effort to convince him I had nothing to do with it.'

'Did you succeed?'

'Yes I did, but it still broke us up. He seemed soured by the whole affair, too agitated to care about anything but business. I was still fond of him, though. I believed in his abilities, I wanted to work for him and, thank goodness, he wanted me. Anyway, after that, he trusted very few people, he looked for moles under every desk.'

'Did he find any?'

'No, that was when he started spying on Futures.'

'Industrial espionage?'

'That's the euphemism I suppose, but what it amounts to is sneaking and stealing. He was after dirt on Futures, and somehow he got hold of their plans for a brilliant new entertainment complex – like nothing that's gone before – and he aimed to launch it ahead of them.'

'But how did he steal it?'

'I don't know exactly, but I do know he took on a so-called security consultant.'

'A private detective?'

She nodded. 'I can give you his name, it's in the office.'

'And what about the complex – is it under way?'

'Yes, still in the early stages.'

'What makes it so special?'

'It involves virtual reality in conjunction with robotics. Ideal for us – thrilling, but compact. You'll be able to meet the abominable snowman, for instance, or fight fire-breathing monsters, or fly across Mars in rocket-propelled sneakers, the only limit's your imagination with this stuff.'

We stopped, and she stared bleakly over the thick grey soup of the Irish Sea: 'That's as much as I know Anna, it's as far as I can go. Llew's gone. I never realised how much I'd miss him.'

'Look Rosie, I need to make sense of all this. Basically you're saying Llew took on Futures and lost?'

She stayed mute, refusing to be drawn to any conclusion.

'I know this might be painful to you, but I spoke to Matthew Whittaker. He couldn't tell me much, but one thing he did say was "Llew Madden was a loser." '

This roused her to anger, as I'd hoped it would: 'Matt never understood Llew. Just because he wasn't an all-American bastard, Matt thought he was weak. Llew was strong, he had principles, Anna. It was Futures that threw him off balance when he found them undermining him, and Matt's goading must've played a part in the way he fought back. Spying, theft, it was all against his nature, but Futures rocked his sense of fair play. He tried to fight dirty, but he was out of his depth. Futures is the shark of the amusement world, it uses its financial muscle to pick off smaller fry and it throws its weight around with the planning authorities to keep expanding the way it does. If Llew had found positive proof of malpractice, and threatened to use it against them, I'll bet Futures would have had no compunction in shutting him up.'

'But Llew was in the same trap himself, if he stole their plans for this new entertainment complex.'

'Exactly – he got in too deep – and that's another

– 34 –

possible motive for Futures to snuff him out.' She bit her lip. 'I really don't want to talk about this any more. All I keep seeing is a sordid fight, with Llew bleeding his life away. No one should die like that. To think I believed this was a fun business.'

She looked back at Mad Mad World's clowns on the skyline with evident distaste. 'Come on,' she said with sudden conviction, 'I've probably given you flu with my ramblings.'

'Are you going to the police?'

'Yes – I'll tell them everything I told you, and when it's finally off my chest maybe I can give up wandering on deserted beaches in the rain.'

'Thanks, Rosie.'

'No . . . I had to do this. I owe it to Llew to try and get things straight. After the funeral I'm going away.'

'Holiday?'

'No – I've had too much of holiday resorts, Northport's given me my fill. I'm going to look for a new job, Anna, somewhere I don't have to watch my back.'

'Metaphorically or for real?'

She gave me a sad smile: 'You tell me.'

Four

D inner at Le Pot de Vin that night did not tell me much more about Llew Madden, but it did about Matt Whittaker – which of course had been his purpose all along.

After my revelatory talk with Rosie, this didn't bother me unduly. He was waiting outside the restaurant when I arrived, his tie distinguishable from twenty paces – a multi-hued dazzler which on close encounter revealed a motif of Popeye and Olive Oyl.

No one could feel threatened with a tie like that. I relaxed and let him butter me up along with the bread rolls he consumed in quantity before we reached the starter. He admired my dress, plain black velvet, short and neat, and I had to allow he had taste. He praised my hair; nothing to write home about, but when upswept, with careless wisps straying artlessly as careless wisps will, then I must concede it can be quite fetching. And he liked my legs, for which I could claim no credit – all my mother's work, but I'll admit she did a grand job.

So I sat and ate champagne-sauced salmon (filet mignon was off) and enquired the pedigree of this discriminating specimen of manhood.

'I'm a mongrel,' he said, growling amusingly into his wineglass. 'My mother's American, father English – they split up when I was young, then did their best to split me, so I spent half my childhood flying from one side of the Atlantic to the other while they sorted it out.'

'A tug-of-love child?'

'Yeah . . . doesn't that tweak your heartstrings?'

'It doesn't look to have done you lasting harm.'

'I was a pretty resilient kid, I made friends easily, had a healthy appetite—'

'Some things don't change.'

'You don't like my body?' His eyes glinted and he pulled a gap between his shirt buttons. 'I have a thinner me inside here if you'd care to explore.'

'I'll stick to the outer you for now.'

'Yes, please.'

'Matt – I'm trying to be serious.'

'So am I. OK, OK, the life and times of Matthew Whittaker, chapter one. When my parents were together they fought like crazy, so I used to escape to fun fairs or amusement parks. Then my grandparents took me to Disneyland and I thought it was Heaven, I never wanted to come away . . . and so I suppose I set out to try and get back there. I've been working in these glorified kids' playgrounds all my adult life. Sad, aren't I?'

'You hide it well.'

'Tears of a clown, my discerning one, they're shed in the dark when I'm all alone.'

'Are you alone in the dark?'

'Yes. Are you?'

And so I told him my story too, skipping a shortfall here, twisting a truth there, waltzing on tiptoe round my early marriage, sozzled husband and his demise, and finishing with my talented and exquisite daughter in a bravura flourish.

'Does she still live with you?'

'No.'

'You're on your own then.'

'Yes, Matt, does it bear repeating?'

'I find it hard to believe my luck, that's all.'

What a lovely, intelligent – nay, minus beard and a pound or seven – surely even handsome man.

I floated out of the restaurant and he accompanied me in my cab home. Then he kept it running on the meter while he gave me a chaste kiss – first rule of the fun business: keep them wanting more.

And so I fell into bed – yes, Matt, on my own – and I realised we had not mentioned Llew Madden at all.

Ellis Clancy certainly mentioned him the following morning. I was in an acute dilemma as I responded to his bark of 'Anna? Whaddya got?'

Rosie's story was dramatic and colourful enough to keep Ellis happy, but was it true? We couldn't go into print alleging dirty tricks on the part of Mad Mad World or Futures without corroboration. And what was I doing when I should have been getting that corroboration? Fluttering my eyelashes at Matt Whittaker while he flattered the pants off me. Metaphorically speaking.

I sighed. 'I have to do some more digging on this I'm afraid, Ellis.'

'Digging? You were given all yesterday to dig – you should've come out in Australia by now. Take pity on me, please, Anna, we're not producing toilet paper, all blank white sheets. I need words on screen. Feed me words.'

He opened his mouth like a gaping baby bird, and I threw him the worm of Rosie's revelations. 'The trouble is, Ellis, I don't have anything to back it up.'

I could see him teetering on whether to go with it anyway, relying on the weasel words we'd used yesterday, until he looked suspicious: 'Wait a minute, who told you all this?' I sealed my lips.

'Come on, Anna, tell me who's your source – it'll be my arse in court too, you know.'

Through gritted teeth: 'Rosie.'

'What?'

'Rosie Monteith.'

'Oh for pity's sake, I might've known. She's throwing you a line to get me on the hook, she wants my balls on a marble slab and cut into tiny pieces. They would be too if Futures slung a libel suit at us, not to mention Maurice Madden. All right, go do your digging, but I can't give you much longer, Anna, I don't have reporters on coat-hangers waiting to be used while you swan round being investigative.'

So that morning I found myself tramping the mean streets of Northport in search of a private dick – sorry, security consultant – whose address Rosie had given me as promised.

The name of Brian Battersby didn't exactly sound the part, but in the underworld in which he worked, it could be a clever cover. I found the place, up some stairs beside a greengrocers' shop, and I pressed the buzzer. No reply. I pressed again, still no answer. I was about to turn away when a short, thickset man came running up the stairs as well as short, thickset men can – breathless and out of sorts.

'Who are you?' he asked between wheezes.

I gave him my name and showed him my press identity card, since security consultants tend to be pernickety about such things. He said nothing and unlocked the door with a bewildering number of procedures, keeping his back to me to shield which key he was using where.

Eventually he was in, and he shut the door on me. Somewhat taken aback, I banged on the frosted glass: 'Mr Battersby, I need to speak to you about Mr Llew Madden – I believe he was a client of yo—'

The door swung back: 'Shut up and come inside. I don't need this kind of noise.'

I sized him up as he showed me into a surprisingly bright office with modern furniture, neat filing cabinets and a bank of computer equipment worthy of IBM HQ. Bald, with a heavy moustache, he blinked painfully in the strip-light. Perhaps he had a hangover, or perhaps I'd read too much Raymond Chandler.

'Who told you about me?' he asked, stripping off his scuffed coat and mangy scarf, yet giving off a scent of expensive aftershave. He sat down behind his desk, transformed into a consultant in a well-tailored jacket, display handkerchief and all. A man of many layers, a chameleon – perhaps that's how he did his job.

I gave him Rosie's name, realising miserably that I was betraying her once more. I told him my difficulty, that she had given me details of Llew Madden's feud with the rival park, and that he had embarked on subterfuge in an effort to fight back. I told him I needed confirmation that this was true before we could print.

As I spoke, his bristly moustache seemed to soften and he actually smiled – fleetingly, it's true, but I felt I was getting somewhere.

'Listen, I'm sorry I was so abrupt with you out there,' he said. 'I've been up all night – surveillance on a wife who wasn't exactly where she should've been. Bread and butter stuff but I don't get Llew Madden's class of caviare that often.'

'So you did do some work for him?'

'Yes.'

I waited for an explanation, but he just stopped.

'You did spy – sorry, carry out surveillance – on Futures?'

'I told the police what I did, I don't have to tell you.'

'This leaves me in a difficult position, Mr Battersby.'

'A difficult position? I wonder if that's what Llew Madden thought when someone stuck a knife between his ribs – "My, I'm in a difficult position, I wish I'd never started this." Take heed, Ms Knight.'

'Are you saying keep quiet about it to save my own skin?'

'I'm saying leave it to those who protect their skin in uniform.'

'The police?'

He nodded. 'I think that's sensible, don't you, in view of the difficult position? I don't know who killed Llew Madden, I don't know why. I do know he was murdered, I do know I did some work for him, and I do know my wife checked my life insurance this morning. I'm hoping these matters are not connected.'

'But Mr Battersby, surely you want to find out – '

'I want to find out nothing unless I'm paid to. Information is currency, Ms Knight, I'm not going to dig it up for no reward. It looks like the Maddens are leaving it to the police, letting the taxpayer pick up the tab, and I've accepted that. I suggest you do likewise.'

'It takes us forever to get anything out of the police. They won't give us a jelly-baby till they've taken its finger-prints, sucked it clean and wrapped it up as a court exhibit. Can't you at least point me in the right direction? Just tell me whether there was something dodgy going on at Futures? Something Llew Madden found out about? You needn't say anything – just nod or shake your head.'

'I'll nod or shake nothing. Do yourself and me a favour, Ms Knight, don't go any further with this.'

It was obvious he was not going to give. The moustache had bristled up again, the mouth was tight, words clipped, and I realised I was being warned off in no uncertain terms.

Well, perhaps it was too much to expect a security consultant to become insecure at the sight of a tall female reporter in black tights and peach lipstick. But when the tall female reporter also prides herself on incisive questioning, then it's a bit more of a blow to the ego.

I tried a final, below-the-belt ploy: 'Mr Battersby, you know journalists and private investigators can often be mutually helpful, can they not? Is there any company you need facts on, information I can get more easily than you through my professional channels?'

He guffawed, eyebrows raised in interest: 'If there is I'll get in touch. But for now, sorry, no tit for your tat.'

I bade him goodbye and hit the mean streets once again, though they looked a little less tough now that I had met Mr Brian Battersby and his mobile moustache above the greengrocers' shop. He could simply have been a security adviser, telling Llew what alarms to fit, what codes to use. But if so, why had he warned me off?

At the police station Chief Inspector Alex Anderson was too busy to see me, and I had to content myself with the community affairs officer. Trying to pin him down on anything was like playing catch with the Invisible Man. Elusive.

My question: 'Are you investigating a possible rivalry between Mad Mad World and Futures that may have led to Mr Madden's death?'

His answer: 'We're investigating all possibilities.'

'Do they include this feud between the two companies?'

'Feud is a newspaper word.'

'But was there one?'

'All lines of inquiry are being pursued, Anna.'

'Look, I know Rosie Monteith must have told you her suspicions, and I know one of your officers has spoken to Brian Battersby. Are you investigating the allegation that Llew Madden saw Futures as his worst enemy, was convinced they'd done the dirty on him, and was prepared to fight back to save his business?'

'I can't confirm what you've said. All I can say is nothing's being ruled out.'

I paused, and tried another tack: 'Have you found the murder weapon?'

His face brightened: 'No, but we do know it was an unusually long blade – at least nine inches. Most knives are no more than about seven or eight. It was non-serrated and sharply pointed.'

'Sounds like my mother's old carving knife.'

'It could well be a household implement of some sort.'

'So your lines of inquiry now include every kitchen drawer in Northport?'

'We'd like – with your invaluable help – to ask the public if they see such a knife discarded, anywhere unusual—'

'Don't tell me, could they get in touch with you without delay?'

'Right. Oh, and by the way, the coroner's due to open the inquest on Madden at 2.30 p.m. next Monday.'

'To be adjourned immediately no doubt.'

'That's not for me to say.'

'Anything else for us?'

'Only unqualified admiration.'

I might have smiled had I not heard this merry quip ten times every day from various police stations as I did the routine calls.

Once back at my desk I persevered, ringing Matthew, who was gratifyingly pleased to hear from me, but who merely whistled in disbelief when I asked if he knew anything about Rosie's story.

I then tried the holy of holies, getting Matt to put me through to Maurice Madden in his inner sanctum. Mr Madden, sounding weary and frail, was perfectly polite but absolutely adamant his son was involved in nothing underhand. He had been disappointed about the TV studio tour, he said, but that's the way of the world in business. With poignant pride he told me that the proposed virtual reality and robotics complex was solely his son's creation, and he was obviously affronted that I could suggest otherwise. I felt sorry to have injured his feelings and pressed no further.

Ellis was not pleased.

Five

Ellis was seething. My profitless searches only served to convince him that Rosie had tried to foul him up with a false trail of inter-company dirty tricks, and he took out his resentment on me for being duped and wasting precious writing time.

I tried to forget his publicly voiced opinion to the effect that I indulged in solitary sexual practices, and that I'd better get my finger out – if I still could – and give him some copy instead of engaging in carnal congress with private detectives. Except he used shorter words.

It's called equal opportunities – a woman has an equal right to be slagged off by a jumped-up pillock in the same language as a man. Well, I took it like a man, and sulked off back to my desk, damning him with oaths he couldn't quite hear.

Whatever he said, I didn't believe Rosie was that devious, but he put the heavy boot on further digging by diverting me for the rest of the week to the lowliest magistrates' court, a minor ministerial visit and the unfair dismissal of a rock-roller.

However, there were bright spots: Matthew Whittaker did sterling service in salvaging my jaundiced view of the male species. He took me to see the latest Disney cartoon, and we followed it up with a visit to a wine bar. When he left me on the doorstep – with rather more than a chaste kiss this time – I was so lulled by his easy companionship (and three glasses of Chardonnay) that I promised to cook dinner for him on Saturday.

Come Saturday I became a regular housewife, wheeling my trolley round the supermarket, cleaning the flat (well, elevating the dust for a while) and making enough dinner for three, hoping to freeze some for later in the week like any good housewife should.

'Mmmm-mmmm' murmured Matt, diving into the *boeuf en daube*, and the freezer went hungry.

Well, I never was a good housewife. Good housewives don't press their best sheets and polish their toenails, hoping to get lucky with a man they met barely a week before.

Did I get lucky? What do you take me for, an idle tittle-tattle? Well, since you force it out of me, I have to confess the evening had its moments. Suffice it to say that he was surprisingly agile for a man of his size, and he made an excellent pillow for my weary head between rounds. Mmmmm.

By Monday morning I was raring to go. Ellis's weekend had evidently not been as restorative as mine. As I entered the newsroom he was sitting fixed to his computer screen, as though he had never left. Did he have weekends, I wondered, or did he haunt the office on a Sunday like a lost soul, waiting only for Monday and his spiritual communion with the copy-flow?

At least there was something I could now do to get back on the Llew Madden story – attend his inquest. It would inevitably be adjourned, a formality so that the body could be released for a decent burial, but the statement of the physical facts might throw up something fresh. It did.

Though Llew's head was burned black, his body had

largely been shielded from the flames by the carpet. He had been in a struggle – there were grazes and bruising – and he'd had sexual intercourse with a person unknown shortly before his death. I wondered if the police thought the two were connected – a rape perhaps, in which his victim fought back? Somehow a rapist didn't match up with the Llew I'd begun to know, through Rosie and the rest. I preferred to think he'd made love, and hadn't had time to wash. Poor Llew, that pathetic smear on his underpants pored over by the pathologist, lab analysts, the police and, by extension, me and the readership of the *Northport News*.

Still, it indicated that someone, somewhere had not come forward to fill in some of those vital hours before he died, despite the best efforts of the police and media.

The coroner briskly dealt with the paperwork and adjourned to a date to be fixed. Until the police had got to the bottom of Llew's killing, or had given up the ghost, she could do little else.

Llew's funeral was a couple of days later. By keeping my head down and doing Ellis's bidding, I had purged some of my sin in the Clancy hierarchy of penance. I moved up to the the level where he accepted my suggestion of attending the funeral with a grunt, rather than blasting me down again to the fiery furnace.

But I was, without question, strictly on parole. I knew Ellis would not stand for any more days out chasing inquiries which, as he said helpfully to the editor, 'produced no more than a mouse-fart in a gale.'

A gale was blowing that morning as I hung at the back trying to be as insignificant as Ellis's metaphor. Funerals are for families, friends and functionaries, they are not for hangers-on such as me, and there was a good chance I would be hounded out of the churchyard – it had happened before.

Jon Spry was with me to photograph the cortège and pick out any special tributes on the flowers. We were there to observe, to note the mourners, to jot down the minister's oration, and to make of Llew's death something more dignified than the wretched image of a stabbed corpse on a beach bonfire.

Llew's father was well liked, well respected in the town, and I suspected many people were there more for him than his son, who had lived away for sixteen years.

The gale abated a little as Jon and I sheltered behind the lych-gate to watch the mourners pass on their way to church: Maurice Madden, who had only last year buried his wife, thin, stooped and grey, leaning heavily on the arm of a younger, taller, fitter version of Llew. I looked again – of course, this must be Llew's brother, the test pilot, Guy Madden.

I had come across a few test pilots in my work as there was a military aircraft plant just a few miles down the coast from Northport where many of our readers worked. In my experience, pilots were neither daring young men in their flying machines, nor *Top Gun* clones homing on targets and women with equal precision – though several played up to the popular myth. They were men of method, repeatedly going through lists of checks and double-checks until they were sure and double sure of every manoeuvre, and then they'd check again. They were highly trained, professional technicians, and just because their techniques included riding a spear of carbon fibre round the sky and occasionally, so it's said, touching the face of God, there was no need to hold them in awe.

Guy Madden looked as though being held in awe was his natural birthright. Oh, he was handsome, with his neat dark hair and military bearing, and he was intelligent – they don't let duffers loose on £20 million-worth of proto-type. He led his father into church, and the other family mourners followed. A line of astonishing cars had rolled up – Llew had belonged to a classic car club – and their drivers joined the column, with staff representatives bringing up the rear. Matt winked in my direction and solemnly indicated his muted tie in honour of the occasion. Rosie stared through me as though distracted.

Jon and I slid into a pew at the back, behind a lone woman who looked detached and on her guard, like us. She was dressed in black, but unlike most of the congregation, she neither wept nor bowed her head when the coffin passed, but kept her eyes fixed upon it with grim intensity. Throughout the service I could see her hymnbook shaking, and she barely sang, merely mouthing the words through tightened lips.

The service drew to a close, and Jon whispered, 'I'm going to go out first, so I can get them coming out of church.' The smell of polish and old prayerbooks was beginning to oppress me, so I went with him.

Out into the gusty graveyard the coffin emerged, borne by relatives of the Madden family, with Maurice and Guy right behind. I saw Guy's eyes narrow at the sight of Jon's camera, and he snarled in a clipped undertone: 'Can't you people leave us alone?' Then, in a gesture quick as a snake, he flicked out a hand and Jon's camera was on the grass.

Jon was too stunned to retaliate – in any case what could he do? But Maurice quietly chastised his son: 'Guy . . . please . . . no more damage – we've had enough.' As I watched Guy turn – erect, tense – to follow his dead brother down the path, I realised he was driven by anger – a fierce rage like a thoroughbred trapped at the gate, goaded beyond endurance.

The strange woman in black joined the back of the line of mourners – the first time I'd seen her full face – and I was struck by the conviction that I had seen her somewhere before. The haunted eyes, the drawn expression tolled a muffled bell at the back of my mind. I positioned myself where I could see her during the final obsequies at the graveside.

She was probably about thirty, but she seemed prematurely aged, in a heavy coat that looked as well worn as her features. Her hair, a faded rust, was drawn back with a black ribbon into a pony-tail, a young style, but she looked pale and shrivelled, as though the youth had been drained out of her. All that seemed to keep her upright was her stare, chained to the coffin. She had watched every bump, every swing as it was carried through the graveyard, and when it was lowered into the earth, her whole body bent as though to follow.

'Ashes to ashes, dust to dust,' intoned the minister, invoking in me the irreverent thought that the ill-fated Llew had had more than his fair share of the former. The prayers finished, Maurice threw a handful of mud on his son's remains. Guy didn't – too messy for him to bear.

The mourners drifted away and the sexton began his spadework, the clay thudding down on to the coffin with dull finality. Jon and I stepped forward to read the cards on the wreaths. One of these was a magnificent construction, a helter-skelter of flowers, sent by the staff of Mad Mad World. I fondly imagined it was Matt who had made the suggestion.

We were just about to retreat for a warming coffee when I noticed the mystery woman coming back. She bore a wreath of white lilies. We stood back while she laid it with the others, crossed herself and then hastened away, running down the cemetery path as if released from a personal prison. The card read: 'From Natalie. Together at last.'

The woman turned out of the graveyard and ran toward the car park which was just over a low wall near us. On impulse I whispered urgently to Jon: 'Can you get her picture?'

She seemed oblivious to our presence, indeed to anything but her need to get back in her beat-up old car – an orange Fiesta with one yellow wing – and drive away from that place. She didn't notice the camera at all.

'Who the hell's Natalie?' asked Jon when she'd departed like a woman possessed.

'I don't know,' I said. 'I can't place the face, it's driving me mad. But I'm going to find out.'

Six

Back at the office, typing away, trying to breathe life into Llew's memory with my deathless prose, Natalie nagged at the edge of my consciousness. 'Together at last' – what did it mean? Could she be a lover? Was she the one whose traces still stuck to Llew's body as he died? Could she be an ex-lover, inflamed by the torch she still carried for him? Perhaps he had rejected her cruelly, painfully – and was the pain enough for her to retaliate with a knife?

I knew she was not his ex-wife, I had identified her in the funeral procession accompanying their grieving daughter behind Maurice and Guy.

Jon brought the picture to my desk, as I had asked him, and the questions still buzzed round it like infuriating flies. I had definitely seen this woman's face before. Natalie, Natalie who? Soon a knot of reporters clustered round my shoulders. 'Come on,' I urged them. 'Surely somebody knows who she is?'

Ellis looked up. To him any huddle of reporters mumbling in low voices could mean only one thing – they were talking about him. He sauntered over. 'What's all this about then?' he asked, as insouciantly as a cobra poised to strike.

'It's this woman, Ellis,' I replied, waving the photo in his direction. 'She was acting strangely at the funeral. She wasn't part of the family or friends or anybody else as far as I could see. All I know is her name's Natalie – from the flowers she left by the grave. She struck me as off balance.'

'Oh, so it's Anna Knight, private investigator, again is it?' he sneered. 'And does Anna Knight, PI think this woman could hold the clue to Llew Madden's mystery murder? Give it here, let me see.'

I thought he was going to dismiss the photo without a second glance, but he did give it a second glance, and a third. In fact he was fascinated. 'Natalie, you say?' he muttered.

'Yes.'

'Her name's not Natalie at all. I can't remember what it is, but I know one thing, Natalie was her daughter.'

'Was?'

'She was killed. Scrawny little thing, glasses. I remember her school photo was printed in all the nationals. It must be about five years ago, the kid was seven or thereabouts. The usual pic – a family in tragedy – was used all over the place. This, unless the old memory bank deceives me, was the mother. Same hairstyle, same eyes. Can't remember the details.'

He scanned the picture as though he could imprint it on his brain and come up with a match. 'Yes!' he exclaimed, like a striker scoring. 'Now I've got it. The kid fell off a ride at Llew Madden's fun park down south. Mother desperate. Blamed guess who?'

'Llew Madden?'

'Bingo. I think you might have yourself a little theory there, Miss Private Investigator,' he grinned, pleased with himself. 'How would you like to pursue it?'

Her name was Penny Worthington, aged twenty-seven, address a common-or-garden semi in Hove, Sussex.

I deciphered this from the blotched fax of a cutting

sent up from the local paper in Brighton, next door to Hove, at my request. The cutting was five years old – Penny would now be thirty-two – but her picture loomed out of the shadowy fax with the same pale, drawn agony of the woman at the funeral. Sitting with his arm round her in the picture, almost holding her up, was a man identified as her husband, Mark. Natalie had been their only child, she had been taken to the local amusement park as a treat for her seventh birthday.

I read the cutting:

'The accident happened as Mrs Worthington took her daughter on the Road-Runner, billed by the park as 'The Thrill-a-Second Crazy Chase'. Riders are held in by a safety bar as the carriages climb, plummet and twist round a series of tight bends.

Natalie somehow slipped from under the safety bar and fell down on to a lower level of track, straight into the path of a following carriage.

Mrs Worthington, her voice broken with tears, is convinced Natalie's death was not just a tragic accident.

'My beautiful daughter would be alive now if that safety bar had been safe,' she sobbed. 'I tell you the bar gave way as we were flung round a corner. Natalie was so light she flew out and I couldn't hold her. The bar clamped down again and I'm the only one who saw what really happened. They tested it and said there was nothing wrong with it. They said Natalie must have been larking about. Larking about!'

The park's managing director, Mr Llewellyn Madden, offered his deepest sympathy to Natalie's family, but he denied anyone ever said she had been larking about.

'That would be completely insensitive,' he said. 'However, children can become excitable on rides such as this, and that is why we never let them on without an adult. We have signs warning parents to ensure their children do not unwittingly put themselves in danger by standing up or leaning out of the carriage.

'Natalie was the victim of a tragic accident. I have a daughter her age myself. No one could be more sorry for her family.'

The distraught couple said sorrow was not enough.

'We're going to sue the park for negligence,' said Mrs Worthington. 'It's not for the money, that'll never bring my lovely daughter back. I just want justice for Natalie who'll never have another birthday again, thanks to them.'

It was pretty heart-rending stuff, as I said on the phone to Jo Daniels, the reporter who sent it to me from Brighton. I had set up an exchange deal with her – we would swop any copy relevant to our areas.

'It gets worse,' replied Jo. 'I have some more cuttings in front of me. The inquest verdict was accidental death – but the Worthingtons were adamant they were still claiming negligence. When it came to court three years ago Llew Madden brought out the big guns, paid a fortune for a QC to represent him, and won.'

'They must have been in despair.'

'Penny Worthington stood on the court steps and screamed blue murder at Llew Madden. She had to be taken away and put under sedation.'

'So what's happened since then?' I asked.

'Well, the Worthingtons disappeared from the scene. I thought they were probably quietly trying to rebuild their lives – until last week.'

'Since Llew's murder?'

'Yes. The Northport police rang, asking for our cuttings like you did.'

So they were already on Penny Worthington's tail. I wondered if they'd kept a discreet watch on the graveyard and noted the pale woman lay the wreath of white lilies. I wondered whether the words on the card were now taken down to be used in evidence.

'From Natalie. Together at last,' I muttered.

'What?'

'That was the message she left on the flowers at Llew's grave.'

'Oooh. Spooky,' mused Jo.

'D'you think Penny wanted him dead?'

'Certainly she did on the court steps. But she was deranged with grief as they say in all the best papers.'

'What, still that upset – two years after the accident?'

'Oh yes. She'd become obsessed, that much was clear as the case went on. Mark was much more together by then. I think he just wanted to put the whole thing behind them. I tracked him down, you know, a couple of days ago when the police began sniffing – I was after both of them, but Penny wasn't there. Eventually he told me they've split up.'

'Because of this?'

'It seems like it. They tried for another kid, but it didn't happen – they had all the tests and there was nothing wrong, but emotional distress can mess up your hormones, and from what Mark said, Penny was as uptight as a violin. She didn't want treatment, she just started brooding. She said Llew Madden had blamed her for not taking care that Natalie was safe—'

'Mothers are always guilty,' I interrupted morosely. 'Even when they're not, someone blames them. Believe me, I've been there.'

'Anyway, Llew Madden became a fixation with her. When he moved back north, she wanted to follow – said he'd do the same to some other poor child if she didn't stop him. Mark put his foot down. He'd had enough. He has quite a decent job here which he's not prepared to give up.'

'So she left?'

'That's right. She's been living in a Northport bedsit on social security, apparently. Mark's been sending her money. He's concerned about her but he couldn't go on the way they were. He says she needs treatment, but she refuses all help.'

'D'you have her address here?'

'I can ask Mark for it. I think he trusts me now.'

'Thanks Jo, and if there's anything I can do for you just give me a bell.'

She came back to me within the hour with Penny Worthington's whereabouts. But she added a rider: 'Mark asks if you can give her a message – she never replies to his letters, you see. He only knows she's still there because she keeps cashing the cheques he sends her.'

'Of course I will, what is it?'

'You're to tell her he'd welcome her back if she wants to come. Tell her he still loves her and there's no one else. Tell her he still means what he said that night on Fox Hill, and he always will.'

'Which was?'

'He didn't say – that must be their secret. He obviously threw that in to make sure she knows the message is genuine.

'Jo, does he know she's a suspect in the murder investigation?'

'He'd be pretty dim if he didn't. The local police've been round to see him, helping their Northern colleagues with their inquiries. I think that's what's brought on this outbreak of let's-kiss-and-make-up. The guy's genuinely worried about her, Anna.'

'OK, I'll go round, see what I can do.'

'And you'll send us the results pronto?'

'Pronto's my middle name.'

By late morning I had found the place: at the end of a side street, a shabby, narrow house that went up four floors; from its upper windows the concrete clowns and ersatz towers of Mad Mad World must have been visible. I presumed that had been Penny Worthington's prime consideration.

The front door opened as I approached and I thought my luck was in. A small man emerged, looking furtively down the street. He scuttled out and was heading across the road as I caught up with him.

'Excuse me,' I said. 'I couldn't help noticing you come out of that house. Could I ask you if—'

'Sod off.'

'My name's Anna Knight, I—'

'Listen darling, I'm not looking for any more business, all right?'

'I don't know what you—'

He stopped, ferret eyes biting into me: 'You from the police?'

'No.'

'Council?'

'No.'

'Social security?'

'No, I'm a—'

'If you're not one of them I couldn't care less. Sod off and leave me alone.'

'D'you live in that house?'

He gave a nasty snort which was meant to be a laugh: 'They don't have fellas living there, darling. One or two might stay overnight I s'pose, but that's extra. Satisfied now?' And he hurried off, hunching his shoulders against further interference.

I approached the front door again, this time with a sinking heart. Had Penny fallen so low she had to sell her favours? But surely she was getting enough money to survive without that.

A spent-looking woman, make-up smudged, smelling of talcum powder, answered my knock. Although she opened the door only a crack I could see she was too weighty to be Penny.

'Hallo,' I said, as brightly as I could. 'I'm not from the police or anything official. I'm looking for Penny Worthington, and I was told she lived here.'

'Who by?'

'Her husband.'

'What for?'

'He wants me to give her a message.'

She blinked as if her eyelids were too heavy to keep open: this woman needed sleep, her whole being craved unconsciousness. Her eyelashes stuck together and she rubbed them, spreading mascara like a black eye. 'Oh Gawd,' she muttered, looking askance at her blackened fingers. 'You'd better come in off the street while I sort myself out.'

I followed her through a dim hallway to a kitchen at the back of the house. She held her purple velour dressing-gown together as she called up the stairs. 'Penny! Someone to see you.'

A faint voice could be heard: 'Down in a minute.'

The woman came back in: 'Cuppa tea, love? You look perished.'

'Yes, thanks, that'd be great.'

'Just hang on while I wipe this muck off my face. Put the kettle on, there's a love. I'm gasping for one myself.'

She disappeared and I busied myself at the sink with the kettle. The kitchen was clean, if a little careworn, a warm bolt-hole. Its cupboards were of the modern self-assembly school of furnishing – plywood and plastic handles – with washable wallpaper and a cooker scarred with scrubbing.

My hostess came back, her face now white and damp under a freshly-raked frizz of short dark hair. She looked roughly my age, puckered round the eyes, lines beginning to dig in for the duration. Sisters under the skin.

'My name's Janette,' she said.

'Pleased to meet you. I'm Anna Knight.'

She yawned copiously as she fetched teabags and poured the boiling water: 'Aeeaaaw – 'scuse me. Can't seem to sleep much these days. Get up in the morning worn out.' She continued, 'I s'pose he wants her to come back then does he, Mark?' she asked. 'All is forgiven?'

'Something on those lines.'

Janette pulled a wry face, 'I know. They all say that when they get sick of living out of tins.' She offered me a cigarette.

'I don't smoke,' I replied, 'I'm sorry. I gave up. You go ahead.' Why was I apologising? I didn't want her to think I disapproved of what she did, I felt flustered.

Janette couldn't have cared less. She pulled on her cigarette like a vacuum cleaner. I ventured a question: 'Has Penny lived here ever since she came north?'

Janette nodded, closing one eye against the smoke, and sat down at the table opposite me, pouring tea into giant floral mugs. 'I found her outside the station. I was working one night. It was blistering cold, she'd just got off the train and she looked like a little lost whippet. She'd nowhere to go, so I brought her home and she's been with me ever since. She wasn't right, up here,' Janette tapped her head, 'not for quite a while. That business with her kiddie knocked her sideways. It would anybody.'

'Does she . . . does she work at all?'

'Only for me.'

Janette saw my look: 'Oh, it's not what you think. Poor mite, some of my brutes'd crush the life out of her. She just helps keep the house clean and tidy as part-payment of rent. I like a clean house. This is really too big for us – used to be a guest-house but I couldn't make it pay. It isn't easy keeping on top of things when you're a working girl with two kids to keep.'

'Kids?'

'My daughters. There they are, look.' She pulled a photo out of a drawer. Shining morning faces. 'Why do you think I put myself out – for the good of my health? No, it's so we don't have to scrape and scrimp every penny. Those two won't have to go shelf-stacking instead of doing their homework. I want them to stay on for their exams and get good jobs. Not like their mother. A decent start in life.'

She gulped her tea and stared at the table: 'I'll miss Penny if she does have to go. It's not just the rent, although

Gawd knows we can do with it. I like a bit of female company – you know, not kids – another woman. Some of these men can make your skin crawl, it helps to have a laugh about 'em. I feel safer too, somebody else in the house. I hope she tells her husband she's staying.'

The door opened: 'Don't worry, I'm not going back to him, Janette, I've told you before.'

I stood up to greet the incomer. Her hair was tied back tight and severe, she wore an over-large tracksuit which drowned her bony frame, and she carried a damp cloth.

'Not another detective,' she said, ignoring my out-stretched hand and crouching to open a cupboard under the sink. 'I've told you all I know.'

'No, I'm not from the police, Penny, I've brought a message for you, from Mark.'

She stood up slowly, a bottle of bleach in her hand, and for the first time looked at my face. 'Who are you?' she asked.

'You don't know me. I'm Anna Knight.'

'Anna Knight? Course I know you. D'you think I haven't read the local paper with these stories about Llew Madden? Your name's been on every one of them. You're a reporter.'

'Yes, but—'

'You think I killed him too, don't you? That's why you're here.'

'I genuinely don't know who killed him, Penny.'

She glanced at me suspiciously, then sank down on to a chair and started ripping the label off the bleach bottle. 'I wanted him wiped from the face of the earth. I wanted him blasted out of existence. I wanted him scoured out and flushed down the sewers like the germ he was. But I didn't kill him.'

'She's right,' interposed Janette swiftly. 'I told the police. That day they say he was murdered, the Thursday, Penny was right here with me. In fact we never left the house from Wednesday to Friday. We're doing a bit of decorating upstairs, see – I took the Thursday off and we stripped the paper off one of the back bedrooms, didn't we? And then we had a night in watching telly, just us and the kids.'

'Did the police believe you?' I asked.

'I dunno,' said Janette huffily. 'Makes no difference if they did or not, it's the truth. I wish it wasn't, in a way – I wish Penny had someone else who could back her up. In my line of trade, well, I'm what's called an unreliable witness. But I'm the only one she's got so they'll have to make the best of it.'

'You're the best,' comforted Penny quietly, touching her hand.

'Yeah, well, someone's got to look after you. You didn't do yourself any favours, following him around like you did.'

'I just wanted him to see me. To remind him about Natalie. So he'd never forget.'

'All right, but on top of that sending those letters. Oh, girl, talk about asking for trouble.'

'What letters?' I asked.

'Oh, she only sent him whole notepads of the stuff, like she just spouted now, about wanting him – what was it? – wiped up and flushed down the lavvy?'

'The sewers,' smiled Penny.

'Same thing.'

I studied Penny. Janette's warmth seemed to thaw her out, but I guessed it would take very little from me to freeze her up again. I'd better take advantage while I could.

'Anyway,' continued Janette, 'nothing was more likely to bring the boys in blue sniffing round as soon as he coughed it. Penny said she wanted him dead, and he was dead. What more did they need? They couldn't scrape up enough to charge her with but they're working on it.'

A rap at the front door broke into our talk. 'Oh Lord,' said Janette, rolling her eyes. 'That'll be my twelve o'clock and I haven't even put my face on.'

'You go and get ready,' said Penny. 'I'll show him into the front room.'

'You are a love. Give him a whisky if he wants one. He's not one of the nutters.'

Janette ran upstairs and I nursed my tea until Penny came back. 'She seems to be a good friend to you, Penny,' I said, hoping to keep the embers glowing in Janette's absence.

It seemed to work – Penny's pinched face softened as she washed the tea mugs: 'She was there when I needed her,' she said quietly. 'Like a guardian angel.'

'I really do have a message for you, from Mark,' I said. 'Don't you want to hear it?'

She shrugged, and so I told her. I thought her eyes winced when I mentioned Fox Hill, and that Mark still loved her, but she quickly suppressed it.

'I can't go back,' she said, wringing a tea-towel with controlled anguish. 'Don't you see, every time I look at him I see Natalie, she was so like him, everything about him reminds me of her. I wanted him to come with me when I moved up here, but he wouldn't, and that practically broke me apart. Now at last Llew Madden's gone and I'm making a new life for myself. I didn't think I could. I love Janette, I love the girls, and I think they love me. They need me. Mark doesn't.'

'Then do him a favour, Penny. Tell him, write to him, ring him – anything – but let him know.'

She nodded, 'I suppose you're right. To be honest when I left him I blocked him out, I lost all feelings except for hating Llew Madden. Janette stuck by me. She's a good woman, you know.'

'I know,' I smiled.

'You going to put all this in the paper?'

I sighed: 'I'm not out to accuse you, Penny, or anybody else, that's for the police to decide. What would you want me to do?'

'Yes, print it. Tell them about Natalie, people need to know. Tell them he damn near destroyed my life as well as hers. I admit I sent those letters, but I didn't kill him. Promise me you'll put that in.'

'Of course,' I said, rapidly pulling out a pad to make notes.

'I know you've a job to do,' continued Penny. 'I got used to you newpaper people with all the fuss after Natalie died, and then the court appearances and argy-bargy with Madden. But . . .' she tailed off, forehead creased with worry.

'What's bothering you, Penny?'

'Janette and the girls, I'm bringing all this aggravation on them – police coming round, now a reporter, I s'pose there'll be more where you came from. They don't deserve—'

'I've no intention of giving away your address, and I wouldn't dream of getting Janette into trouble.'

She did not look convinced, and I heard a dirty laugh as Janette popped her head round the door before going in to her client: 'Don't worry, love, Janette's quite capable of getting into her own trouble. And getting out of it. You live and learn. Anyway 'bye love. Per'aps we'll be seeing you again some time?'

Perhaps they would.

Seven

I could readily imagine Ellis sharpening his clichés for the kill: 'Bad Penny Turned up to Haunt Mad World Boss'. No, that was unfair, he would not call her bad just for the sake of a catchy headline. He'd just wish her behind bars so that he could.

I wrote the story as factually and unsensationally as I could, refusing to tart it up to satisfy his demands for 'colour'. I missed out Janette entirely, stating only that Penny was living in a bedsit in Northport, and I gave prominence to her denial of guilt. But as I unravelled the tale of the dead child, the agonised mother, the legal battle, the marriage break-down, the tailing of Madden, the hate-mail – well, it needed more colour like a lorryload of Dulux.

Added to that, we had broken the story – we were able to make money by selling it to the tabloids: Ellis's tip-off had hit pay-dirt, and he was smug as a Cheshire cat. When my copy reached his computer he summoned me to bask in the glow of his screen, as if to say, 'This is my beloved tip-off, in which I am well pleased.'

I did not set too much store by this, knowing his blessings could just as easily turn to curses, but for the moment I was the Chosen One, and I was rewarded with the ceremonial dishing out of a perk. Perks are not ten-a-penny for most reporters, whatever the popular impression of us as a bunch of freeloaders may be. The features editor normally reserved restaurant reviewing for himself, but he was off sick with food poisoning, and so the onerous task was bequeathed to me.

I was delighted – a dinner for two at the Cadillac Café awaited my pleasure, all on expenses, no questions asked. It was an upcoming restaurant purveying Californian food and wines of impeccable refinement. And to show both sides of American culture it also boasted a bar shaped like a pink Cadillac with Mickey Mouse at the wheel. Who could I ask to be my guest the following night but Matt Whittaker?

'I'd love to,' he said, and then balked.

'Do I detect a "But" coming on?'

'I'm sorry, Anna, there's nothing I can do about it. I'm personnel manager and as long as there's personnel here I'll manage it. I have to be entertained by a pensions executive who will no doubt be scintillating about deferment revaluations and additional lump sums. He's an additional lump I wouldn't wish on anybody. Could we make it another night?'

'Sorry, the deadline decrees this date only.'

'Well, may I decree a date with you later in the week?'

He might, he did, and I rang off.

Who else could I invite? Shelley needed cheering up – Lord knows, she had bought me dinners enough when she was Queen of Comedy, Mistress of Mirth, First Lady of Laughter, as the compere's patter went. Now the patter had gone and the ex-mistress of mirth needed jollying along.

Even in eclipse, however, Shelley could still make heads turn in a restaurant. Her hair was blonde as any bottle could make it, her limbs brown as any tanning lamp could toast. With her sparkler earrings and gym-honed body sheathed in a red dazzler of a dress, she still knew how to put on a show. I was proud of her, yes I was. Despite her premature departure from school, despite her insistence on appearing in trashy shows and flashy nightclubs, and her deliberate deafness to my sensible warnings, she had made a success of being a comedian, short-lived though it was, and I had to hand it to her.

The problem had been, she was too cruel with her jibes – no good-natured guffaws greeted her jokes, no belly-laughs reverberated, no tears streamed down aching cheeks. She had played on the humour of embarrassment: she picked on men's failings, and men soon tire of being reminded of these. She made fools of them, and women soon tire of being told they married fools. For a time it worked, the sexual sparring provoked an outbreak of shock and titillation. Then it wilted like the male organs she had mocked for lack of staying power. Ironic, really.

She toyed with a leaf of lollo rosso and drank yet another glass of Napa Valley's finest.

'Ma, do you think I'm like my father?'

'You must be, you didn't get that noble nose from me. I'm strictly peasant stock.'

'I don't mean in looks.'

'You're stubborn enough – he could have won prizes in the mule of the year show.'

'I mean am I like him – a failure?'

I couldn't speak – answers blocked my throat. What should I say? 'He wasn't a failure'? – an untruth by most standards. 'He was a wonderful rumbustious, wild-hearted man, but if I'd never met him I'd have saved myself a lot of grief'? – a truth that would wish her out of existence. I swallowed. She wasn't really talking about him or me, she was talking about herself.

'It's not a life sentence, Shelley,' I replied gently.

'It was for him.'

'That's because he wouldn't lift his eyes off the floor long enough to look through the prison bars. Let's face it, he was mostly too pickled.'

She took another drink: 'I can understand him, you know? That's what frightens me.'

I had to jerk her out of it. This was told-you-so time, and let the cowboy boots fall where they may.

'Look, I know your heart was always set on the stage, but if you hadn't been so impatient, if you'd gone to acting school as I wanted, you'd have a training to fall back on now. It'd make you more flexible, more marketable. Do you see? It's not too late, love, you have talent, they'd still take you.'

'Oh God, Ma.' The wineglass went down on the table with a splash. 'I don't need that argument all over again. I didn't want to go to drama school because it's all so arty-farty. Dad tried to be an Artist, with a capital A, and look what it did to him. Screwed him up so tight the bottle broke.'

'He wrote novels, he didn't act.'

'Correction: he wrote a novel, one outpouring of his soul that got published, and the rest were rejected for the scrap heap. When the cheers stopped for his one book what good did art do him? It never fed us – you did that – it never clothed us either. All art did was send him spinning into the bar, saying cheers to himself when no one else would.'

'That wasn't art's fault. Your father's trouble was he was too thin-skinned: one rejection made him bitter and two made him despair. After that he gave up altogether. Rejection's not a monopoly of the art world though, Shelley, you can get bitter in a working men's club when your jokes are thrown back in your face.'

She shoved her plate away, sulky. That charge hit home. Fighting talk was the way through to my material girl.

'Shelley, the lesson your father never learnt is you don't let the bastards grind you down. You haven't given up – look at you – even when you're low, no-one but me would know it. You're a born actress. Think of it – no jokes to make up, only lines to learn, other people to share the burden. Course, you probably wouldn't earn as much money. Sometimes you wouldn't earn any.'

She laughed scornfully. 'So what's new? I haven't been earning any for the past six months, and my bank manager won't let me forget it.'

She bit her lip, and slowly a dawn of enlightenment began to break through: 'I've been doing it the hard way, haven't I? A one-woman oompah band, that's me, trying to write with one hand, play a tune with the other and bang the big bass drum.'

'At last, I think she's got it. Boom boom.'

I laughed, she did too, and the tension was broken. 'Don't put your daughter on the stage, Mrs Worthington,' the old song echoed worryingly in my mind. At least I had a daughter. Penny Worthington didn't. What had I to worry about?

We dawdled long over mountainous desserts, and it was after midnight when I paid the bill, careful to pocket the receipt. As a waiter helped Shelley into her coat I noticed a man at the back of the restaurant look up. I thought no more about it – the phenomenon of men staring was common in Shelley's company.

We emerged into the night air. It was crisp, refreshing, and we decided to walk to the taxi-rank to clear the fug from our brains. As we rounded the end of the street I saw, out of the corner of my eye, two figures about a hundred yards behind us, coming in our direction. A flicker of danger crossed my mind.

'Let's cross over,' I said to Shelley.

We did, and they did too.

'Let's cross back.'

'What's wrong with you, Ma? You're supposed to follow the white line to show you're not drunk, not keep zigzagging over it.'

'Those men are after us.'

'What? Oh, I see.'

It was late, the street was deserted, the resort slumbering in its winter woollies. Their footsteps rang on the pavement, gaining on us. There was no doubt about it, we were being tailed.

'Go away,' I called, trailing the words over my shoulder. They took no notice. I clutched my handbag tight and began to look for cover. It was no use banging on a door: this part of town was all shops and offices, closed down for the night.

Shelley turned round: 'Listen, I don't know what you think you're playing at, but stop hassling us.'

It had no effect. A male voice came back: 'I'm not playing. Stop, I want a word with you.'

'Yes, and I'll have a word with you, prickbrain!'

'Shelley!' I hissed, alarmed.

'Well, what would you call them?'

'Bigger than us. Come on, it's fight or flight time. Let's run, the taxis are only round the next block.'

But there were none on the rank. 'There's a phone-box on the corner, ring the police,' I panted, out of breath.

Shelley, her young lungs stronger than mine, grabbed my arm and pulled me in her wake, but the footsteps were swiftly catching up. My heel caught in a crack in the pavement and I twisted my ankle. Shelley was propelled onwards by sheer momentum. She stopped, but before she could help, I felt the weight of a male hand on my shoulder.

'Don't you touch my mother, you bastards!' yelled Shelley, giving an ear-rending scream as she leapt on my assailant, kicking him in the groin, almost pulling his arm out of its socket, and grappling him face down on to the ground.

I readied myself to intervene before his companion could attack. But he was standing, stunned as I was, absolutely immobile.

'Well I must say, you asked for that,' he berated the prone figure. Then he turned to me, 'I'm most terribly sorry – I told him we were frightening you, but he wouldn't listen.'

'I only wanted to talk,' came the muffled voice on the pavement. 'I couldn't remember your bloody name.'

Shelley laughed: 'Remember it now, dumbnuts? Or do I have to beat it into you?'

His companion stepped forward to extract him from her clutches. 'Come on, we've done enough harm for one night. We've had far too much wine for our own good. It's just, when he caught sight of you leaving the restaurant, he would follow you. He's not usually such an idiot, are you, Guy?'

The prone figure rolled over, and Guy Madden's perfect features, marred by a fast-rising bruise on his cheek, gazed up at me. 'Don't call me an idiot,' his voice was slurred, but the anger was no less threatening. Then he creased up in pain.

'Come on, Guy, let's go home.'

'No, just – you – ' his attention was directed at me. 'You're the reporter? You rang my father? He told me – aaagh – he's not well, he couldn't remember what you said. About Futures. Are they gunning for us?'

'I – I don't know. You tell me.'

'I can't. Llew kept too many secrets.'

'Rosie knows about it.'

'She's gone off sick – won't answer my calls.'

'The police then?'

'Hah!' he gave a hollow laugh. 'Get as much out of them as milk from a bull. But I – oww – those Futures bastards! Damned if I'm – going to let this go.'

'Gu-y-y,' his companion was wheedling now. 'You're going to have to let it go for now. Horizontal on the pavement is not the place to hold a conversation. These ladies are cold and we've frightened the life out of them. The least we can do is leave them alone.'

A black taxi came trundling down the street, and he hailed it, opening the door for us, then passing the driver a banknote.

'Have this one on me, ladies. Oh, by the way,' he addressed me, 'what is your name?'

'Anna Knight.'

'Please don't think too badly of him, Anna, he's had a hell of a lot on his plate recently.'

'He's not the only one,' muttered Shelley, slamming the door.

Eight

'Anna, I'm at my wits' end. Penny's gone.' The smoke-rough voice of Janette was on the phone, with a pub's lunchtime noise in the background.

'Gone? Back to her husband, you mean?'

'No, that was the first place I thought of. She's disappeared. Can you meet me at the Clifton Arms in town? That's where I'm ringing from. I daren't even use the phone at home.'

I had arranged to meet Matt for lunch, but she sounded so distraught I put him off and made for the pub. I saw Janette's short, dark frizz hunched over a corner table. She was alert, on guard, an empty glass in her hand. I asked if she wanted a refill. 'Just an orange juice please, love,' she said. 'I need to keep on my toes right now.'

I came back with the drinks and she lit a cigarette, expelling smoke as she talked: 'I can trust you, can't I? You didn't put me in the paper and you could've done, I appreciate that. Thanks.'

'No problem.'

'You see, I believed Penny was innocent, or I wouldn't've done it.'

'Done what?'

'Given her an alibi.'

'You mean it wasn't true?'

'Oh yes it was true – partly.' She glanced round, edgy.

'Come on, Janette, if you want my help you're going to have to tell me the full story.'

'I mean, I did take the day off and we did strip the back bedroom, that's how I remember it so well – it was a nice break. But . . .'

'Penny wasn't with you all the time, is that what you mean?'

She nodded. 'I remember it because he came to pick her up at night, and that was unusual.'

'He?'

'Fella she's been seeing – he only usually came during the day. Well, love,' she winked a mascara-laden eye, 'I may not be Mastermind but I do know fellas. Daytime matches mean only one thing – he's playing away.'

'Married, you mean?'

'As both ends of a pantomime donkey. Oh, she never said 'owt about it, but I knew. Anyway, when Llew Madden's murder came out all over the papers, I knew something else, there'd be coppers crawling up our drainpipes the way she'd been carrying on – I told you.'

'Following him round you mean, and the letters?'

She nodded, and drained her drink as if parched: 'Penny went down on her hands and knees for me to say she never went out the day Madden died. Said she didn't want this fella dragged in. I told her she was off her head, no man's worth being banged up for, specially not to save his face. She wouldn't listen, so I had to protect her from herself.'

'You lied to the police.'

She laughed and shrugged. 'I'm not short of practice. Goes with the job. I don't owe them no favours.'

'No, I suppose not.'

'But you owe me one. You wouldn't've got your story if I hadn't let you in the house.'

'I'm aware of that, Janette, that's why I'm here.'

'Right, anyway when you'd gone Penny seemed to go to pieces. Went to her room, I couldn't tempt her to eat or nothing, she was just getting more and more wound up. I thought she was working herself up to tell the cops the truth, so I tried to egg her on. Then yesterday the phone rang. I answered it. It was her fella, I could tell his voice, but she wouldn't speak to him, she was shaking by this time. I begged her to tell me what was going on, but she said it was best I didn't know. And then she went.'

'How?'

'What d'you mean how? Packed her bags and left.'

'No explanation, no note?'

'Nothing. Just said she was sorry and rushed out the door, tears streaming down her face. Well, I couldn't run after her, I was half-undressed with a bloke screaming he wasn't getting his money's worth.'

'Do you know the man's name?'

She shook her head: 'Like I said, awaydays – they're called darling or Mr Smith or bastard – they don't throw proper names around to pin 'em down. She just called him "my friend", I never even saw his face. All I saw was the back of his head once. I was coming downstairs and they were going out the door – he had a funny kind of bald patch, more of a hole in his hair, like a monk's . . . you know?'

'Tonsure.'

'That's it, and he was wearing a sheepskin jacket that'd seen better times. It had a big rip on the shoulder and it looked too tight for him – reminded me of a teddy with the stuffing hanging out. I remember thinking, well love, I hope he's a better prospect from the front 'cos he don't look too good retreating.'

'So . . .' I pondered, 'have you told the police anything about this?'

'I can't, Anna, I'm up to my neck in it already. I lied

to 'em – and coppers don't like lying, they're funny like that. I've my business to think of, my girls to support.'

'They'd shut you down, you mean, if they found out?'

'For starters. They're only being soft now because they think I'm co-operating. Look, I never have fellas in the house when my kids're there, but that wouldn't make no difference if they were really out to get me. I don't want to lose my kids, Anna, it'd kill me. I have to tread careful, you see what I mean?'

I sighed. 'I understand that, but you'll only get yourself in deeper trouble not telling them, Janette, you're better coming clean now, because they'll probably find out eventually – don't you see that?'

She tensed: 'I'm not going to the law and that's final – I promised Penny I wouldn't, and I don't rat on my friends. Anyway, if they do find out I'll tell 'em I got the days muddled up.' Then her eyes narrowed. 'You're bloody well going to grass on me, aren't you? I should've known I couldn't trust you. Scum like me aren't worth helping, that's what you think, isn't it?'

She rose to go, and I grabbed her arm: 'No – no – please, Janette. I won't grass, you're never scum, please don't walk out. I want to help. Do the police at least know Penny's gone?'

She looked at me warily. I gazed back with what I hoped was the utmost sincerity, and it appeared to work. She sat down heavily: 'They're gonna find out soon enough. They came yapping at my door this morning, asking for her. I made an excuse, said she'd gone to Manchester, shopping. But I can't keep wriggling her off the hook. I'll have to tell 'em she never came home.'

'She might, though, she might have changed her mind and come home even now.'

Janette gave a despairing look: 'No . . . I don't think so, not the way she left. She took everything. I just had the feeling she wanted to disappear, take herself and all her belongings away from me, because she thought it was dragging me and the girls into more and more bother.'

Then she gripped my hand: 'Help bring Penny back, please Anna, help me make her go to the cops and clear up this whole mess. That poor girl, after what she's been through, my heart breaks every time I think of her.'

'I'll do what I can, Janette, but I can't promise miracles. I can't just take time off and look for her, but I'll ring the hospitals, the Salvation Army and such.'

'I've thought about what you could do,' she said with sudden animation, 'that's why I asked you here. I thought you could put a story in the papers, say I've been mugged or something, all my money stolen. If she read it she might think I've really been hurt and come back.'

'But it wouldn't be true.'

'Oh, and I s'pose everything's true that goes in the papers is it?' she sniffed. 'I could get someone to do it, you know, hide my money, rough me up a bit, make it look real. I have friends who wouldn't ask questions. I told you Anna, I'm at my wits' end.'

'Let's leave it for now, all right? I'll try and track her down every way I know before we have to resort to that . . . Listen, Janette, I have to ask, do you think she might've gone into hiding because she killed Llew?'

She didn't answer. 'I just want her back where I can look after her. She's not safe on her own, not safe.'

A man, bearing a burning bush, stood outside the office on my return. On closer inspection, the bush turned out to be a profusion of garish red roses, and the man behind it, Guy Madden. I'd had time to stoke up a fair steam of resentment over what he'd done to Shelley and me, and I was not going to let him off lightly.

'I came to see you,' he said (straight in, no effusive greeting such as 'Hello'). 'Your colleague told me you were out for half an hour, so I said I'd wait.'

'My colleague shouldn't have been so honest,' I replied. 'After last night I'm out to you all day, every day.'

'There's no need to take that attitude, Anna.'

'No? When you never even said you were sorry? You left all the apologies to your friend.'

'He's rather good at apologies. I'm not, I'm afraid. Look, take the flowers. They're by way of a peace offering. I need to talk to you.'

'I guessed so. If you didn't you wouldn't be here, with or without roses. If you think I'm dumb enough to tell you all I know in exchange for a bunch of overblown floribunda then you're very much mistaken. You terrified us. We thought you were muggers or maniacs.'

'I know.' He put a hand up: 'I concede it was a stupid thing to do. But I came off the worse for it – look at me.' He touched his grazed, purpled cheekbone. 'I can still hardly sit down and I've got a stinking hangover.'

I stood silent and cold, refusing to offer him pity.

'In that case,' he retorted, 'if you're too hard-faced to forgive a man for getting rat-arsed when his brother's been murdered, then I'm obviously wasting my time.'

The banked anger flashed out as it had at the funeral. He threw down the flowers and turned on his heel. 'I know something the police haven't told you,' he taunted over his shoulder. 'I had hoped we could exchange information. I was wrong.'

Curse the man. Waving that dangler in the air, knowing I couldn't help but bite. It was a scene played a thousand times on TV soaps: a couple argue, one stalks off and the sucker begs the stalker to return.

'Wait!'

Yes, the magic word he had wanted was out of my mouth before I could stop it. And he wouldn't wait, he darn well wouldn't. He just laughed and kept on walking away.

Look children, look at Anna run, fast as her feet can carry her, to see what nice sweeties the man might have. He was easing his undercarriage delicately into the driving seat when I caught up with him. This slight performance made me take notice of his car. It was a daffodil-yellow Jaguar E-type, its sinuous lines so perfectly preserved and polished I could have knelt down and worshipped the road it stood on. All right, all you style snobs, a naff car in a naff colour, but when you see one up close, the earth moves, it's like sex on wheels.

'You like it?' he asked, his voice inviting now. 'Want a ride round the block?'

Oh foolish girl, she glided into the passenger seat, drawn by his siren song. The horsepower thundered into life and we were off – not just round the block, but on to the dual carriageway out of town and joining the motorway.

'Guy! I cannot do this. I have work to do.'

The Jaguar roared. Guy was silent.

'Where are you taking me? Stop this at once.'

Silly, silly girl. 'She was last seen, Chief Inspector, getting into the car of a strange man outside the office. No, no one's seen her since then.'

Guy laughed at last. He was good at that. Laughing so you knew he did not mean it. A substitute for those apologies he was bad at. I had well and truly been taken for a ride.

'Sorry,' he said. Did I hear right? Guy Madden, sorry? 'I got carried away. This car has that effect on me, you see, still new to me. I can hardly believe it's mine.'

'New or not, Guy, turn round at the next opportunity or I'll slit its precious seats with my nail-file.'

I reached in my bag and held up the said instrument, a long, sharply pointed, diamond-hard number, deliberately acquired for such emergencies.

'Ssss – nasty. We'll have to do what the lady says, babe.'

Why did he have this knack of making me feel small? He did turn round, and on the way back I tackled him about the police. What had they withheld from me? He pinched the bridge of his nose as if in pain: 'Can we discuss it tomorrow,

Anna? To tell you the truth, I really am feeling lousy. Come to my office.'

'Your office? At the aircraft plant?'

'No, no, at Mad Mad World. I've taken over Llew's old desk. In fact I'm rather sliding into his shoes. This little beauty was Llew's too,' he patted the steering-wheel. 'The Bible said thou shalt not covet thy neighbour's ass, but it said nothing about coveting thy brother's E-type. I would have died for it from the moment he brought it home.'

'But what about ... I mean, surely you can't just take it?'

'He left it to me – he knew how much it meant to me. I used to tell him he shouldn't keep it locked away – an animal like this needs to be driven, daily, to display its full power. I used to moon over it like a frustrated lover – built in 1967, a 4.2-litre, six-cylinder engine, the shape streamlined in a wind tunnel, designed to race at Le Mans. When the solicitor read the will I was utterly overwhelmed.'

The thought of Guy being overwhelmed stretched my credulity. He was an egotistical, spoiled brat too used to getting his own way.

But if I wanted the boy racer's goods it looked as though I would have to trade mine. I did not say I would meet him the following day, I merely took his phone number and said I'd get back to him. I felt a vicious pleasure at keeping him on hold. I was not a machine, like his car or his aircraft, conditioned to obey his every wish.

Call me a slow learner if you will, but the playground law had been dinned into me at last. Strange men are dangerous, Anna. 'Just say No.'

Back at my desk, bruised floribunda arranged in a jar, my first task was to ring Jo Daniels in Brighton. I told her of Penny's disappearance and asked Jo to contact me the minute she surfaced down there.

I was sure Penny would not wander for long. She needed support, she was still too frail to cope on her own, of that I felt certain. She would probably go to familiar surroundings – maybe she'd turn up at a guest-house in Brighton, or the home of a relative, even Mark. When I'd finished telling Jo all this, she just said one word: 'Snap!'

'What?'

'I have a missing person for you too.'

'What – relevant to the Llew Madden case?'

'Relevant? You could even say in bed with him for a long while.'

'A lover?'

'I doubt it somehow. His name's Rodney Zale, Llew's one-time sleeping partner, businesswise.'

'I've never heard of him.'

'Then I'll tell you a salutary story. As a young man Rodney Zale made a mint out of a second-hand car business, then he sold up to live a life of leisure. But after a few years leisure got a bit boring, so when Llew came along looking for backers for his amusement park, Rodney took a fancy to the idea and came up with the goods. He didn't do much, in fact he preferred to stay in the background, but as the park grew successful, he backed Llew to the hilt. Then, one day, a little girl came to celebrate her seventh birthday, she tumbled off a ride, and people began to think the park was unsafe. So Llew spent lots and lots of money proving otherwise, but the gloss had gone off the park, and people still stayed away. And one day it came to pass that the park failed to pay its bills, the bailiffs were at the door and the big bad wolf of a receiver came to gobble up all their worldly goods.'

'Is that when Llew came back to Northport?'

'Exactly. Llew was fine and dandy – his family rescued him, as he knew they would, Llew was in clover. But Rodney Zale was a ruined and bitter man. He sat and brooded in his rented hovel, and he blamed Llew for putting him there.'

'How long's he been missing?'

'Since just before Llew died. He was in the habit of going off two or three days at a time, so his landlord didn't think anything of it until he got behind with his rent. But when the flat was opened, Zale'd done a moonlight, and no one's seen him since.'

'What do the police say?'

'They'd like to speak to him in connection with their inquiries.'

'I'll bet.'

'Listen, I'll fax you the full story if you like.'

'Great. Meanwhile, can I ask you a favour? Hang fire on publicising Penny's disappearance until it's official. I don't want to get my contact in trouble. It shouldn't take long. I'll get back to you either way first thing in the morning.'

'Mum's the word.'

I guessed it was. Janette's mothering instinct for Penny had got her into this mess, and mother-love stopped her getting out of it by coming clean with the police. A guardian angel, Penny had called her. But she was no saint, just a mum who'd sold her body but not her soul.

Would I sell my soul to Guy Madden tomorrow? Well, it may be a bit shop soiled, but I'm sort of attached to it. Guy Madden had the look of a man who ate unwary souls for breakfast – I'd see him choke before he had mine.

Nine

M y persona was distinctly non grata with the police. Chief Inspector Alex Anderson himself came out of his office to rebuke me when I called at the police station next day. I was to blame for scaring off Penny, spiriting away their prime suspect.

'Didn't you think of what harm you were doing?' he ranted. 'The girl's nervous as a rabbit, she was bound to take off.'

'Why?'

'Why, Miss Trusting Soul? Because she's hiding something. I suspected it all along, that's why I left her alone, gave her a bit of rope.'

'What, to hang herself with?'

'Aye, and she would have done if you hadn't interfered.'

'Anyway, what d'you mean, hiding something?' I asked innocently.

'Her alibi's been blown. Someone came forward, said he'd seen her near Llew Madden's house.'

'She often watched his movements though, didn't she?'

'Yes, but come on – she was seen there the night we believe he died.'

'On her own?'

'Yes, on her own – why?'

'Oh, I just wondered,' I mumbled. Evidently they had not discovered the existence of her secret lover. 'How did this person identify her?'

'Saw her photo in your paper . . . all right, so you did do us some good. But you shouldn't've tackled her face to face.'

'It wasn't me that lost her.'

'Hmph.'

His voice betrayed lost patience. Some lowly DC had obviously been blasted from his office carpet for that slip-up.

I pressed home my advantage: 'Is there something you've not been telling us, Chief Inspector, something about Llew's death? You can keep it off the record if you want to. You know I've always respected that in the past.'

'You've been told all I want to tell you, and what I don't you'll probably go hunting for yourself. I know there's not much I can do about that until we press charges, but I warn you, Miss Knight, I do not look kindly on journalists who interfere with our investigations, because ultimately you interfere with justice. Do I make myself clear?'

He did. It was clear that I'd burned my boats as far as confidential briefings were concerned. The chief inspector was determined to leave me stranded on the shore.

I had asked the question hoping I would not have to deal with Guy Madden, but now I had little choice.

I drove away from the police station and on to the promenade, turning in the direction of Mad Mad World. Low clouds over the sea threatened rain. The tide was in, thrashing over the sea wall. A grey, chill day, with a squally wind, not the best time to go jogging, but someone was pounding along the wide asphalt separating the road from the sea. Her back was toward me, blonde pony-tail lashing from side to side with each step. Was it? Could my daughter be out in this weather – numbing cold, scything wind, and incipient rain ready to soak her to the skin at any minute? She'd catch her death.

She was on the opposite side to me as I drew level with her. Yes, it was Shelley, running as if her life depended on it instead of just a shapely thigh. I honked my horn, intending to pull over and give her a lift as soon as the traffic was clear. But she kept on, as if she did not hear me. I tried winding down my window to shout, but the wind whipped my voice away.

Cursing my thoughtless child, I crossed into the other lane and adopted the behaviour of a kerb-crawler, earning honks and flashes from cars going in the other direction.

Surely she must hear or see such a commotion? But no – run, rabbit, run – blind and deaf to all entreaty. Well, if she insisted on pursuing strength, beauty and pneumonia, who was I to argue? Stubborn she was born, and stubborn she remained.

It was then, when I was about to turn back onto my appointed route, that at last she looked towards the road, as if waking from a trance. Still running, looking for the source of the disturbance, she ran too close to the railings, failing to notice the approach of an enormous wave. It was the time of the highest tides of the year, and the wave crashed all its Irish Sea rage over the rail, flooding the promenade, knocking her off-balance. She slipped, fell and, before she could recover, another wave had deluged her, dragging her under a chain across a beach-ramp, and pulling her down into its maw.

In the same instant I was out of the car and dashing for the rail. When I reached it she was thrashing in the water, being rolled back and forth in the force.

'Shelley!' I screamed, unhooking the chain and clipping one end of it to my belt. Water filled my boots – all right, Shelley's boots – as I slithered to try to reach her, the waves tossing her up and dragging her back in the dreaded undertow. Her eyes were terrorised. I shouted again.

'Shelley! Grab my arm!' She tried, our fingers touched, and she slid away, pulled back in the torrent.

'Again!' I called, and someone else, a man, on the ledge above me, shouted down to her, 'Catch this!'

A lifebelt flew out towards her, its rope unfurling behind. It hit her square on the chest, and she looped her arm through it. He pulled, I held out my hand, she grabbed it, and between us we heaved her, gasping all three, up the ramp and on to level ground.

She coughed, racked into spasm, bringing up half a lungful of sea water, which was half a lung too much for me. I cried, deep, shuddering sobs that left me weak.

The man turned out to be a bank manager, who belied the nature of his calling by being kindly and compassionate. He wrapped us up in his car rugs and drove us to hospital, where Shelley was examined and X-rayed while I shivered under a blanket and drank a gallon of tea. Finally Shelley was declared none the worse for her ordeal, all bones present and correct, but as with all concussed bodies they wanted to keep her in overnight just in case.

I approached her bed after she'd been cranked upside down and thumped by a physio to clear her passages of any remaining brine. She looked a wreck.

'You'll never make a mermaid,' I remarked.

She gave a wan smile: 'Thanks, Ma.'

'Don't mention it.'

'No, I mean really, thanks for dragging me out. I thought I wanted to . . .'

'What?'

'For a minute, when I was running, I thought I wanted to run straight into the sea and never come out.'

'Shelley! For God's sake.'

'But when I was in there, with the noise and the cold and the water up my nose and in my mouth, I couldn't take it. I wanted to live, I knew I wanted to live.'

'Trust you to nearly die finding that out. You always were such a drama queen.'

But I was wrong, she was not overacting, not now. Bereft of her make-up and artifice, she presented her naked face to me, and it was worn out.

'Shelley what's wrong? I thought we sorted you out the other night. You came out fighting – you threw a man to the floor.'

'I didn't want to burden you with it, it's not fair.'

'There's no such thing as fair with your own flesh and blood. That's what we're here for, to pick up each other's pieces when no one else will.'

I smoothed a strand of her limp hair and asked, 'What's at the root of this, Shelley?'

'I've got myself into trouble,' she said softly.

'What kind?'

'Money . . . what other kind is there? Look, the mortgage was a huge mistake. I bought the apartment at the peak of the market, I thought it was an investment, I thought I'd be earning tons enough to meet the payments. But then the work fell away, the property market slumped, and I couldn't sell the apartment for love or trading stamps. I've been falling behind with the payments for months, I've tried talking to the bank, I've sold everything I can, I've taken out loans and only got myself into a worse state. And the letters kept coming, getting more and more threatening, until this morning . . .'

'Repossession?'

'I have to be out in a week.'

'How much do you owe?'

She told me a sum that made me wilt.

'I wish you'd told me earlier, Shelley, I really do.'

'It didn't seem fair. I should've saved my money when I had it instead of squandering it on parties and pictures and hangers-on.'

She had a point there.

'It just seemed,' she went on, 'that everything I'd touched turned to ashes. I know you did your best to restore the old ego the other night, Ma, and it worked for a few hours. But I came crashing down again soon enough. My career at a dead end, up to my ears in debt. That letter this morning was the last straw, I just put on my running shoes and ran.'

I weighed the possibilities. My flat was tiny – just a bedroom, bathroom and living-room cum kitchen – which was a boon to me after living for years in a draughty old Victorian monstrosity, but too small to accommodate a prodigal daughter.

Besides, if Shelley lost her apartment she really would have lost everything she'd ever worked for.

'I'll give you some cash to hold them at bay until you can sell, and then I'll pay off whatever you still owe,' I said firmly. 'You might have to live with two sticks of furniture and a Calor-gas fire, but better that than a furnished dive with an extortionate rent.'

'No, Ma, I couldn't.'

'You could and you will. You know I made a profit out of the old house. I was saving it for a round-the-world trip but the world can go round without me for a while longer. If it makes you feel any better we'll make it an interest-free loan – all right? You can get a grant or a loan to go to drama school, then pay me back when you start earning wages, and not before.'

She gave a weak grin: 'You're going to get your way on that come hell or high water, aren't you?'

'For goodness sake don't mention those – I've had hell and high water up to here, I'm so sick of hell and high water, I've a good mind to call the physio back to thump those words out of you.'

She was giggling by now, but she looked tired.

'I'd better go,' I said. 'Leave you to sleep without worrying your pretty little head over quite a lot. I . . . ummm . . .' I looked down at my feet, 'I'm afraid your cowboy boots took a salt bath. Don't worry, I'll dry them out and polish them up. It'll add character.'

'Keep them, Ma, I know you like them.'

'Really?' I kissed her, inordinately pleased.

I took a taxi home, changed the boots and my damp clothes and went to rescue my car – still parked unlocked on the seafront. I thanked the goddess of maidens in distress and continued my interrupted journey to Mad Mad World.

But as I drove, I considered again my gesture to Shelley. My nest egg would hold off the bailiffs, and I could continue to subsidise her from my wages for the time being. But if no grants were forthcoming and I had to support Shelley through drama school, we'd both be in trouble.

It had rained by now, and stopped, though the roads were still very wet. An overtaking van sploshed filthy spray on to my car, and I raised my voice in solitary anger, like you do. But my words trailed away as I saw, through my smeared windscreen, an arresting sight in the other lane.

Driving towards me was a beat-up orange Fiesta with one yellow wing. Penny's car, could it be Penny? It passed. I had as much chance of seeing the driver as seeing a miner when the pit-lights went out. There was nothing for it but to turn round and put Guy Madden on hold once more.

Ten

Two cars had interposed themselves between me and my target by the time I'd found a side street, executed a wobbly reverse and taken up hot pursuit.

The orange Fiesta, its cracked indicator winking, turned off the promenade up a shopping street. I followed suit, knowing that at the top of the street was a set of traffic lights, invariably on red, where I could draw up alongside.

But the patron saint of green lights was with them and not with me. The signal turned to amber as I approached and I dithered – should I shoot through or not? At the last minute cowardice became the better part of valour and I stood on the brakes, to the wrath and hoots of the driver behind.

The orange Fiesta with the yellow wing carried on over the crest of the hill and could be seen no more. By the time the signal changed and I charged over the hill it was a speck in the distance, but old never-say-die Anna would not give up.

'Excuse me,' I muttered under my breath to fellow drivers as I dodged in and out of my lane, overtaking, pulling back, veering out, 'Terribly sorry, I don't normally drive like this.'

Apologies notwithstanding, I drove like a sales rep in the latest fleet model, late for my next appointment and ruthless as hell. I cut in front of pensioners tootling at a snail's pace, I gave taxi-drivers a lesson in dodgem skills, and was swerving past a police van when I realised I'd better slow down.

Nevertheless the orange Fiesta was now just one car ahead of me. I was nearly there. Just keep my nerve, one more overtaking and ... it was pulling away from me, accelerating, fleeing. Had Penny seen my antics? Did she know my car?

Without warning the Fiesta ducked into a side street and I had no alternative but to squeal round the corner, tight on its tail.

There were houses on either side, and miracle of miracles, sleeping policemen at regular intervals – a play-street – bless those slumbering humps. The orange Fiesta was bumping over them, and I bumped too, foot still on the accelerator, praying that my saggy springs would survive the ordeal. The Fiesta was even older than my Metro, it had no option but to slow down. In fact, it stopped.

I pulled up in amazement. It had parked outside a house, and the car-door was opening. Penny?

Not Penny. A large, gangly, spotted youth, with a face as livid as his red hair.

'What the 'ell d'you think you're playing at?'

I eased myself out of the driver's seat and stood up to meet him on level terms, although his eyes were a level or two above mine. 'I – I'm sorry, I thought you were someone else, someone I'm looking for.'

'Yeah, and I'll come looking for you if you try such tricks again. Blimey, you came after me like a bat out of hell.'

'Well, as I said, I can't apologise enough. Look, could you just tell me, have you bought the car recently? Only it's so like my friend's, I wondered ...?'

'What you saying? You think I stole it from yer friend, eh? You think I'd steal a heap of rust like that?'

'No, no, I didn't mean that at all.'

'Well I bought it yesterday, fair and square. Wish I hadn't if idiots like you are gonna be up my exhaust all the time.'

'Who did you buy it from?'

'What's it to you? None of your business.'

'I really do need to speak to my friend, you see, and I don't know where she is.'

He stood, radiating dumb insolence.

'Look,' I delved in my purse. 'I'm sorry for the inconvenience, I'm sorry I chased you, I hope this might be some recompense.' I proferred a five-pound note.

He took it tentatively, looked me up and down, said, 'Dave Barnett, car mart,' swerved on his heel and disappeared through the door of his house as though he feared I might grab the note back.

I got back in my car and heaved a sigh of relief. At least it was something, a slight lead for my pains.

Could I face Guy Madden after all that had happened that day? No way. Mr Mad Mad World could wait, until tomorrow, when my world was not quite so mad, and I'd had a stiff bourbon and a long, dreamless sleep.

Thankfully I was still trailing clouds of glory as far as Ellis Clancy was concerned. If I'd told him I was going to pursue Rosie's story with Guy Madden he'd have put down obstacles straight away, but if I said I was on the tail of his pet suspect, the missing Penny, he would loosen the leash.

In addition, I'd turned out to be a Clancy heroine of the first order, not only creating copy but starring in it. The bank manager who'd helped rescue Shelley had rung the paper, not knowing I worked there. 'Mum Pulls Drowning Daughter from Disaster,' went the headline, together with a photo of washed-out Shelley propped up on pillows, and a sheepish head-and-shoulders of me. Normally I'd shrink from such mawkish stuff, but I could see my halo positively gleaming in Ellis's eyes. I took advantage of his temporary blindness and hot-footed out of the office, tossing a casual, 'Back later. Don't wait up.'

So, at last, Guy Madden waited at my journey's end. He was standing in the park entrance as I arrived, wearing a ski jacket over a heavy sweater and thick cords. Hardly office wear, but then Guy would shun such niceties. He knew best, and cobblers to the rest.

I hailed him with a cheery 'Good morning, Guy, how are you today?' just to see how he'd react.

He ignored the question. 'You know how to keep a man waiting,' he stated tersely.

'Unforeseen circumstances – I did ring.'

'I know. A veritable Anna Knight in shining armour – rescuing the lovely Amazon who put me on the floor. I saw the story.'

And I saw that he was looking at me with a new regard, even a grudging respect. Was it my imagination, or did his gaze then slide over my shoulder, as though he were wary of anyone following me?

'Come on,' he said. 'Walk and talk.'

Walk and talk – sing and dance and do a merry jig to his beck and call? 'I'm not a wind-up doll, Guy,' I blasted at his retreating back. 'Slow down, what's the hurry?'

Workmen high up on painting platforms looked down as we passed, no doubt amused at the sight of swaggering Guy Madden with a woman in his wake. A barked order I'd once heard on a drill square came echoing back in my mind, 'Left right, left right – come on lads – bags of swank!' Guy Madden had bags so full of swank he almost burst out of his Puffa jacket.

He did a left turn and I quick-marched to keep up, so that when he abruptly halted I cannoned into his shoulder.

'Wait here.'

He rolled up a creaking metal shutter, and I found myself in front of a shooting gallery, rifles at the ready, prizes of fluffy rabbits and teddy bears on the shelves. Guy lifted a rifle and handed it to me, imitating the tones of a fairground barker: 'Come on, little lady, try your eye on this. Look at those lovely bunnies – just waiting for you to put your arms around them.'

As I took aim, he lifted a second rifle, and I realised this was a contest. A contest I did not want. Why were such men in competition all the time? Macho men, show-offs, men who'd crush you under their size tens to show who's boss. Ugh!

I channelled my anger into my sights. All right, if that's the way you want it, we'll see who comes out Top Gun.

I fired, my shoulder blasted six inches back, and a black spot appeared satisfyingly near the bull's-eye. He raised an eyebrow, and took aim. Bang – a plaster dog shattered below his target.

I fired again. Blam – a hit, within the outer ring. He steadied his barrel and pulled the trigger – bam! A notch appeared on the edge of the cardboard. He gave me two more pellets, I slammed them in and let rip, one after the other. The first missed completely, the second hit the bull, just off centre. He followed – a hole appeared in the cloth behind the target, and – kerpang – a ricochet off a shiny trophy. He put down both his weapon and mine.

'Congratulations, Anna Get Your Gun,' he shook my hand. 'You win today's star prize.'

He vaulted over the barrier and took hold of a particularly fat rabbit of a virulent pink, presenting me with my hollow victory. He'd let me win, of course he had, and like a fool I'd played for real.

Nestled between the rabbit's startled ears was a photograph. 'Go on, look at it,' he pressed, 'that's what we're here for.'

It was a Polaroid, a quick snap for instant gratification, though what could be gratifying about its contents I could not imagine. The picture showed a desk, with papers strewn all over the place, and a filing cabinet, open, with more papers and office paraphernalia spewing out of it.

'Come on, Guy, stop the show business, what is this all about?'

He pulled down the shutter and began to stride about once more: 'We reached a bargain, Anna Knight. Fair exchange, I've shown you a sample of my goods, now you give a taste of yours.'

I put my foot down, in fact both of them. I stood stock-still, refusing to obey orders. The ghastly pink rabbit rather undercut my aggressive stance. I stifled a smirk. Mutiny in the ranks. Guy Madden was not pleased. Obstinate subordinates must be punished. He wheeled, strode straight back to me and I half expected to be hauled along by the arm, willing or not.

'If you won't walk I can't make you,' he said, in a low tone of veiled impatience. 'But you'll only get cold and I refuse to talk inside. OK?'

'But why? This is ridiculous.'

'Because your ears, my ears and the fluffy pink bunny's are the only ears that must hear this conversation. Do I make myself clear?'

The man was clearly suffering from paranoid delusions.

'You think someone's following you, or bugging your office?' I asked, frankly amazed. His glance darted around, as if he suspected the laughing clown on the hurdy-gurdy to be cocking its lug-hole to his every word. It was so absurd I fell into step beside him, in the hope of exploring other aspects of the fantasy.

We were passing the Lumberjack River Run, a rollicking ride in which people sat in hollowed-out tree trunks and were whisked over cataracts and waterfalls. Staff were tending to the hidden tracks.

'All right there, men?' shouted Guy, the boss, the commanding officer.

'Fine,' replied an overalled technician. 'We've just

about finished the checks. Want to give it a test run, Mr Madden?'

He looked at me, shrugged, and answered back: 'Why not?'

I let him go, but he turned and gave me a wry smile: 'Fancy a ride round the block? Come on, trust me. We'd look pretty silly belting down the motorway in a tree trunk.'

And so I squeezed myself into the back of a hollow log behind a test pilot. Life throws some odd experiences my way sometimes. The log trundled on its appointed way, snaking between boulders with aplomb, and I began to think this wasn't a bad way to spend a day.

'Now,' called Guy, over his shoulder, 'what have you got to tell me about Futures?'

'Precisely as much as you've told me about the police and their lack of candour.'

'You won yourself the picture, now win yourself some information. Give and take – ouf!' he exclaimed as the log lurched round a particularly sharp bend and began a steep ascent.

'All right. Llew suspected there was a Futures mole on the Mad Mad World staff, stealing information.'

'What kind of information?'

'That's the end of our broadcasting for today. Folks, tune in again when we've thrown more light on this week's mystery picture.'

'The desk was my brother's. What do you see?'

I picked the photo from the rabbit's grasp and studied hard, trying to ignore the fact that we were now perched on a high scaffold above a lake, where make-believe swamp monsters waited to open their jaws.

'It looks like a perfectly ordinary desk which has been hit by a tornado.'

'Of the human variety. Now your go.'

'Llew believed Futures muscled in on his studio-tour plan when he was on the brink of clinching a deal. Your turn.'

We rounded a bend and were heading for a brink ourselves. Guy steeled himself for the plunge. I prodded him hard as we edged toward the noisy torrent. 'Llew's house was burgled,' he shouted.

'Futures snatched the studio contract from under his nose,' I shouted back.

'Nothing was stolen,' he called.

'Llew fought back,' I returned.

'Only his papers were ransacked.'

'Whoo-AAAA!' we whoaaed in unison.

The log tumbled over the precipice and we plunged headlong into the lake, emerging in a tidal wave at the bottom.

'The break-in happened the day Llew died,' he said in the midst of the backwash. 'The police think the two incidents are connected.'

'Llew was digging for dirt on Futures,' I replied. 'And he stole some of their plans.'

'Stole?'

'Mmmm – ' the waves were receding, 'plans for the new complex you're building. Virtual reality?'

'I see . . .'

We entered calmer waters and the log bumped back to the embarkation platform.

'All right, Mr Madden?' asked the foreman.

'Perfect,' he smiled, helping me ashore.

As we walked away from the Lumberjack River Run I filled in some more details for him and he handed me a large clean handkerchief to soak up the drips.

'Are you game for another ride,' he said at length, 'or has your enthusiasm been dampened?'

'I'm OK,' I replied, surprisingly invigorated. 'You took the brunt of the splashes up front.'

'Mmmm – I have a knack of acting as fall guy, it seems,' he said oddly.

'Guy, what's going to happen to the park?' I asked as we continued walking.

'I'm taking over where Llew left off. I looked up to my big brother, you know.' He looked at me challengingly. 'The sad thing is I can tell you, and I never told him. He was always a gentleman, he had the knack of making people like him. I never did. He had loads of friends, I didn't. I sort of resented him for it. I even used to pick fights, just to provoke him. I suppose you think that's terrible.'

'Terrible or not, it's common – jealousy between siblings.'

'Well I was jealous, that's what made me turn away from the family business. I didn't want to be compared with him. He thought I didn't care, and we kind of shut each other out. We were just beginning to get over all that, and now he's dead. It made me do some serious thinking. If he'd trusted me more he'd have told me what was bugging him. I could've helped. The least I can do now is make sure the park survives even though Llew didn't.'

'But surely you can't do two jobs at once – this is a full-time commitment. What'll happen when you go back to flying planes?'

'I'm not going back,' he said firmly. 'We're not here to talk about that.' Anger had flashed into his face again and I realised the issue was closed. This man was as volatile as a bag of Semtex.

We came to a Viking longship, and he opened a concealed door in its side. Nothing was what it seemed in this place, for when the lights flashed on I found myself entering a room full of mirrors. Wobbled mirrors, distorted mirrors, mirrors that made me look ten feet tall or small as a dwarf. A giraffe-necked freak with a Humpty-Dumpty body appeared by my side, and I realised it was Guy's reflection.

I addressed the freak: 'Why have the police not told us about the break-in at Llew's house?'

He spoke back to the dwarf: 'They're playing a waiting game. If they keep the break-in a secret, but pick up someone who spontaneously speaks of it, even to deny all knowledge – then obviously they can clap him in irons.'

We moved, and he became a wasp-waisted soubrette with a mountainous bosom. I asked the bosom, 'Do they have a suspect?'

He replied, to my beanpole, 'They have, but they won't tell me who. In any case I don't think they're covering every angle.'

'Why?'

'Because they refuse to pursue Futures.'

We moved again; he squashed into a thick pancake, I grew hips like humps on a dromedary. 'Look,' he continued, 'I think they've got a pre-set idea who did my brother in and it doesn't involve Futures. They say they've looked into it and drawn a blank. They've ruled it out of their investigation.'

My image transmuted to a slender, exquisite ballet dancer – oh for a mirror like this in my bathroom: 'So who are they pursuing?'

'I've told you, I don't know,' he said impatiently, now a goggle-eyed fly, his arms spread like black wings. 'They don't tell me everything. I'm only the brother of the murdered man, what do I count? Anyway, enough of this. The mirrors are only an amusement to keep people occupied while they wait for the ultimate experience.'

'The ultimate?'

He pulled back a screen and I followed. A fairground horse stood before me, shiny black with a gold mane and red flared nostrils. It was fixed to a plinth with wires leading up its hooves. 'Meet Mephistopheles,' Guy said, 'your mount for an adventure beyond your dreams.'

I climbed into the fine-tooled leather saddle, and he produced a pair of gauntlets and a winged helmet with a heavy visor which he lowered over my head. In complete darkness I felt him put the gauntlets on my hands.

'Take the reins, ride him around, get used to him,' Guy encouraged me.

Lights flashed and when my eyes became accustomed to the brightness I found myself in a Tuscan landscape. The horse plodded under me, I could see his ears twitching in front, and I felt the reins pull taut as he moved his head from side to side. In my other hand I felt a heavy weight, and when I looked I saw it held a lance.

'Now, get ready for take off,' said Guy.

The horse speeded up until he was galloping, and suddenly he left the ground and we were soaring above the trees, over hills and down valleys, his mane flying in my face. I laughed in sheer exhilaration. 'This is fantastic,' I heard my voice echoing inside the helmet.

'This is the ride you now tell me Llew stole from Futures,' came Guy's voice. 'Well, they may have originated the idea, but Llew made it his own. He based this scenario on a fairytale he used to tell me as a kid. Look up.'

Clouds scudded above me, and Mephistopheles raised his head to leap through them. I looked to right and left and saw that the horse had wings. A golden eagle appeared out of nowhere to look me in the eye. I ducked and the horse swooped away.

'To Futures we're probably easy meat, you know,' called Guy. 'The break-in at my brother's house, and his suspicions of a mole – it strikes me what could be behind all this is a hostile takeover bid. They need confidential information on the state of our business, that's why they wanted copies of Llew's papers.'

I was concentrating – I'd spied a handsome youth below me, tied to a tree. The youth wore a crown. An imprisoned prince – I must dash to the rescue. As Mephistopheles plummeted landwards I managed to ask, 'Why?'

'Because we're an annoyance, because they know we wouldn't play ball for a friendly takeover, and because we have a prime site on the seafront which they want.'

I'd landed with a thud, and Mephistopheles was galloping towards the struggling prince – but as he skidded to a halt I saw smoke billowing from my right, and smelt a fetid odour of fire and brimstone.

'Ugh! What's that?'

'Dragon's breath,' said Guy matter-of-factly.

Flames leapt towards me, and I saw behind them a mighty monster, a red winged beast with scales and lashing tongue and eyes like the devil. 'Use your lance,' instructed Guy.

I raised my arm and began to fight the monster. Mephistopheles danced under me, swerving me away from its claws.

'What're you going to do about it?' I managed to gasp.

'First, get my evidence.'

'How?' I ducked a blast of flame.

'Same way they tried to get it from us. Two can play dirty.'

'But Llew tried that. Look what happened to him.' The dragon was crouched like a lion, readying itself for the kill. It leapt at my horse.

'Llew should have confided in me, he was too straight for their nasty predatory games. I'm not, and I'll stop their manoeuvres. I'll take them to court and grind their reputation in the mud. Mad Mad World is our property, and they'll grab it over my dead body.'

I thrust my lance into the dragon's breast. Blood flew into my face, and the monster collapsed under my horse's hooves.

The prince's ropes broke free and he knelt at my feet. A job well done, I thought.

'Have you killed it?' asked Guy.

'Dead as a broken dream.'

Guy laughed and lifted the helmet from my head: 'Come on, you must need a hot coffee, dragon-slayer.'

I dismounted, and paused: 'If you can't make headway on your own . . . I'm willing to help.'

Anyone who could thrill me like that deserved something in return.

Eleven

G uy opened the lift doors and we ascended to the upper floor of the yellow submarine. After my ride on Mephistopheles I was still not sure where reality ended and fantasy began, half-expecting mythical beasts to appear in the office corridor.

'The project's still at the experimental stage,' Guy was explaining. 'As we develop it I want to play around with my own scenarios, see if I can do even better than Llew.'

A bearded bear charged from a door without warning, barging me into the wall. 'Anna!' exploded Matt Whittaker, 'I really should look before I blunder. But I couldn't have wished for a more lovely collision. I'm sorry, did I hurt you? I have pretty soft bumpers though, don't I? Here, let me brush you down.'

He did so, and Guy looked on over his shoulder, amused.

'Hmm – your jacket's damp. Still a little moist around the gills from your sea rescue?' asked Matt, and kissed my cheek. 'I'm glad you came, I desperately need to talk to you. Where are we going for lunch?'

'I didn't come for lunch with you, Matt, I'm sorry. I'm here to talk to Guy.'

His face fell, heavy as a flat-iron, as he noticed Guy for the first time: 'Oh, I see. Well, catch you later. Call in on your way out.'

'I will.'

I felt a heel, and yet, why should I? I'd done nothing to regret. It was just that a *frisson* of jealousy had raised the hairs on Matt's neck, so lightly it was barely detectable. But with the bat-like sonar of a lover, I had picked it up. I called over my shoulder, 'Matt! I can squeeze in a sandwich if you like.'

He turned round, patted his girth, and smiled: 'You know how to reach a guy's heart – I'll squeeze a sandwich with you any time.'

Guy sat with his feet up on the desk in Llew's former office like the very picture of a managing director. I told him so, and he said, 'Why not? It's what I am. Captain of the yellow submarine, and I'm not going to see it founder. You hear that, whoever you are?'

He addressed the walls, and I imagined he'd be climbing up them if this paranoia got out of hand. He poured coffee and asked if I'd like a dash of brandy. After dragon's breath, who wouldn't?

Once we'd drunk it he took me to another part of the site, ostensibly to see the demolition of one of the park's oldest rides.

'I haven't yet managed to get hold of that security consultant Llew hired,' he said worriedly as we left all possible range of snoopers.

'Brian Battersby? I hope he's more open with you that he was with me.'

'He's playing hard to get. Makes me suspicious, but I'll give him one more chance.'

I asked what other scenarios he had in mind for the virtual reality and robotic complex and we spent a pleasant ten minutes discussing inter-galactic Armageddon, sinking ships in shark-infested seas, and the foulest ghouls that ever leapt from a dank dungeon.

I was genuinely interested, but I was conscious of my promise to Matt: 'Look Guy, I really should be going.'

'I'll be in touch, Anna. Thanks for your co-operation.'

'The pleasure was mine.'

What was I saying? I had to remind myself this man had nearly assaulted me in the street and abducted me in his car. He was self-centred, wilful, and maybe half mad, but that was part of the fascination.

'Don't forget your rabbit,' he called, and came after me, leading me back to his office to thrust it in my hand. I couldn't get rid of the darned thing, could I?

'Who's your friend?' asked Matt, looking at the fluffy toy, as I entered his lair.

'He's an English cousin of Bugs Bunny. What's up, doc?'

'I'm in need of a shipmate, Anna,' he pleaded with the soulful eyes of a man all at sea. 'A friend to help me through these turbulent times.'

'Oh yes?'

He changed tone to the rat-tat delivery of Groucho Marx: 'I'm also willing to pay this friend a considerable sum of money – how d'ya like them cookies?'

'Pay?'

'Come on, honey, let's grab a sandwich and I'll spill the beans.'

We went across to a steamed-up sandwich bar and perched on stools, Matt ordering a double-decker with extra everything, and I a smorgasbord of dainty delicacies – we are what we eat.

'I'm offering you a job, Anna.'

I nearly choked on my bean sprouts.

'Why?'

'Because we need a new public relations supremo, and I think you're supreme.'

'Rosie really is leaving, then?'

'Past tense. She left after the funeral. She was so cut

up after Llew's death, she collapsed – on the edge of a nervous breakdown. She didn't want to have anything more to do with Mad Mad World so we paid her a month's salary and that was that. A month's salary is not insignificant in this post, Anna.'

'How much?'

He told me a sum that made pocket money of my current earnings, plus car, plus perks that made me wilt with envy.

'Interested?' asked Matt, chewing his way through the double-decker like a starved locust. 'I have free rein to recommend who I want, and we need someone fast, to plan a campaign for next season. You are my someone, Anna, I want you wrapped up in time for Christmas.'

Two conflicting armies were battling in my brain. I needed the money – no doubt about it – bailing out Shelley was going to destroy my savings, with no guarantee I would ever get them back. Besides which, if I had to support her through a drama course there was a fair chance I'd be running into a slough of debt and despond myself. Mad Mad World's money would keep us both above the waves.

But on the other hand, a PR person was a sales rep in sharper clothing: selling the company to the public, always putting the best face forward, hiding the faults, playing the company tune. Journalism's for people who take a sadistic pleasure in undercutting such flim-flam, exposing faults, blowing raspberries at hypocrites. People like me. All right, Ellis was a burden, but one I could bear – he was, after all, a man who suffered no fool gladly. And as a PR person I'd have to play the glad fool.

'Can I get back to you?' I asked weakly.

'Sure, think it over. Listen, if you're worrying about the park's future – don't. I was wrong about it going under now Llew's gone. Since Guy Madden got fired from the aircraft plant he—'

'Fired?'

'Sure . . . oh gosh, I've said something I shouldn't. I

forgot you're still on the outside looking in. That's a story to you, isn't it?'

'Certainly is. Tell me more.'

He wiped crumbs from his fingers and covered his eyes, ears and mouth, 'I am a wise monkey, I never said a word, and I will deny all knowledge of any words you say I said.'

'But you'll tell me.'

'Nope.' And his eyes gleamed, knowing he held a secret I wanted.

'I'll ask Guy.'

'Not if you value your skin, you won't. The subject is not to be broached on pain of detonating a fifty-megaton Madden bomb. I know, I tried it. I hit the ground in a thousand pieces.'

'You've done a pretty good job of putting them together again.'

'Cemented with sandwich spread and the company of a good woman.'

'You'll have to tell me who she is.'

'You're good at your job, Anna, and you'd be good for us too.'

But would they be good for me? Should I do it for Shelley's sake, or stay put for mine? Ach! I couldn't handle the arguments in a sweaty sandwich bar.

We went out into the biting wind, and I took my leave of Matt, wishing Rosie had had the stamina to stick with her job and not put me in this predicament. She'd taken flight from the *News* over Clancy and she'd fled Mad Mad World over Llew. Man trouble. They weren't worth running your life around, Rosie.

However, I had to run my life around a man this afternoon, and I hoped he wasn't going to be trouble. Dave Barnett's car mart was my destination, armed with a photograph of Penny plundered from our files.

I threw the pink rabbit into the back of my car and set off. The rabbit sat goofily in the rear window, distracting me in the mirror, reminding me of Guy. Fired? From being a test pilot? What catastrophic misconduct had he been guilty of? I was intrigued.

I found the car mart on the outskirts of town. It looked more like an automobile graveyard than a second-hand car business. The models on display were rattle-traps and old bangers, heaps of rust held together with spot-welds and masking tape. A stubble-chinned man in a donkey jacket sat in a draughty shed which had a secret life as an office.

'Excuse me – Mr Barnett?'

'That's me. What're you looking for, love? I can give you a fair trade-in for your motor – looks in good nick.'

Good nick my car was not, but I wasn't there to argue the point.

'Actually I'm not here to buy a car. It's about a vehicle you sold the day before yesterday. An orange Fiesta with a yellow wing?'

'What about it?' he looked suspicious.

'It's just that I need to trace the person who sold it to you. She's a friend, I've lost touch. When I saw someone else driving her car I asked him where he bought it and so I came to you.'

'What if I can't remember?'

'You keep records, don't you? Did she leave an address?'

Now he looked defensive: 'What're you really here for?'

'To trace my friend. It's genuine.'

'Look, when I bought it for scrap that's what I thought it was worth. Wasn't my fault some geezer comes along and takes a fancy to it afterwards. If he wants to drive round a heap of scrap, it's his lookout, not mine.'

'I'm not interested in how much you paid her.'

'You're not?'

'No. Look,' I showed him the picture. 'This is the woman I'm after. Penny Worthington.'

He rasped his chin with a greasy hand and shook his

head: 'No – that's not her. The woman who came here was fatter-faced than that. She'd short hair, and dark, not that reddy colour. It was all done up in those tight little curls – you know – look like a pan-scrubber.'

My shoulders sank.

'Same name, though,' he added, trying to help, running his finger down a grubby record book. 'The only address I got was on the papers she gave me. Here it is – down Sussex way.'

'Hove?'

'That's it. Any help?'

I couldn't say it was, but I thanked him anyway.

A fatter-faced woman with short dark hair? Could it be Janette? And if so, what game was she playing with me?

Twelve

I rapped on the door of Janette's tall house with some impatience. I could understand why she had lied to the police, but why lie to me? Why beg me to look for Penny when she'd obviously had contact with her to sell her car? I stamped my feet, waiting for a response from the silent house. Perhaps Penny had left her car behind and Janette took it upon herself to sell it. No – I could not believe that. But I didn't know what to believe any more.

I was about to walk away from the house when I looked up and saw the edge of a curtain lift in an upstairs window. A familiar face peered down to steal a peek at the impatient door-rapper. It was Janette. I waved. The face disappeared and shortly I heard bolts being drawn back.

She opened the door a crack and hustled me through to the kitchen.

'Have you found her, have you any news?' she asked. She looked haggard, and without her business make-up, raw and vulnerable.

'No, Janette, look I need a serious talk with you.'

I'm fairly good at clipped tones and a severe expression when I want to be – it comes of steering a daughter through troubled teens. Such headmistressy disapproval was too much for the raw and vulnerable Janette.

'Don't you come the lah-di-dah with me,' she exploded. 'I've had it up to here what with social workers and the rest of the nosey parkers. I can't work, my lodger's run off, I'm gonna be had up in court, the bills get redder, and now the ruddy taxman wants his pound of my flesh. I wish people'd stop treating me like a criminal, I was only doing what I thought was best.'

She was trembling. She was wounded and I'd barged in with the salt rub. I put my hand on her shoulder and eased her into a chair. 'I'm sorry, Janette, I'd no idea you were so upset.' She allowed herself to be soothed, and when I'd made a pot of tea she'd calmed down enough to tell me what had happened.

The police had set the full wheels of state in motion to crush Janette's business when they discovered she had been lying about the alibi. Magistrates, social services and the Inland Revenue were called in for a piece of the action. As a result she was holed up in fear. They had not yet spoken of taking her children, and she was keeping her head well down to deny them that possibility.

'To cap it all,' she finished, 'Penny's bloody fancy man rang just before you came.'

'The married man, you mean, her lover?'

'Huh, lover? I had another word for him,' she snarled. 'O'course he wouldn't give his name, but I know his voice. He was after her, thought I'd know where she was. I told him she didn't want to see him no more, that's why she'd gone away. And then I scared the poxy pants off him. I said I knew what he looked like, and if I get my hands on him I'm gonna drag him to the cop-shop myself, because it's not fair on Penny, it's not fair.'

'Why did you say that? You said you'd never seen his face.'

'I know, but I'd recognise his back view all right. Besides, I wanted to put the wind up him, he's yellow as a bowl of custard, expecting her to cover up for him, and I was at the end of my rope with the whole business. Penny should've dropped him in it in the first place, instead of getting all wound up and running off like a scared rabbit. The trouble is the longer this goes on I keep thinking they'll find her, you know, hanged or drowned or overdosed somewhere – she's so high-strung, cops on her back – it might all have got too much for her. Anyway, I slammed the phone down on him and you caught the backwash. I'm sorry.'

'No, no, don't worry about that, I'm just concerned that all this is getting on top of you. Can you manage?'

She smiled ruefully, rallying her old spirit: 'Oh, don't worry, good old Janette'll manage somehow. I've got to, for my girls. At least it's forcing me to take a holiday from pleasing fellas, isn't it? Can please myself for a bit now. I'll bounce back, gal, don't you worry, my hide's made of rubber – it has to be.'

At last I broached the subject of Penny's car.

'What?' she responded, with genuine dismay. 'I'm supposed to've sold it to a fella I've never even heard of? Not unless I've been sleepwalking, love, and that's gospel. The last I saw of that car was when Penny ran out of here and drove it away. You have to believe me, Anna, it's the truth, as I live and breathe.'

Truth was relative, I reflected, in Janette's case. She'd believed Penny's innocence was true, and she'd lied quite forcefully to support it. But clearly she was still desperate about Penny's welfare – and there was no hollow ring to her voice when she denied selling the car.

In that case, the chase of the orange Fiesta with the yellow wing had led me nowhere but a dead end. All I could do was turn round gracefully and get back on the main trail.

I spent the evening on my own trying to decide whether to take the money and trumpet the glories of Mad Mad World, or to stay on roughing it with the *News*. Trumpeting glories with my tongue in my cheek would not be comfortable. On the other hand, perhaps I could tolerate a little tongue cramp if the alternative was living in a garret on cheese and a crust – just as I was approaching my prime.

Matt's offer was one I really should not refuse. I slept on it, and woke depressed, which puzzled me until I remembered what I'd slept on. This was one mighty hard pea, princess. I would not rest easy until I'd swallowed it or spat it out.

There was a note on my desk: 'Please ring Marianne Knatchbull. Beware – she's on the scrounge.'

And so I rang Marianne, who was not on the scrounge, at least not for herself, but for her charity, Journey of a Lifetime. She wouldn't say exactly what she wanted on the phone, but implored me to join her for lunch, *chez* Knatchbull. I hadn't had a better offer that morning, and an invigorating blast of Marianne might cheer my careworn spirits, so I said of course I would.

My rust-scarred Metro positively slunk on its springs as I parked it behind the Bentley on the gravel drive of Highfield House. Compared with the Knatchbulls I was like the beggar at the gate, and yet Marianne was asking for favours: there was a power attached to my lowly state.

A subdued Marianne greeted me at the door, her face flushed and puffy – was it with cooking or weeping? I could not tell, for a labrador bounded on to my chest at that moment, licking the kind of welcome I'd hoped for from Marianne. Her remonstration with the dog bordered on tears. Crying was undoubtedly going to break through, but she mounted a staunch defence against its first onslaught.

'They should put dogs like this on the National Health,' I smiled, pretending I hadn't noticed her discomfort as the dog threatened to wag its tail off. 'Even when you feel lousy and look worse, he'll always be deliriously happy when you come through the door. It's a tonic just to look at him.'

'You're right,' replied Marianne, stony-faced. 'Loyal, that's what a dog is. Pity his master's not the same.'

So that was it. Barnaby had gone again. Woe is me, to be a mattress for my friends to fall on and bounce off.

We went through to the morning room, which was decorated in shades of yellow, with winter sunshine flooding in through the long windows, and flowers in Chinese bowls. It was a room designed for brighter moods than Marianne's, and maybe that's why we were eating there – to bolster her failing resources.

I was obviously part of the bolstering stratagem too, for Marianne was refusing to give in to her tiresome emotions. 'I want to get straight down to business, Anna,' she said as we sat down at the table and a housekeeper bustled in with a steaming tureen of homemade courgette soup. 'Thank you, Maggie, I can manage the rest. It's time you were getting off home.'

Over soup and chunks of rough-grained bread, game pie, fruit and cheese, Marianne launched into her attack. 'You know Journey of a Lifetime positively eats up money. It's not like a scanner appeal with a definite end – it's ongoing, children keep going down with dreadful diseases and it's our declared goal to fulfil their wildest dreams.'

I nodded assent.

She went on, 'One of our biggest moneyspinners over the past year or so has been Survival of the Fittest.'

I knew this – it had appealed to the business community's basest, sharpest instincts. Survival of the Fittest was an assault course for hyper-fit workaholics. Two competing businesses in the same field would challenge each other to spend an evening locked in combat in a giant indoor arena. Each team would do anything it could to win the prized Leaping Lioness – a bronze sculpture of an animal at the peak of its powers devouring a hapless wildebeest.

Brute strength and quick wits were essential, but cheating and sabotage were also allowed to add spark to their competitive fires. No one wanted to be the wildebeest; everyone wanted to be top of the heap. The winners were allowed to keep a copy of the Leaping Lioness to show off in their promotions and crow over their defeated enemy.

Aggression, self-aggrandisement and ruthlessness were sheened in the gilt of charity fundraising, and everyone was very proud of their efforts. Even the losers gained an edge – they were given the chance to fight another day – and another competitor was lined up for the fray. They adapted, got mean, and were damned if they'd lose again.

Money rolled in through sponsorship, tickets and cash donations on the night. Survival of the Fittest had become a wildly popular spectator sport, each team bringing its own partisan crowd to trade insults and raise cheers at the ringside.

I was interested – indeed more than interested – in what Marianne was going to ask me, for Survival of the Fittest was staged at Futures, and that set my investigative pulses racing.

'Of course, we could advertise,' Marianne was saying, 'but that would cost money that would otherwise go to the charity, and I believe a feature in the editorial columns, with pictures, would have much more impact. We're in need of a boost: we've covered most of the firms on the Liverpool end of the coast, we now want to interest those in Northport and all points between.'

'You want me to write an article on Survival of the Fittest?'

'Oh, Anna, how kind – that would be the most marvellous gesture.'

'They're held monthly, aren't they? When's the next one?'

'Ahhh,' pondered Marianne, 'we have a slight hiatus at the moment. You know we have two professional team-leaders, a man and a woman, to rehearse the participants and help plan strategy?'

'Uh-huh – they have fierce-sounding names don't they?'

'Bulwark and Viper, yes. Unfortunately – or rather

fortunately for her – Viper has become pregnant, and can't risk rope-swinging and belly-crawling much longer. We need a temporary replacement before we can start the challenges again.'

One word leapt out at me from what Marianne had said: 'professional'.

'These team-leaders are paid for their labours?' I asked.

'Yes, that's Futures' contribution – plus a generous discount for the hire of the arena. Futures is very keen on Survival of the Fittest, it was one of their executives who originated the idea – you've met her, haven't you? A friend of mine, Liza Boyd-Adams – and she does all the accounting for us. It's a big help, but then they get publicity out of it and I suppose there's some tax jiggery-pokery involved. One never gets something for nothing, does one?'

I wasn't really listening – I was more interested in Viper's maternity leave: 'This temporary replacement: what are the requirements?'

'We're on the lookout for a strong, young, fighting-fit woman, preferably with experience of performing to the public. The public loves a good show – bread and circuses for the masses.'

'Marianne,' I grasped her arm with anticipation, 'I know a strong, young, fighting-fit woman with tons of experience of performing in public. And she desperately needs a job before going to college.'

'Then send her along to the auditions next Wednesday, my dear. What's her name?'

'Shelley Chantelle. Actually that's her stage name, which I loathe. She's really Shelley Knight.'

'Aaaah.' And Marianne gave me a knowing wink. 'Say no more, lovey. If she makes the grade, it's the least I can do for all your help.'

We retreated to a sofa for coffee. The bounding labrador, who'd been exiled to the garden while we ate, came snuffling at the french windows. Marianne got up and let him in. 'All right, Tigger, you've served your punishment. I can't stay angry with you for long.'

She rejoined me on the sofa, her hand scratching the dog's head with affection: 'What am I to do with him, Anna?'

'Oh, he's still young and full of energy. He'll grow out of it.'

'Grow out of it? As he's got older he's got worse.'

It took me a second to realise that while I was talking about Tigger, she was talking about a much older dog – her husband.

'I take it he's gone back to . . .?'

'Yes, he's gone back,' sighed Marianne, lacking the energy even to summon up an insulting nickname for her rival. 'There were phone-calls, you see – emotional, tearful phone-calls late at night – well, he's not a man of iron. She obviously thinks a great deal of him. He went. And yet he came back here yesterday, ostensibly to pick up some clothes, but to be honest there aren't many left for him to pick. He sat with his head in his hands in the kitchen, and said he didn't want to lose me. What am I to make of that, Anna, I ask you?'

'Sounds like he wants to have his cake and eat it,' I said, ever the hard-head when it came to other people's men trouble.

'He always was a greedy man, my Barnaby. Oh I can see I'm not everything he needs, of course I can, but it still hurts.'

'No one can be everything to another person. No one's perfect, Marianne, not you, not I, not Barnaby nor his girlfriend. You mustn't blame yourself for this, whatever you do.'

'No . . . I suppose you're right, none of us is perfect. But as things stand, none of us is happy either. I miss him when he's not here, she misses him when he's not there, and he misses whoever he's not with at the time. Life's a bitch sometimes, isn't it, Tigger?'

The dog wagged his tail, the picture of happiness,

and he was still just as happy when I took my leave, bounding around after a stray wood-pigeon on the drive. As I drove away, Marianne took him in hand, holding him tight by the collar, putting up a robust front for the outside world once more.

I shuffled among my cassettes for a suitably triumphant tape to match my mood – ah, a blast of the *Fanfare for the Common Man*. As it blared out I gave thanks to Marianne, for now it looked as though I could remain as common as I pleased. If Shelley got the job, and I did a bit of moonlighting – selling copy to the nationals, on Survival of the Fittest, for example – we could manage without Mad Mad World's glittering prizes. The road opened up before me, blessedly free and clear, and I sped down it, surrounded by the sound of golden horns.

Thirteen

F utures shone on the horizon like a vision of the celestial city. Silver domes, golden towers, ivory spires grew out of the green and pleasant land. Flags of many nations fluttered and danced in the breeze, though citizens of more penurious countries might have looked long and hard for their proud pennant.

The site, on a flat plain where once a farmer eked out his set-aside subsidy, could be seen from miles around. Signposts declared its imminence from a network of motorways, billboards promised unearthly delights, and children's mithering began a hundred miles away: 'Are we there yet, are we there yet?' repeated like a mantra.

Finally, when Futures was conjured into reality, expectations were running riot. Yes, exclaimed the parents with relief, we are there. Bright, shining, full of hope and excitement, its outer walls a continuous shopping mall, its interior a fury of high-technology super-rides; this was not just an amusement park, it was the ultimate escape, the antidote to depression, the silver lining on the clouds of gloom. TV commercials spotlighted visitors who spoke in tones of wonder, viewers greened with envy and plundered their redecorating money for the privilege of breathing its air.

And as an added kick this enchanted, electric city gave a seductive boost to the national psyche. 'Sod me!' as Shelley exclaimed when we saw its munificence in the distance, 'eat your heart out, Walt Disney.'

Why then, did I feel such an alien as she and I broached the turnstiles? The rides were in full swing, the shops were radiating a come-hither glow, the lines snaked patiently, confident of joys to come – and it seemed that I alone wanted to turn right round and run screaming from its very portals.

With every step I took into this earthly paradise, I seemed to grow increasingly freakish, until at length I felt I had three heads and eyes on stalks. I was not of these people, I did not think like these people, I had come from a distant planet named Silence, and all I wanted was to climb back in my Metro and hide.

Unlike Mad Mad World, Futures would not conceive of closing in the winter; it opened all year and much of the night. Closure time was death, for when no money changed hands, what was the point of Futures' existence? Clatter went the ticket-machines, clink went the coins, rustle went the banknotes, beep went the tills.

Drawn to the sound, adding their own cacophony, came the populations of three conurbations, all within an hour's reach by car. Fun-seekers, shoppers, the idling rich and not-so-rich watched longingly by the idle poor, they coursed into the heart of Futures and pumped out again replete with booty. We were now on the runway towards Christmas, and Futures' emporium buzzed with the build-up of a spending frenzy. I moved among the noise and the lights, the prattling families, the nipping children, trying to protect my three heads, trying to shade my stalk-eyes. I truly was a freak: no one else felt this way – even Shelley was enraptured, all bland face and silly grin.

I had to carry out my duties before people noticed my alien presence and ejected me to the outer wastes where I belonged. At length I spied the entrance to an epic-scale glass golf-ball which was the indoor arena. 'Shelley!' I shouted, 'The Cosmosphere. It's over there.'

'What?' She was captivated by a gigantic merman – half-man, half-Loch Ness monster – seducing her into his subterranean cave with fawning flips of his fishy tail.

'Shelley—' I had to drag her away, the merman's burblings reverberating in my extra-sensitive ears. 'Here. Look. One Cosmosphere, Journey of a Lifetime for the use of. Marianne will be in there. You should be in there, showing off your supple sinews for Survival of the Fittest.'

'Right,' she said, grasping her kitbag and pulling herself together at last. 'Wish me luck, Ma, I need this.'

'We both need it, love,' I replied with regret. 'Break a leg.'

'Will you come back here when you've finished whatever you have to do? I may need someone to pick up the pieces of my shattered ego.'

'Nonsense. When I get back here I expect to see your ego flashing like a beacon on top of this overblown blister.'

We separated, and without Shelley for cover I felt even more conspicuous heading for a block that looked like the space-ship in *Close Encounters of the Third Kind*. I was so sick of close encounters of any kind, I drove my way through the double doors and shut myself in. Ah, blessed relief: a low hum, a scent of herb-meadows, and a soft light to soothe the shaken soul.

'Good afternoon,' greeted a uniformed man in a glass box. Was he real? Or was he a clever animation like the merman? No, he had real crumbs on his moustache. It was lunchtime – a real sandwich lay in front of him.

'Hello,' I smiled, hoping my extra heads were shrinking. 'I'm here to see Tim Hetherington, public relations, he should be expecting me.'

'Take a seat, I'll call him down,' said the uniformed man, hastily secreting his sandwich.

Tim Hetherington appeared, a plump, squat smoothie with a hairy jacket which left green wisps in its wake. 'Right, we'll just get you badged up and we're on our way,' he smiled.

And so I was labelled – stamped as an outsider with the word 'VISITOR' displayed on my chest in black and white for all the world to suspect.

Tim Hetherington had to use a swipe-card to gain access to the inner sanctum. We were entering the very nerve-centre of Futures, its heart and brain, the seat of all its wisdom. Swipe-cards, security men, an electronic fortress. How the hell was I ever going to find anything in here? I could have been glowing green I was so glaring a pariah, I might as well have stood on a chair and cried, 'It's me, I'm guilty, I'm a spy, I'm an infiltrator, take me to your dungeons.'

In fact, 'Take me to your leader' was what I said, hoping flippancy might be a stock in trade of Futures men.

Tim Hetherington, to give him his due, laughed like an automaton: 'If you mean the company chairman I'm afraid you're out of luck. Mr Burchill is away on business. In any case it's Survival of the Fittest you've come to talk about, isn't it? He has very little to do with that particular project. You asked to see Liza Boyd-Adams, the financial director. After all, she gave birth to the idea and nurtured it to what it is today.'

I was shown along thick-carpeted, heavily foliaged corridors into a large office, plush but not ostentatious – a quiet taste had been at work in its expensive furnishings. Liza Boyd-Adams had yet to return from lunch, and Tim Hetherington, infuriatingly, sat like a toad on a rock by my side, immovable. As we waited I tried to read a report upside down in an in-tray – but even eyes on stalks have their limitations.

I noted the waste-bin and its crumpled papers, I noted the personal computer console, its make and type of software, and I noted the shredding machine – all targets for the would-be spy still out in the cold. We waited, and we waited.

Finally, joy of joys, Tim Hetherington got off his rock and announced, 'There must have been some delay, I'll go and see what's happened.'

He left. Immediately I sprang up, scanning the in-tray for any mention of Mad Mad World, or Madden, or competing parks, or takeover plans. No dice. I leapt towards the computer: all praise to the fallible Ms Boyd-Adams – she hadn't switched it off. I punched it into life, gaining access to the directory without problem. Scanning the file names wasn't much help, but I didn't have time for deeper probing. I pulled a diskette out of my bag, hoping against hope I could download something of use onto it. I pushed it in. I pressed buttons, selecting datafiles almost at random, praying the copy instructions were ones I knew. Quickly, quickly, oh Lord, how slow can these high-speed machines be? 'Copy complete.' Pull the disk out, slam the machine back to idle. Voices approaching, getting louder. Run to shredder, lift a sheaf of swarf from the receptacle. Laughter, closer. Twist to waste-bin, shovel crumpled balls of paper into my bag, along with tissues and sweet papers and – ugh – cigarette ash. And finally, the door opens, and I'm sitting in my chair, three heads, stalk-eyes, ash settling around my shoulders, and I say, 'Good afternoon, Ms Boyd-Adams, glad to see you again. I'm grateful you could spare me some time.'

'Please, call me Liza,' she beamed. 'Ah yes, I remem-ber, we met at the bonfire where that body was found. Dreadful business.'

She was tall, glossy-haired, fragrant and perfectly poised. She wore a suit that would have cost me a mortgage, and fixed me with a violet gaze that made me suspect tinted contact lenses. But who was I to judge, almost caught red-handed rooting in her files? She shook my red hand, and brushed a smear of ash from her palm. That penetrating violet gaze again: oh God, arrest me now, end this agony.

But no, she calmly sat, toad by her side, retelling how she thought up Survival of the Fittest as a one-off event to help Marianne's cause, and how its growth had astonished but pleased her immeasurably, and how much money it had raised for those darling little children whose lives were blighted. It was like listening to a TV commercial, and I let it wash over me, my hand automatically taking shorthand notes.

Finally she stopped, and I realised the interview was over. Liza Boyd-Adams shook my hand once more, addressed my glazed eyes with her tinted ones, and I was leaving, two steps behind Mr Toad. They were letting me go, I was being released, faster, faster, down the corridor, away, free and clear – but no!

'Ms Knight,' her voice pulled me back like a bird on a chain. 'Wait a moment, please.' My shoulders sank. I waited for my bag to be grabbed and turned upside down to discharge its incriminating evidence.

'Do you, Anna Knight, plead guilty to stealing a binful of rubbish and half a disk of useless material?' 'I do, yer honour.'

But those were not the words I heard. What she really said was: 'They're auditioning a new team-leader for Survival of the Fittest, I'd like to see the candidates myself, I'll take you over there.'

And so we lost the toad and I found myself entering the glass dome of the Cosmosphere to sit high up in the stands and watch Shelley battle it out with half a dozen others to be Viper's stand-in.

Liza Boyd-Adams gave me a running commentary as they climbed the precipitous Peak Too-Early, dodged blasteroids lobbed by the wily Spin Doctor, shinned the tail of the Boss from Mars, and crossed the River of Diminishing Returns by clinging to a frozen cash-floe.

This was purgatory, and I was serving my time, forced to sit beside my innocent victim and be nice to her, despite my three-headed infirmity and ever-reddening hands.

'I have to admit, I really enjoy this,' smiled Ms Boyd-Adams, clapping a hand to her mouth as one girl came to grief on the relentless wheel of the Rat Race.

'Actually, I have to admit something too,' I replied. 'My daughter's on trial down there.'

'Really? How thrilling. Don't tell me who she is, let me guess.'

She perused the competing specimens of womanhood, now negotiating the slippery slopes of Mount Burn-Out and emerging through the Tunnel of Vision. She guessed the skinniest and mousiest of them all. Deeply unflattered, I put her right.

'Ah!' she exclaimed, as Shelley executed a particularly thrilling leap across the Chasm of Debt, 'now I see. How could I have been so blind? She is magnificent.' Yes, she was, I took a vicarious pride in that praise.

'Do you attend many of the Survival of the Fittest events?'

'Oh, yes' she smiled – a smile that would not shame a toothpaste ad – 'I come to them all. My work involves so much wading through figures, and so much humdrum administration, it bucks up my spirits to come here. It's such a boost to know that everyone's having fun *and* raising money for a good cause. I love it, I love working with the charity team, particularly Marianne.'

She was intense, as all high-flyers are, but she was so overwhelmingly nice with it, gushing over with enthusiasm. A nice, sincere, good person – and I had rifled her mail, broken into her personal files, and stolen her fag-ends. What kind of a worm was I?

A worm who produced a team-leader, that's what. Shelley was even now being singled out as the victor down there in the arena. Marianne stepped forward to give her a hug and Liza burst into applause on my behalf.

I blushed, the model of a modest mother: 'That's my girl.'

Shelley and Marianne looked up and spotted us. They both waved and came running up the gangway.

'We're saved, Ma,' gleamed Shelley, breathless. 'I can tell the bank manager to stuff his threatening letters up his—'

'Shelley, this is Liza Boyd-Adams, financial director of Futures, and creator of Survival of the Fittest.'

'I'm honoured,' returned my daughter with the airy handshake of the newly successful.

Marianne interposed: 'Liza will be paying your wages, Shelley. She does all the accounts for Survival of the Fittest, in her own time. We really are deeply indebted.'

'Oh, Marianne, please' returned Liza, 'it isn't a chore, it's a pleasure.'

Shelley had little patience with mutual admiration societies: 'Well,' she announced, 'all I need now is a name that'll sock it to the opposition.'

I cast my mind back to Guy Madden, sprawled on the pavement under her feet, and the name he later used to express his submission: 'How about Amazon?'

'Good! Yes,' enthused Liza, 'Amazon and Bulwark. Beauty and the Beast. I'm sure we can market that.'

As we came away I managed to slip a word of thanks to Marianne. 'Don't even mention it, dear,' she responded. 'She was the best of the bunch. Such vitality, she'll have Viper looking to her laurels.'

A good job Marianne hadn't seen her half-drowned in debt and depression. 'Anyway, it's I who must thank you, Anna,' she went on. 'I felt better after our talk the other day, it helped me put this infernal triangle of my marriage in perspective.'

'He's still away then?'

She nodded: 'I'm coping, my dear. I sometimes think that's what I was put on this earth for.'

Fourteen

G uy Madden was waiting for me in the corridor outside his office, nerves pulsing in his too-perfect face, ready to pounce. 'Anna, we need to discuss what you got at Futures. We can't talk here, come down to my car.'

'Guy, does it ever occur to you to ask people politely instead of giving instructions?' I grouched. 'I've just driven back from there hell for leather through the rain. Don't I even merit a cup of coffee?'

'You'll merit a gallon of Gold Blend if you've got what I need, but let's get business out of the way first.'

I sighed deeply and accompanied him to his car. It was still raining. We dashed across the car park to the yellow Jaguar, and hurtled into it, steaming up its insides. Guy leaned over to dump his briefcase on the back seat, peering warily out of the windows as he did so: 'Did anyone follow you from Futures?'

'Follow me? I don't know, Guy, I was too glad to be getting away from the place. It scared me rigid doing this for you.'

'You didn't notice any suspicious characters, any cars that kept appearing in the rear-view mirror?'

'Guy, it's bad enough your having a severe case of the willies without trying to pass them on to me.'

'Perhaps they let you go deliberately. With stuff they wanted me to see – a false trail.'

'If you're saying I'm the booby set to trap you then I'm going home now. I don't need this. I put my neck on the line for you, I'm as wound up as a contortionist's jock-strap, the least you could do is look at what I've brought and say one little word your nanny should have taught you.'

'What?'

'Oh forget it. Here.' I unzipped my bag, poked around, pulled out my booty and a cloud of cigarette ash joined the steam. Sweet papers and tissues tumbled out, besmirching his precious classic car.

'What is this? I thought you were a journalist, not a bag-lady.'

'Oh you'd noticed I have a profession? In that case you should've noticed I also have a good name, and I'm darned if I'm going to lose it carrying out your dirty work again.'

'The disk, the disk,' he pressed with impatience.

I gave him the disk, vowing never again to help a vain man in his hour of greed. I wiped the steam from my window and stared out at a man in a light-coloured mac standing at a bus stop across the road, getting soaked. I knew how he felt, a wretch at the mercy of an unfeeling force.

Guy had pulled a laptop computer from his briefcase. The disk slotted in, he pressed buttons, and column after column of accounts hit the screen. 'All hail to mighty Mammon, look at that,' he breathed. I looked; it meant no more to me than a Sanskrit tract. 'Liza Boyd-Adams must be dealing with a budget that could run a Third World country.'

'Right. She's powerful – and she plays the part to the hilt. But not all hard-heads are heartless, Guy,' I said pointedly. 'Liza genuinely puts a hell of a lot of effort into helping Marianne's charity. She evidently has a conscience. Oh, sorry,

I forgot, you're not familiar with the word, are you? It means suckers like me who do something for nothing.'

'Ach!' he muttered, deaf to my lecture. 'This is no use. It's their catering accounts – d'you know 6000 tons of French fries and 10 million bread-buns were stuffed down the throats of Futures customers last year?'

I felt like stuffing the whole lot down one man's throat at that moment. He was pounding the machine like a one-finger pianist, crazed by its refusal to play his tune. My gaze wandered again, watching the man in the mac, his coat-flaps spreading wings in the wind.

Guy grunted: 'More.'

'Pardon?'

'It's all very sobering finding out that my annual food profits would barely match Futures' for a month, but no earthly use as far as their takeover plans are concerned. I need more. What else have you got?'

I held out my bag of detritus – he could jolly well rummage for his own rubbish if he wanted it that badly. He extracted a ball of paper, dismissing it after a short glance, delving deeper into the pile and salvaging a bundle of paper-shreds. I had been careful to disturb the shredded sheets as little as possible, and some of the sliced edges of this one still clung together, the paper fibres sticking like Velcro. He closed his laptop and carefully laid the strips on its cover.

One by one he straightened them, moving one line here, another there, edging them into a semblance of order and then sat looking at it for several minutes, so engrossed he seemed to forget my presence.

'What is it, Guy?'

Silence. I peered over his shoulder. All I could decipher from the jiggledy page was the name of Futures' chairman, Jolyon Burchill, and a figure that looked like £100 million. Hardly peanuts, even for a man of as many mansions as J.B.

'Ah-hah' was his only utterance.

'Guy, what does it mean?' I demanded with mounting

frustration. 'I feel I've earned the right to share in any result from this, don't you?'

He turned. He kissed me hard. I was so stunned I simply pursed my lips and kept them pursed, tight, refusing to let him in.

'There,' he said. 'That shut you up, didn't it?'

I unglued my lipstick, unclamped my tongue and rasped, 'If you think that's what kisses are for I'm having nothing more to do with this.'

'Anna,' he touched my hand. 'I know what kisses are for. That one was for thank you, and this one . . .' he leaned forward and brushed my cheek gently with his lips, 'is for sorry.'

'Careful, that's twice you've used that word to me.'

'Mmmm – I don't want to get too used to it.'

'So what's brought all this on? I'm aware I'm not getting something for nothing. I take it that of all the bumph I managed to bring back, that mangled mess of paper is of actual use to you.'

'It's not what I wanted, but yes, it could be useful. Forgive me for being such a brute. Sometimes I'm so focused I forget all manners. I repeat, I'm grateful for what you've done.'

'What is it then – proof they're eyeing you for a takeover? Is that what the £100 million's all about?'

He gave a hollow laugh, shaking his head: 'Heavens above, Mad Mad World would have to be paved with gold for that. No, it's part of a confidential memo from Mr Jolyon Moneybags Burchill to Liza – the sort labelled "Read and Destroy". The gist is that a large amount of cash is to be quietly spirited out of the country.'

'Why?'

'I'm guessing that what governments don't know about, they can't tax.'

'You think Futures is cheating the Inland Revenue?'

'Ah no, maybe that'd be too difficult a scam to pull, even for Jolyon Burchill. But his personal finances are a different matter. He made his fortune in the music business, right? He always maintained he'd keep his recording empire, then suddenly he changed his mind, sold out to his main rivals and said he was going to concentrate on Futures.'

'Oh yes, the £100 million – that's what the papers said the deal was worth. So?'

'His rivals wanted the company so much, I believe it took extra sweeteners to persuade him to part with it. Look, this memo mentions the £100 million, which must be being dealt with above board – but here he's informing Ms Liza Double-Barrel about the timing of a further injection of cash for her to oversee. Its destination is his own personal offshore trust. See here: phrases like "utmost confidentiality", "deny knowledge of this transaction". Now I want to know what that's all about, because it seems to me Burchill wants to keep everyone – including the taxman – blithely ignorant of this particular capital gain.'

'Why would he do that, though? He's rich.'

'But the rich always want to get richer. Besides, he's an empire-builder, Anna, maybe another part of his empire's draining his resources. He's such a secretive so-and-so, we don't know. What I do know is this could be my blocker, I could threaten to expose his tax evasion if he tries to muscle in on Mad Mad World. Burchill's a bully, he'd respond to bully tactics. The problem now is getting proof. Let me see if there's any more bits of this memo in there.'

He sorted through the remaining litter in the bag, cast it aside in exasperation and continued to stare at the ripped strips as though he could spirit his desires out of their broken lines.

At last the bus had arrived for the man in the mac. I sent him a mental farewell, soulmates through adversity. But when the bus departed, the man was still there.

'Guy?'

'Mmmmm – hold this carefully for me, will you? I want the shreds to stay touching until I can stick them together. I'm sure I've some Sellotape somewhere.'

'Guy,' I persisted, doing as he asked, 'that man across the road. I think he's watching us.'

Immediately he was galvanised. His eyes narrowed. Swiftly he finished taping the shreds as I told him about the bus, all the time thinking: This is crazy, I'm getting as paranoid as he is.

'I'm probably wrong – it could just've been the wrong service,' I concluded lamely.

'The hell with that. Even if it was, you'd get on it in this rain, wouldn't you? Just to get out of the wet?'

'He couldn't be any wetter.'

'We'll see about that.'

He handed me the precious document, reached for the keys, turned on the engine, and I had an awful vision of a man in a mac being chased down the promenade by a mad yellow Jaguar.

'Guy, please. If you're going to play Avengers let me out of here.'

'You sometimes talk to me like a child.'

'What d'you expect?' I glared at him meaningfully, and praise be, he got the message and turned the engine off.

'I thought test pilots were supposed to be steady, unflappable people,' I said. 'Why let a sodden man in a mac get to you?'

He gave me a penetrating look and I thought for a second he was going to tell me how he lost his job. Instead he smashed his fist against his classic steering wheel.

'I am being watched, Anna. It may seem to you like I'm over-reacting, but I can feel Futures on my back at every turn. Why d'you think I hide in here to look at this stuff?'

'If you really believe that why don't you hire your own watcher? Did you speak to Brian Battersby?'

He nodded. 'No good. He's one of them.'

'What?' I gasped, incredulous.

'Why else would he say he's too busy to work for me, too busy even to tell me what he did for Llew? Futures must have put him on their payroll to keep him quiet. Either that or he was always working for them.'

'Then hire someone else, there are more security consultants than Brian Battersby. Better ones too.'

'How could I trust them? Futures has more hush-money than me.'

He looked at me with sorrowful appeal. Help me, I'm a lost boy all alone in an evil world, the look said. I'm not paranoid, it's just that everyone's out to get me. If I was his friend, his only trustworthy helpmeet, he must be desperate. I wasn't happy to be the scraping at the bottom of his barrel, but I sighed: 'You really do need to get to the root of this business, don't you? For the sake of your sanity, if nothing else.'

'There's nothing wrong with my sanity,' he spat with sudden venom.

'No, all right.' Lord help me, I was soothing him. Any minute now I'd be offering to put hot-water bottles in his bed and make him cocoa.

'Look,' he continued, trying to contain his animosity, 'I need more evidence. I've got to break into Futures myself and get rock-solid proof if I'm to accuse Jolyon Burchill of tax evasion. He'd sue me to kingdom come if I made an error.'

The last word seemed to catch in his throat like a poisoned apple. He adopted a beguiling expression, like a noble martyr. And like an idiot I was beguiled. Yes, brothers and sisters, I admit my foolish weakness for the noble martyr. He was wronged, he was an underdog, his brother had been murdered, and he was built like Flash Gordon. I took the apple and bit. 'Don't start talking about break-ins, Guy, you'll only get yourself in trouble. I'll see what else I can do.'

'You've done enough. All I've done is fanny around letting them put the wind up me. I need to fight back.'

'You've no idea of the level of security, Guy, you'll land yourself straight in jail. Look, there's no point in taking such risks until you know for certain whether Futures has designs on Mad Mad World. I'll be seeing Liza Boyd-Adams again when I go to watch this insufferable Survival of the Fittest for my article. I'll talk to her, try and make friends with her, maybe catch her off-guard and see if she lets something slip. But I cannot and will not get up to any more dirty tricks on your behalf.'

You do talk bilge sometimes, Knight, I reflected afterwards. If you think sucking up to Liza Boyd-Adams isn't a dirty trick, you're a pitiful innocent. You're in the dung-heap, sister, and you've just dug yourself deeper, so don't start complaining if you don't like the smell. You could have left it with Madden and let him get on with it, but no, you clung on, you brought it home and dumped it on your own doorstep, so you'd better take a shovel and start digging your way out.

I could not put off a certain duty any longer. I had to inform Matt I didn't want to be public relations manager for Mad Mad World. I went straight to his office after leaving Guy, anxious to get it over with.

I was sure Guy himself couldn't care less who did the job, as long as they did it perfectly, the personality didn't matter. But to Matt the personality was the be-all and end-all – to wit, he wanted me, and his bulk deflated like the Hindenburg when I gave him the disappointing news.

As a result he turned me down when I offered to cook a consolation dinner. I saw he felt lonely at Mad Mad World and he'd seen me as a fellow conspirator in pricking management pomposity.

Well, he could prick away with someone else. I couldn't be all things to this man, or indeed any man, as I'd said to Marianne. He turned round and stared out of his office window when I said I had to go.

'Look, Matt,' I tried to be conciliatory, 'I don't want this to create ill-feeling between us.'

'There's no ill-feeling, Anna,' he replied to the window. 'At least not on my part. On yours I fear there's no feeling at all.'

'That's not true! I'm just not public relations material. I'm not sugar and spice and all things nice. I'm more of the slugs and snails and puppy-dogs' tails variety.'

'It's OK, I understand, you're happier rolling around in the gutter press with the rest of the slime.'

'At least in the gutter I can look up and see stars.'

'We have stars too.'

'Yes, I know, but to me they're tinfoil and glitter-dust. Artificial. I need the real thing, Matt.'

At last he turned round, and I saw there was sadness in his eyes, and that was the real thing. 'I'd better go,' I said.

'I'm not stopping you.'

Guy was passing in the corridor when I shut the door.

'You never did get that coffee,' he said. 'Come into my office, you look badly in need of refuelling.

'Thanks,' I said. 'Actually I feel like a louse because I've just told Matt I don't want your blessed PR job.'

'He'll get over it,' replied Guy. 'PR people started lobbying for the job as soon as news of Rosie's departure went round the grapevine. Most of them are experienced – they'd be better at it than you.'

'Gee thanks.'

'I'm only saying you're far more use to me in your present capacity than you would be on my staff – pax?'

I nodded grudgingly, and drank his coffee to the dregs.

Fifteen

'Listen up, everybody!'

Everybody in the newsroom, far from listening up, cringed behind their screens when Ellis Clancy slammed into gung-ho mode. Undeterred, our commander soldiered on: 'Anna, this involves you, get up here where you belong.'

Up there, by his side, was the last place I belonged, but Ellis was in no mood for backchat. It was late afternoon, that day's paper all done, but a news conference for the following day was imminent. He was a man with a mission and short on time.

He charged ahead: 'Anna, as you know, is a soft touch – sorry, I should say a kind soul – when it comes to doing favours for Marianne Knatchbull. This time she's promised to write a feature on Survival of the Fittest. Marianne wants Northport companies to get into this charity thing. Believe it or not, I'm not as charitable as Anna. My view is, they've been getting something for nothing out of us long enough.'

Oh Lord, I thought, here goes, he's going to stymie my feature – my first chance of freelance cash. I couldn't possibly try to sell it if he put his foot down. That was an offence punishable by demotion to the lower ranks of fillers and flower shows.

'If we're going to give them free publicity,' Ellis went on, 'we might as well squeeze our own concertina at the same time. We're not a benevolent fund, as I must remind certain people before I sign their latest expense claims.'

Was his eyebrow raised at me? Yes, it was. Well I'd had to embellish the truth a little – debt-ridden daughters not being cheap to run.

'The nub of all this,' resumed Ellis, 'is that we'll be the first Northport firm to slam into Survival of the Fittest. We'll be up there, starring in our own headlines. I've just been on to our so-called rivals at the *North West Sentinel* – they're keen to thrash us and the feeling's mutual – so I need volunteers to fight for the honour of the *Northport News*. All volunteers will be rewarded with a day off, a month free of weekend duties and my undying regard until they drop their next bollock. Plus, if we win, there's a bottle of your favourite poison from my own pocket. Now, you can't say I don't offer a decent bribe. Anna, take names, get it organised. I only want winners.'

Needless to say, Ellis classed himself in the latter category, and was the first name to go down on the list. Well, he was young, and burly, but he was about as fit as the wooden leg of the desk where he sat all day. If all else failed, Ellis could sit on the opposition and bombard them with his armoury of insults and expletives.

I made straight for the younger end of the newsroom, the lads who played five-a-side soccer twice a week, the girls who swam and lusted after cricketers, and bowled a mean googly themselves, given half a chance. We needed ten. The prospect of earning Ellis's public scorn was enough to press-gang nine into my merry band. The rest were either scornful enough of Ellis to endure his pricks and arrows with disdain, or apologetically too fat, old, smoke-logged or drink-sodden – and in one unrepentant case all four.

'Anna, I don't see your name on there,' said Ellis when he returned hot and grouchy from his meeting.

'But I'm writing the piece.'

'So, you'll write a far better one if you take part, won't you?'

'Ellis, I couldn't normally give a damn about my age, but surely I've earned the right to draw the line at prancing about on an overgrown adventure playground.'

'Oh hark at Miss Prim. Dear me, slap my wrist and write a hundred lines: Anna Knight's an old has-been.'

'Listen, Jane Fonda's older than me, and I don't suppose you class her as a has-been. Just because I don't have her time, money or physique, it doesn't mean I need a Zimmer frame.'

'So what? I don't have Arnold Schwarzenegger's time, money or physique – but I'm in there.'

Arnie's teutonic determination was certainly in there too, and I wasn't going to win this particular battle of wills. With ill grace I added my name to the list, and Ellis grinned, letting all volunteers off early as a sign of his approval. I got my coat ready to hasten home, hoping that by some miracle an Olympic athlete might have joined the staff by tomorrow.

As I went out through the front office I noticed a familiar figure at the classified ads counter. 'Janette? What brings you here?'

'Oh, Anna, hello love,' she gave a battle-worn smile. 'I've just been putting an advert in for a lodger – the more the merrier – cash is tight nowadays, love, I don't mind admitting it.' She lifted a couple of heavy carrier bags full of groceries, and tottered a little on her spiked heels.

'Here, give me one of those,' I said. 'I'll give you a lift home if you like.'

Her face brightened at this small gesture: 'Would you? Only the girls'll be back from school soon, the bus takes forever, and I don't like leaving them on their own too long.'

I took the seafront route, which is usually quieter and quicker than any other in winter. As we passed Mad Mad World I had to stop at a pedestrian crossing while a man with a toolbox hurried across. Janette was prattling on about food prices, how she was having to seek out the cheapest supermarkets, cutting back to bare essentials – 'I'll be hanging out the teabags to use again before I've – my God, it's him.'

'What?'

'The bloke with the toolbox. It's Penny's fella, I'm sure of it.'

He was walking away from us, and the bald spot on the back of his head was clearly visible, while the fur of his sheepskin coat spilled out of an L-shaped rip on his shoulder.

'He's going into that car park, Anna,' seethed Janette. 'Follow him, follow him.' I needed no urging, but it was a right turn and a line of traffic was coming the other way. Janette coud hardly contain her frustration.

'Come on, get out the way,' she raged under her breath. 'You can make it after the bus – now!'

I swung the Metro round into the car park. It was well set back from the road, behind a miniature golf course, closed for the winter, and it was deserted.

'Damn,' cursed Janette.

A movement caught my eye, and I noticed, behind a toilet block, one lone van. A chugging noise rent the air – its engine being turned over. 'Got him!'

Janette delved into her shopping bags, came up with two large bean-cans and burst out of the door, running to the van with the stiff gait of the stiletto-heeled. I got out to follow. She was banging on the driver's window with her baked beans.

'Get out, get out now! I know who you are, you yellow-bellied snake, you! Why don't you go to the police and tell'em the truth instead of hiding behind Penny Worthington's skirts? If you came out with it, she'd come back.'

The van lurched into life, reversing with a skid. As

the driver changed gear Janette took aim and bowled one of her bean-cans straight at the windscreen. It whitened like instant frost and the engine stalled. A fist punched through the frost, spattering glass everywhere.

Janette would not give up. She threw herself at the driver's door, pulling at the locked handle, screaming, 'Get out and face up to me like a man!'

He was desperately trying to restart the engine, but it stubbornly refused. In exasperation at the noise from the bonnet and the beating woman at his shoulder, he flung the door open, bowling Janette into a wire-mesh fence. A fence post broke under her and she lay on the ground, gasping for breath.

I ran over to help her, but she shouted, 'No, Anna, watch out!'

I'd no sooner heard her than the tarmac flew up to meet me, my feet tripped by his shoe at my ankle. He loomed over me.

I lashed out in fury with the only weapon I had – my car keys – ramming them towards his face. But these were what he wanted. He grabbed my arm, yanked it away from him, trying to prise my fingers from the keyring. Blood seeped from the hand he'd used to punch the windscreen, dripping into my face as I lay under him. I hung on, and as we wrestled Janette shouted, 'Leave her alone! Go fight someone your own size.'

Then she flung her other bean-can at his head. It hit his sheepskin-padded shoulder and bounced off, catching me full on the temple. My ears rang, my grip loosened, and in that moment he grasped the keys and was gone.

The Metro screamed with abuse as he booted the accelerator. He was taking my car. Overcome with anger I picked up the broken fence-post and tried to spear it towards the windscreen. It missed, but he instinctively ducked, wrenching the wheel blindly in my direction. I tried to leap away, he tried to evade me, but we both got it wrong and the wing brushed my body, spinning me into the toilet block.

Pain seared through my head as I hit the pebbledash chin first, grating my way to the ground.

He swerved away, out of the car park, and I gingerly fingered my jaw, which seemed to be swelling up like a mammoth's mumps.

Sixteen

Janette was crouching over me as I lay, still spreadeagled in the car park. 'Gawd, Anna, are you all right? It's all my fault, I wish I'd never set eyes on the so-and-so.'

I was all right, or so I thought, barring a swollen face and a headache heavy as thunder. I creaked myself up into a sitting position, trying to decide whether I should go to the police or to a doctor first or, as I'd rather, just crawl home to bed and shut out the world.

When I tried to seek Janette's advice, the decision was made for me. I could not open my jaw. I was forced to bray like a bad ventriloquist, and I'd be no use to myself or anyone else until it was locked back in its socket.

Janette quickly took my welfare in hand. A woman with a dog was cutting through the car park on her way back from a walk on the beach. She quailed at the sight of Janette – broken-heeled, laddered-stockinged – hailing her over, but she approached, overcoming her caution when she saw my state.

The dog thought I was great fun, a giant bone, trailing droplets of tasty blood. As he yelped around me, his mistress, a timorous, retired soul, tried to cow him into submission while listening to Janette's colourful rendition of what had happened. Between them they helped me to my feet and ushered me towards her car, parked on the promenade.

As I eased myself into the passenger seat I could see Janette was getting agitated, and I knew she must be worried about her daughters. My communications were little more than painful grunts, grimaces and nods, but through sign language I managed to convey to her that she'd no need to come to hospital with me. She was within walking distance of her home, but our new-found companion insisted on dropping her off.

In the car, Janette suddenly turned to me: 'You'll be going to the police after this, right?'

I nodded.

'You tell 'em who he was and why we wanted to get him. I know I promised Penny I wouldn't breathe a word, but I'm damned if I'm going to keep my mouth shut after this. He's nothing but a rat.'

I left her waving at me from the doorstep, angry and shaken and minus her shopping apart from a battered bean-can, but otherwise unharmed. As my helper dropped me off outside Casualty I expressed gratitude with a mime show worthy of Marcel Marceau, and she drove away, the dog still watching in frustration through the rear window, pining for my blood.

I don't know which was the worse, the agony of the doctor forcing my jaw back into place, or the sound it made. Wrench, crack, creak, click.

'There,' he said with satisfaction. 'How's that?'

'Sickening,' I said, surprising myself with an articulate word.

'We aim to please. Now, the nurse here will clean up those nasty grazes and the NHS can chalk up one more successful treatment as per ye Patient's Charter.'

'You're surprisingly cheerful for a harassed house-man,' I ventured slowly, testing out my restored power of speech.

'Ahhh, you've got me at the beginning of my shift. Try me the day after tomorrow and I may not be so gentle.'

'No thanks.'

'How did you get into this scrape, anyway?'

'A man and I had an argument over my car keys. He won.'

'Have you told the police, or was it your husband?'

Cynical housemen can wear a patient's patience. I bade farewell as soon as I'd been cleaned up and jabbed against a plague of infectious diseases. I smelt like an antiseptic factory and looked as though I'd done six rounds with Frank Bruno.

The police were rather more sympathetic. Actually, by this time, I was not so much upset as angry that this man had steamrollered over us; angry that two women were not up to stopping one pig of a man. The woman officer listened patiently as my anger spilled out all over the interview room.

Two cups of sweet tea and a cigarette later (yes, gentle readers, I gave in to the demon weed) I was deemed safe enough to be let loose on Chief Inspector Alex Anderson.

He stood up as I walked into the room. 'Do you want the good news or the bad news first?' he asked in his gentlest Scots burr.

'Today's been all bad news, I could do with some good.'

'Well then, we've found your car.'

'That's good news? I was hoping to get a decent replacement on the insurance.'

'If that's all the gratitude we're—'

He broke off as my legs seemed to wobble under me and I thumped down into a chair. 'I'm sorry,' I said, 'forgive me. I've been so angry it's driven all the thanks out of me. I'm damned if I'll let the bastard have that satisfaction. I am grateful, really. I'm quite fond of that old car.'

His voice dropped to a gentler tone. 'The bad news is we haven't yet found the bastard, as you put it. He dumped the car at the railway station. We're bringing it in for fingerprints.'

'Blood too. There'll be blood on the door, and probably on the steering wheel. He cut his hand when Janette shattered his windscreen.'

'That was very public-spirited of her – blood's meat and drink to the forensics.'

'Hmmm – I doubt she was thinking of that at the time. What about his van? Surely you can trace him through the registration number?'

'We could if it was registered in his name. It isn't. I've just had a message through. Apparently it's still in the name of the previous owner, who looks nothing like your description. Your man paid cash for it a few days ago and it looks like he gave false particulars. No go, I'm afraid.'

'He had a toolbox, and he was walking away from Mad Mad World – he could've been working near there.'

'I'm asking Mad Mad World for details of their employees and contractors,' he sighed. 'We could have made a hell of a lot more progress if Penny Worthington and Janette Jones had told us the truth about this in the first place.'

'I know. Janette was labouring under a misplaced loyalty to Penny, I'm afraid. She wants to tell the truth now, this business has shaken it out of her.'

'When did she tell you?' His eyes became icy.

'This afternoon,' I lied quickly. 'She had to tell me why she was so keen to stop this complete stranger.'

'Janette's version is he was a husband having an extra-marital fling with Penny, who didn't want to get dragged into a murder inquiry, am I right?'

'Well yes, but from his behaviour it seems to me there's more to it than that.'

'Mmmm,' he nodded, raising an eyebrow knowingly.

'Do you know who we're looking for?'

'Let's just say I have my suspicions.'

'For pity's sake, who?'

'That's as far as I can go at the moment, Anna. Let's not forget who you are.'

'I'm a member of the public who's been run over by some maniac who stole my car, and I want to know who he is.'

'You're also a member of the public who writes for the newspapers, and I cannot implicate anyone until I have the evidence, all right?'

I sighed. The painkillers were beginning to wear off, my jaw was aching and I didn't have the strength to battle another intransigent man that day. Let them go hang themselves on their own virility.

'I'll get someone to drive you home, Anna,' he said kindly. 'I'll give you a ring when you can collect your car.'

'Thanks.'

'No – I should thank you. You've had a hard time of it, and I'm grateful you've been so open with us.'

'Don't mention it, I hope I can say the same of you some day.'

'We'll get there, Anna, trust me. We're on to him now and we'll get him in the end.'

One favour my assailant had done me was to put me out of the running for Survival of the Fittest. When I told Ellis on the phone what had happened he seemed to think I could still take part – 'It's your legs and arms that do the business, not your jaw' – but when I turned up at the office next day and he saw my purpling cheek and blackened chin he had second thoughts.

k   'Blimey, that mush won't look too good above a leotard. Nah, sorry Anna, you'll spoil the corporate image. Get me a substitute.'

Jon Spry happened to flit by at that moment, his flowing ringlets tied back, and in another moment he'd been grabbed by the pony-tail and hauled up before Ellis as my prize. 'This one's young and good-looking, squire,' I said.

'He'd be worth a tasty sum at the flesh market.' Ellis looked up, said 'Done!' and returned to his keyboard.

'Wait a minute, what's this all about?' enquired the object of our desires.

'We want your body, Jon,' I said, as he put up his hand in protest. 'Sorry, but you've no say in the matter. Your company needs choice and handsome specimens to fight on the front line of the circulation war, and you've just passed the fitness test.'

'Don't tell me I've been volunteered for Survival of the Fittest.'

'He's bright too,' I threw at Ellis.

'He'll do,' grunted our leader, and that was that.

And so, a few days later, I joined the coach party got up to support the *Northport News* in its self-styled battle of the giants with the *North West Sentinel*.

Actually there were several coaches involved, for Ellis had taken the opportunity to liaise with the promotions department and flog the spectacle of a local newspaper war for all it was worth. A host of readers joined our cause, less out of loyalty than in response to a cut-price ticket deal and the chance to glimpse the glory that was Futures. Nevertheless they swelled our ranks most gratifyingly, and Ellis, his eyes ablaze with enthusiasm for this prized fillip to his curriculum vitae, lost no time in melding his troops together in a series of war whoops, moving from coach to coach at each loo-stop. By the time we arrived, the supporters were ready to go over the top for their paper's champions.

Futures did not seem quite such foreign ground to me as before. I was camouflaged among our own partisan group and felt a little more self-assured. Of course people did stare – my purple patches had now blossomed a bilious yellowy-green, and my chin still bore black blotches – but I no longer felt the dreaded three heads and stalk-eyes syndrome that had afflicted my earlier visit.

The tall, polished figure of Liza Boyd-Adams was

easy to spot, right by the door of the Cosmosphere, overseeing the tickets.

'Don't forget,' she announced to the passing queue, 'the second half of the evening is an auction of promises and I want everyone to give as generously as they can, the charity needs your money.'

Ellis smirked: 'Don't worry, we'll deliver the goods – after we've thrashed the Sentinels.' The team cheered as they disappeared to the changing room for their pep talk.

The *Northport News* had drawn Shelley – or rather Amazon – for its leader, while the *Sentinel* was massed behind the formidable force of Bulwark. The teams had been rehearsing separately all week, and now Ellis felt they were a finely honed slaughter machine.

I waited until Liza took a seat, for I had obliged myself to carry out a little more intelligence-gathering on behalf of Mad Mad World. Then I slid into the seat beside her and gleamed my best, most friendly smile. 'Good Lord, you look absolutely terrible,' she recoiled. 'What on earth happened to your face?'

'I had an argument with a car, and the car won.'

'Dear me, I am sorry, I didn't mean to be so rude.' Her veneer of composure was swiftly in place. 'I'm glad it doesn't appear to have stopped you working. What a varied life you must lead.'

'That's one way of putting it. Listen, Liza,' I got out my notebook, 'I really need to ask you some more questions for my article. You see, I believe, if I market this well enough, I could sell it to the nationals, or perhaps a women's magazine – the way you and Marianne have succeeded with this event is really quite phenomenal.'

She seemed abashed, toying coyly with a stray lock of her glossy chestnut hair: 'How wonderful of you to say so. But one thing you must understand: our interest in this is not simply philanthropic. The charity aspect is most important, but it has to make business sense too. From a strictly business point of view, it's a question of promoting our core product

with these charity spin-offs which at first might seem periph-
eral, but which in fact bring in an influx of extra visitors who
all spend cash when they're here, and spread the word when
they leave.'

'I'm sure other parks could learn a lot from your
approach – Mad Mad World at Northport, for instance. Do
you know it at all?'

'I – uhhh – of course. Doesn't everyone in this part
of the world?'

'What do you think of their operation?'

'Obviously it's a much older-established business
than ours. It has suffered perhaps from a lack of innovation
in the past few years.'

'Do you study the competition? "You" meaning
Futures?'

'Every business has to. That's what this event is all
about – competition between rival firms.'

'Has Futures studied Mad Mad World?'

She blinked her violet eyes.

'I only ask,' I went on hurriedly, 'because it is our
local amusement park, and of interest to our readers. It might
be old, but it still has a following, and it's on a prime site. I
imagine all it needs is redevelopment by a more innovative
management and it could become a much more aggressive
competitor in the market. What do you think?'

She gave me a long, penetrating stare, and said coldly,
'I thought you wanted to ask me about Survival of the Fittest?'

'I'm just trying to get an overview of your thoughts
on competition between rival companies – it is, after all, the
driving force behind Survival of the Fittest. Of course this is
only a game, but in the outside world successful companies
often take over their rivals. Is that an expansion strategy
favoured by Futures?'

She gave her most brilliant, defiant smile: 'I'm sorry,
I really must get back to the ticket office. Most of the
audience seems to be in now, we'll be starting soon, and I
have to supervise the takings.'

'But can we talk more later?'

'Of course,' she said, oozing openness and generosity. 'I'll come back to watch the latter half of the confrontation. After all, I mustn't miss Amazon's first performance. You must be very proud.'

She left, a professional to her polished fingertips, the picture of grace under pressure. To be honest, I'd hardly given a thought to being proud, so intent I'd been on probing deep into the enemy territory of Ms Boyd-Adams's employers.

Nevertheless when the lights dimmed and heavy, striving rock music began to blast around the Cosmosphere, I looked up into the spotlight where my daughter stood, strong, beautiful and omniscient in this pleasure-ground, and my heart lurched. Her hair streamed long and wild, her muscles gleamed under a green bodysuit, she flexed a bow and shot a flaming arrow into the crater of Mount Burn-Out, which leapt into flame like a roused volcano.

'Amazon!' hailed the deep voiceover, 'Queen of the Jungle! Mistress of all she surveys! Leader of the *Northport News* challenge team! Amazon, we salute you!'

A crescendo of cheers rallied and echoed round the Cosmosphere: 'Yo, Amazon! Yo, Northport!'

A second spotlight shone, this time on a human tank whose biceps matched my waist, and who looked tough enough to sprinkle iron filings on his Sugar Puffs. He wore a bandanna and a pirate patch on one eye, and his body was contained in little more than leather thongs.

'Bulwark! Bastion of the barricades! Mountain of muscle! Leader of the *North West Sentinel* challenge team! Bulwark, we salute you!'

'Yo, Bulwark! Yo, Sentinels!'

Amid a flurry of ticker-tape and razzmatazz the two teams ran on, Ellis resplendent in a leopard-print Lycra leotard that made me and the rest of the staff curl up in mirth.

'Amazon – ready?' boomed the disembodied voice, 'Bulwark – ready? Let battle commence!'

The battle launched with a game called Aim High, a cross between basketball and rugby, in which the teams did their utmost to foul and tackle their opponents. The first team to score a goal won the right to head off with the glittering gold ball and start the assault course. The other team's task was not only to follow them but to snatch the ball from their clutches by fair means or foul.

Aim High got off to an exciting start – Bulwark charged through, flattening the Northport team with sheer bulk; Amazon zipped hither and thither, nipping through gaps that hardly seemed there, urging her flattened team to get up and at the Sentinels.

Inevitably Bulwark scored, and the Sentinels powered off in his wake to scale Peak Too-Early, a vertical cliff face. The whole of the course was embedded in the Ball Park, heaps of coloured rubber balls to soften the landing of fallers by the wayside. Ellis roared with fury at Bulwark's early lead, lobbing rubber balls to fell a Sentinel who quailed at the very sight of his red and spitting face.

Amazon split her team in two to bring the Spin-Doctor's armoury to bear. Half the Northports tackled the Sentinels from behind, the others pelted them from the top with the Spin-Doctor's blasteroid gun, and by the time Bulwark neared the summit Ellis was waiting. He leaned down to grab the ball from under Bulwark's thong, and was gone.

He leapt on to the tail of the Boss from Mars and his team-mates followed after. But the Spin-Doctor was now aiming at the Northports and Bulwark was swinging the tail with all his might. Ellis, to his infinite shame, dropped the ball. A great cheer went up from the Sentinels' crowd as their team homed in to clutch it to their collective bosom and sally across the River of Diminishing Returns.

Amazon forged in, leading her stalwarts to set up a ferocious tidal wave by rocking the frozen cash floes. The Sentinels, trying to cross by straddling a giant bottle labelled 'Liquid Asset', wobbled until Bulwark's weight tipped the balance. Splashdown. Ball gone, Amazon grabbed it and was out on the other side, heading for Mount Burn-Out.

A smoky heap of polystyrene coals formed a perilous scree which she had to clamber. Slipping backwards, she wavered and tossed the ball to a team-mate. A Sentinel intervened, and the prize was lost. Ellis was in a frenzy. Hurling himself on the hapless opponent he tackled him to the floor. They both slid down the slope and Ellis overbalanced. The Sentinel broke free and his team-mates surrounded him like bodyguards.

They reached the top, tossed the ball over the flaming crater and leapt down to cross racketing gangplanks called the Movers and Shakers. The Northports shook these with wild abandon, but the Sentinels clung on and reached the other side. Their target was a giant hamster-wheel, the Rat-Race, but Amazon was already there, pounding the padded treadmill, refusing to give the Sentinels an inch. The ball had to be thrown through a chute in the wheel before the Sentinels could carry on. Thwarted, they bombarded Amazon with coals from Mount Burn-Out. She fell, but Jon Spry leapt on to take her place. A coal slipped under his heels and, slap! He tumbled into the Ball-Park.

Bulwark filled the gap and leapt on to the Rat-Race, bashing the ball through the chute where a Sentinel was waiting to catch it. But Ellis came from nowhere, leaping to snatch it from the air before the startled Sentinel could react.

Ellis screamed down to the crystalline Tunnel of Vision, clambering through on hands and knees, when suddenly he was gone – pitched through a hidden trap door into the Chasm of Debt. He cursed and howled, holding the ball above a rising tide of crazy foam. Bulwark roared like an enraged bull, galloping towards it, but Jon Spry swerved in front of him, tripping him into the chasm, and Amazon soared over both of them, grabbing the ball from Ellis's outstretched hand as she flew.

The Northports charged after her, lifting her shoulder-high for the final challenge. The Sentinels tried to maul her down, but with a mighty heave she threw the ball past the snapping Jaws of Defeat straight into the arms of Major Deal. The military mannequin's eyes lit up, his hat flew off and bells sounded. Amazon had won! The *Northport News* had won!

No longer Amazon but my own Shelley, triumphant over her own adversity, she waved at me as she was carried on a victory lap by her jubilant team-mates. The inhabitants of the Cosmosphere cheered their congratulations into the night sky.

So it was understandable that I didn't hear the commotion outside, didn't hear the alarms and shouts until a man ran in like a fleeing gazelle, leaping seats into the centre of the Cosmosphere, followed by a great charge of louts bawling and baring their teeth in a mass invasion. They poured over the assault course, skidded on the crazy foam, flung missiles from the Ball Park. A thin blue line of security guards followed, the thrill of the chase in their eyes as they clutched the nearest of the hooligans by their scruffy necks.

Shelley sprang from the shoulders of her team-mates, sprinting to catch up with the gang-leader as he headed towards a fire exit on the far side of the Cosmosphere. She launched herself from the Ball Park fence to land on his shoulders. He twisted, turned, threw her heavily to the ground, and she was left holding his denim jacket while he slipped through the exit, losing himself in the crowds outside.

She lay, breathing heavily, but motionless. I ran over.

'Shelley? Shelley, are you all right?'

'I'm fine, just a bit stunned, that's all,' she panted. 'I still don't quite believe what I saw. He had glasses on and a heavy stubble, but Ma, I'm sure it was Guy Madden.'

'What?'

'Yes, yes it was. I'm going to tell the security men.'

'No, no don't, Shelley. Please don't. I'll tell you why later on. Just give them the jacket and have done with it, OK?'

Seventeen

The coach swayed as its cargo of celebrants heaved each other on board for the homeward journey, singing and chanting and trumpeting their exploits to anyone who would listen.

Ellis, blown up with pride like a hot-air balloon, bounced along the aisle, still wearing his leopard-print leotard under his shirt and trousers. He crowed as he flung his arms round his team-mates on the back seat, addressing them like a platoon of grunts after their first battle: 'We slaughtered 'em, we totally wiped them out. That lump of meat they call Bulwark – huh!' he clicked his fingers, 'I've more brains in my plonker. He was dead, the moment he picked up that ball and ran.'

The faces of the team shone up at him, planets to his sun, basking in self-adulation, basking – indeed – in Ellis-adulation, a phenomenon previously unknown in the ranks of the newsroom. They relived every move of the action with minute precision, arguing over details, punching each other with mock-indignation, and dissolving in laughter at their own derring-do.

The singing went on, the back-slapping continued, and as we trundled our way home a call went up for a loo-stop due to the intake of triumphal lager that had found its way on board. I was grateful for this respite, for I had been lost in my own ruminations, staring through the window, as Ellis pointed out to his comrades, 'like a stiff at a wedding'. The general consensus was that the best place for a loo-stop was the next pub, thus allowing the crew to replace the liquid ballast they were due to bail out.

We rolled up outside the Sitting Duck, and I got off the coach in search not of drink but of fresh air and a little peace from the clarions of war.

So Guy Madden had been too impatient, he had tried to infiltrate Futures with a troop of hooligans. Was the man quite deranged?

I circled the car park, and as I turned round the back of the pub, I pulled up sharp. A yellow E-type Jaguar was parked in the corner.

Immediately I braved the steamy, smoky swelter inside the Sitting Duck. Locals had been drawn into the camaraderie of the *Northport News* party, grinning as they heard the tall tales of our victory – 'What're you drinking, Tarzan?' – addressed to Ellis, whose shirt-buttons had been undone lower and lower to expose his manly leotard.

'Pints of jungle juice all round,' came the call as they all congregated round the log fire of the fuggy bar. I ventured further, scanning each table, dodging under the dartboard to find a cold, spare room at the back, normally used for families so that children should not be exposed to the decadence of adults drinking alcohol.

Huddled over a glass, on his own in the corner, sat Guy.

He looked up, narrow-eyed, defensive, then puzzled: 'Is that you, Anna, or a walking Picasso?' It's surprisingly flattering to be compared to a masterpiece, even when you know he means the one with the nose in the wrong place and a pair of unmatched flatfish for eyes.

'Nothing so valuable as the latter I'm afraid, Guy.' I walked towards him. 'I just suffered a slight face rearrangement when someone shot off with my car. I'm OK now, just a bit more colourful than usual, and he dumped the car at the railway station.'

Guy relaxed with relief, ignoring my gory visage and beckoning me to sit down with a chivalrous gesture: 'A sight for sore eyes, anyway. Where did you spring from?' His breath gave off a strong scent of Scotch. How long had he been drinking?

'From Futures,' I returned, emphatically, 'the same place you sprang from. I was in the Cosmosphere when you took a flyer and gave my daughter the slip.'

'You were there? Shelley recognised me?' The defences sprang up again.

'Don't worry, I begged her not to tell anyone, and I don't think anyone else caught sight of you.' He had taken off the spectacles, but his thick dark stubble still changed the face I knew. 'What on earth were you doing? Don't tell me you and that barmy army had been trying to break into the office building.'

He tossed back his drink in one gulp. There was no throat-catching so, as I'd suspected, it couldn't have been his first.

'I need another,' he said. 'What can I get you?'

'Guy, I should go easy, if I were you. The car, remember?'

'How could I forget?' He gave a very uncharacteristic leer. 'My precious beauty. Don't worry, she'll purr and she'll growl and she'll find her own way home.'

'Not with you at the wheel, she won't. How many have you had?'

'Not enough,' he snapped, getting up. 'You want a drink? A man could die of thirst while Anna Knight makes up her mind.'

'It is made up, Guy. I'll have an orange juice and I'll drive you home.'

'In your little banger?' he sneered.

'I came on the coach, with the *Northport News* mob. I'll drive yours.'

'You – ' he pointed a wavering finger at my face – 'are a star. A sterling woman of the finest calibre. Guy Madden salutes you. Where've you been all my life?'

'Get the drinks, Guy. Sterling women of the finest calibre know a drunken question when they hear one.'

He wound his way very carefully to the bar, and returned with even more deliberation, determined not to spill a drop. As he sat down heavily, he asked, 'You don't believe I got into the Futures offices do you?'

'They're protected like the Royal Mint. Of course I don't believe it.'

'Why not? It's true.' He exhaled decisively as another shot of whisky hit his stomach.

'But how?'

He lifted his sweater and slapped his stomach, hard and masculine. 'Punch that – go on.' I had a vision of several Scotches erupting in my lap, so I softened my fist and merely skimmed his shirt.

'Ha – ' he returned with satisfaction. 'Strong as steel, you see?'

'You don't mean to tell me you barged your way in with sheer physical force.'

'Oh ye of little faith,' he drew himself up in indignation. 'Go on, do it again. Harder, harder.'

I punched seriously this time, and he grabbed my fist and opened it, pressing it flat against his solar plexus. He was fit, I had to acknowledge that, and I felt his heart beating faster under the muscle. 'I'm impressed,' I said, taking my hand away as wanton thoughts perked up at the back of my mind, sniffing and snouting and muddying the issue, as is their wont.

'Good,' he replied. 'I'm glad I've impressed you. Now I can tell you that it doesn't take Superman to get in there.' He lowered his voice to a stage whisper. 'It takes a weasel who'll stoop to bribery and corruption.'

'You bribed someone to let you in?'

'Ssshhhh!' He put a finger to his lips, looking round for skulking listeners in melodramatic fashion. 'I prefer to call it shrewd opportunism. A freelance computer programmer who's been working with me on virtual reality has also done some work at Futures. They were slow payers, and they quibbled over what he'd done. He moaned about this and got friendly with a particular security guard, who, it turned out over a pint or three, was similarly cheesed off with his employers. He'd just got divorced, was deep in debt, and he kept being passed over for promotion. I asked my friend to test the water, to see if this guy'd play for a cash injection in return for a little blind-eye turning, and he did.'

'So you managed to get into the admin section?'

'I tagged on behind a group of contract cleaners and mosied through as if I was part of the staff.'

'Did you get into Liza Boyd-Adams's department?'

'Yes.'

His drunken loquacity had suddenly dried up. He stared dumbly at his empty glass. 'Would you like another drink?' I asked quickly.

'Yes!' he rapped the table. 'I need another bloody drink.'

'A small one this time, I think?'

'Are you trying to nanny me, Anna Knight? Or are you just too skint to buy a man a decent mouthful?'

'I'll buy you however many you can take. But if I'm taking you home I want to make sure I don't have to carry you.'

He lapsed into a smile, leaning near and breathing Scotch in my face: 'That might be fun, nanny. You could carry me up to bed, you know, and kiss me and Teddy goodnight.'

'No, Guy.'

'You don't trust me?'

'Oh, I trust you, but Teddies can often become heaving monsters crazed with lust, in my experience.'

He gave a snort: 'All right then, I'll just take a single, and me and Teddy'll have to make our own amusements.'

At this point Ellis Clancy's head appeared in the doorway: 'Any more waifs and strays? Ah, Anna, all passengers are advised to go straight to passport control – the Northport flight is due to depart in two minutes.'

'It's all right, Ellis, I'll be making my own way home.'

His eyebrow raised and he winked as he looked at Guy. 'I see, picked up a little extra baggage during our stopover, did we? Don't worry, your secret's safe with me.'

He disappeared, and I heard his departing voice: 'Hey gang, Anna's only pulled herself a bloke while we've been yakking. She's not backward in coming forward, eh?' A gale of laughter gradually subsided as they filtered out into the night, and I waited till they'd gone before approaching the bar.

I'd hardly put the drink down on the table before Guy picked it up and threw it down his throat, shuddering as it restored his blood-alcohol quotient.

'We'd got to the point where you were inside Futures, inside Liza Boyd-Adams's office,' I prompted. 'What happened then?'

His mock-lust gone, his face strained, he ground his fist into his hand and spoke low: 'It was difficult, there were cleaners round, and I was supposed to be a staff member who knew what he was looking for. I got into her room and tried to get into her computer. No dice. I looked round to see if she'd made a note of her password anywhere. I began opening drawers. Then a woman wandered in with a vacuum-cleaner. I grabbed a wad of papers and just looked at them blindly. The woman went and I started trying the computer with variations on Boyd-Adams's name. I must've tried every combination until finally one worked. I got in, and saw a filename "Madmad". I called it up . . . A complete profile of our business, from the management structure to the financial status, key personnel, market position, and an analysis of our strengths and weaknesses. It contained stuff they could only have got from Llew's files.'

'Is it real proof of a takeover plan?'

'No. It's only proof they're thinking about it, and that they're total bastards who'll break the law to get the information they want.'

'Did you manage to get a copy of the file?'

His fingers tightened around his glass until I thought it would break: 'No time. Bloody woman.'

'What?'

'The bloody woman came back.'

'Who, the cleaner?'

'No, Boyd-Adams.'

'She caught you?'

'Huh, she didn't have time. Never enter a room without first deciding how you'll get out in a hurry. I'd already unlocked a window. I heard someone say, "Hello, Liza", as she came along the corridor. I slammed the computer off and took a dive.'

'But it's one floor up.'

He nodded: 'I took a victory roll through the rose bushes and legged it. Then Liza set off the alarm. My trusty security guard came pounding after me, baying for my blood. You know, I reckon he set me up. He told me to come in on a night he knew Liza Boyd-Adams'd be around, just so he could play the hero and nab me, and get his promotion.'

'Does he know who you are?'

'No, he thinks my name's John Dunn, he's never seen me without glasses.'

'And how did John Dunn end up in the Cosmosphere?'

'He ran straight for the crowds, thinking he could mingle. There was a line of hard-looking young men, bored, waiting for one of the rides. They saw me being chased, they ganged up against the security men and created a diversion, then they ran, loving every minute of it. I dodged into the Cosmosphere, hoping to lie low in the audience, but they saw me go and charged after me. I ended up dashing hell-for-leather into the middle.'

'And that's when Shelley caught up with you.'

He laughed: 'Do you think I added zest to your Survival of the Fittest? Those hooligans were more frightening than a horde of storm-troopers. They frightened me, I can tell you.'

'It was an arresting finale, I have to say, though it rather stole Ellis's thunder at the time.'

'Anyway my nerves were so shot by then I needed a drink to calm down. I got in the car and drove here.'

'And are you calmer now?'

'I'm glad you came through that door, Anna, that's all I can say.'

'You need someone to watch your back if you insist on these undercover schemes. At least it was worth while. Now you've seen the evidence, what are you going to do about it?'

'What can I do? I'm like this pub, a sitting duck. I just have to wait until the enemy attacks. But I'll be waiting for them, twelve-bores at the ready. I still have that ammunition about the tax dodge, remember . . . if I can make it stick.'

He slumped back in the seat, drained and tired and somehow far more appealing than I was prepared for. I finished my drink, quelling a demon urge to take advantage of a man in his cups. 'Come on, master spy, let's get you home.'

Eighteen

T he voice on the phone was smooth and charming and could be that of no one else but Liza
Boyd-Adams.

'Anna,' she gushed, 'I'm so sorry we were unable to
complete our conversation yesterday evening – you wanted
to ask some more questions about Survival of the Fittest, and
I'm afraid I was unavoidably detained.'

'Oh, don't worry about it for a second, Liza,' I
chimed back – her syrupy style was infectious. 'I realised you
had more pressing things to think about at the time. It can't
be every day Futures gets hit by a riot.'

'Is that what you've termed it in the paper?'

'I'm afraid so. You see our news editor was part of
the team, and he tends to have a vivid imagination when
hooligans threaten to upstage him.'

'I see.'

'Anyway, I can carry on the interview by phone if
you don't mind.'

'Better still, why don't you join us for lunch this
Sunday? I'm having a few people over in honour of my
husband's birthday. Nothing elaborate, just a buffet and
drinks, but Marianne will be there. You could bring Shelley

too – I'd like the chance to meet her in mufti, as it were. We could mix business with pleasure and you can interview Marianne and me at the same time.'

'Fine, yes, I'll look forward to that.'

It seemed she wanted to offset the bad publicity by feeding me dainties and soft soap, but I wasn't averse to that. At least it might give me an opportunity to glean more about Futures' intentions towards Mad Mad World.

The Boyd-Adams abode was a converted farmhouse in a village whose buildings been transformed over recent years from humble cottages for farm labourers to sought-after dwellings for city types with country aspirations. My car was back on the road, and though its fingerprints and blood smears had been scrupulously cleaned up, it still felt soiled, and looked its age as Shelley and I drew up between a BMW and a top-of-the-range Rover. 'Executive toys,' proclaimed Shelley dismissively.

'Come off it, you've played with a few of those in your time,' I returned as we crunched up the path.

'I've learnt the real value of things over the past few months, and it isn't measured in flash cars, homes beautiful and a New Man changing nappies between business deals.'

'I'd take a rain check on the last until you've changed a few yourself.'

She turned to walk backwards, stretching her arms in front of me: 'You know what I mean, Ma. It's all a con, a TV ad-person's concoction, and these people fall for it because they've too much money and too little imagination.

Walking backwards she failed to notice the front door opening at our approach, and our hostess listening as she was condemned as over-rich and stupid.

'Hello, Liza,' I beamed effusively.

'I'm so glad you could make it,' she beamed back resolutely, 'and Shelley, how kind of you to come. I must say I've been bowled over by your Amazon Queen, the role of the strapping savage seems absolutely made for you.'

Shelley gave me a raised eyebrow as Liza led us inside. 'You asked for that,' I whispered under my breath.

We were led into a large, lofty room which must have been a barn when the farm was built. The ceiling was vaulted with beams of oak, the walls were old brick, exposed to reveal their true-brick character, but cleansed of any characterful old animal dung or hay-husks. Dried flowers cascaded from mangers and milk churns, and old farm implements such as scythes and pitchforks were polished and wall-mounted to take a pride of place their makers never even dreamed of.

The room was gently abuzz with Sunday lunchtime *bonhomie*, men laughing over-heartily, lubricated from jugs of real ale, women distracting themselves from thoughts of Monday with glasses of Bucks Fizz or Bloody Mary. A few children bobbed about, using adults as shields in their games of catch and poke.

Liza made her way over to a group of guffawing men: 'Robert, may I interrupt one moment; I just want to introduce Anna Knight, a journalist who's writing about Survival of the Fittest, and her daughter Shelley, our latest team-leader. Ladies, my husband, Robert Moss.'

He was slightly shorter than her, balding and sandy-haired with the beginnings of a paunch, and he looked somewhat uncomfortable in his colour co-ordinated casual slacks and stressed silk shirt.

'Happy birthday, Robert,' I said, holding out a bottle of wine which I rather begrudged him, having a far greater need myself if this house was anything to go by.

'Oh, you're too kind,' he said politely. Too right I was: this party had better be worth my while. Liza left to let in more guests and in honour of my gift Robert extricated himself from his friends and asked getting-to-know-you questions about my job, and Shelley about hers, becoming so animated we could hardly get a word in edgeways.

As soon as he stopped he whooshed away to bring us drinks and peanuts and canapés, keeping up a fast and furious running commentary about the house, the weather, the news – anything to prevent being questioned about himself. I read this unspoken message and let him rattle on until he ran out of steam and joined another pair.

I heard a familiar deep, womanly laugh behind me and turned to greet Marianne. 'I see you've met the human whirlwind,' she said, indicating Robert. 'See what being married to a high-flyer does to a man – makes him run round like a demented gofer trying to keep up.'

'He doesn't seem to be doing too badly,' observed Shelley, indicating the prettified farm museum in which we stood.

'Don't be deceived my dear,' replied Marianne. 'You're looking at a passenger, hanging on to Liza's coat-tails.'

'What does he do for a living?' I asked.

'Oh, he's a clever man, that's the sad thing about it. He was a research physicist at the university until the funding ran dry. They don't have much call for research physicists down at the Jobcentre, so Liza set him up in his next love, science fiction books. He became a bookseller, poor lamb, and hardly makes a bean. Liza provides the beans in this house, and the toast and all the trimmings that you see.'

Liza was calling everyone to indulge in the buffet, which was considerably more extravagant than beans, while Robert, no doubt to keep himself out of circulation, was overheard busying himself in the kitchen with an electric carving knife. 'How much of this fatted calf do we need, darling?' he called to his wife.

'Oh, let me do it, you're not safe,' she smiled and went to wrest the lethal implement from his grasp.

'You see,' commented Shelley. 'That's why New Man is a figment, because women won't let him make a mess of things.'

Robert reappeared. 'It's new,' he said sheepishly, 'and I'm a clumsy oaf – the two don't go together according to Liza.'

As we all descended on the food I noticed a pale, fair-haired boy hovering in the doorway, looking bewildered. He must have been about ten years old. Robert saw him too, and grabbed his hand as a prop to deflect attention from himself. Drawing him gently into the room he helped the boy to heap slices of salmon, samosas and other titbits on his plate. The boy spoke to no one, and when Robert led him to the other children, who were already sitting on the floor eating, the boy hunched away.

Marianne saw me watching, and as the three of us found a nook to park our glasses, plates and bottoms, she said, 'That's their son, Charley. They only have one child, and I think he's enough by the sound of it.'

'He seems very shy – doesn't look much of a mischief-maker.'

She shook her head: 'What's the term the social workers use these days? He has learning difficulties. Educationally challenged. Whatever it is, Charley's not quite right in the head.'

Shelley looked over at the boy with pity. Robert was kneeling beside him trying to calm his fears, but he became more and more agitated, his eyes staring wildly at the influx of strangers. 'Just sit down here, Charley,' coaxed Robert, 'come on, no one will bother you.'

'Naaah!' the boy retorted and whipping the plate from Robert's hand, he up-ended it on his head.

This brought squeals of glee from the other children and embarrassed gasps from the adults. Liza rushed in with a cloth, wiped Robert with one hand and stroked Charley with the other, making light of the catastrophe for both. I thought: bravo, Superwoman – all this and being a financial wizard and charity fundraiser. Futures holds at least one very formidable opponent indeed, Guy Madden.

After we'd eaten, and Robert had covered himself in blushes blowing candles out, Shelley gravitated towards the boy. Instead of cowering on the floor at his mother's feet he looked up, fascinated by Shelley's clouds of loosened hair.

He put a hand up towards her, and she crouched by him, letting him touch and stroke it. Then she pulled a brush from her bag and gave it to him, and he sat quietly brushing the hair down her back, as if the rhythm pacified his inner turmoil.

'That's good, Charley,' smiled Liza. 'Thank you, Shelley, for being so kind.'

'It's nothing,' replied my daughter. But it was something. No one else had approached him, no one else would even try. I saw Liza appreciated it, and guessed that Shelley's earlier gaffe was quite forgiven.

'He still gets a bit upset when we have people in,' explained Liza, 'but I have to keep trying with him, he needs to gain confidence with strangers.' I took a seat beside her as she went on, 'Charley's been at home the past term, but after Christmas he's going back to school – in America. It's a remarkable school, they do wonders for youngsters like him. They use a special teaching technique. Unfortunately it has yet to catch on over here.'

Robert spoke up: 'Which is why we've spent a fortune on fees and fares across the Atlantic.' There was a tetchiness in his voice which, in the light of Marianne's explanation, I could understand.

Liza went on, apologetically, 'For that reason I took him away at the end of last term, thinking we'd try sending him back to a school here, but I'm afraid it didn't work. He regressed so much, he was having fits. I had to take him away, and it just isn't fair on him. He deserves the best, don't you, Charley?' She rubbed his head with affection, 'and he's going to go on getting it.'

Her husband gave a pained sigh, and got up to drown his obvious discomfiture in another drink.

'Well, Anna, that's not what you're here for, is it?' Liza turned her attention to me, and patted the arm of her chair. 'Marianne, come sit by me and be grilled by this inveterate news-hound.'

I did my job. I asked Liza pertinent questions about

Survival of the Fittest, I asked Marianne about Journey of a Lifetime and the debt she owed to Liza and Futures. I asked about the children who benefited, and the trips they went on. And finally, when Shelley gave a long and loud yawn, I realised my questions had dried up, and I was simply expressing my genuine respect for these two women.

Shelley knew what I was trying to do here, and the unspoken message in that blunt yawn was: Stop being a hypocrite, Ma, I know you're only flattering Liza to soften her up, you're trying to help Guy Madden because you fancy the socks off him. Disapproving daughters I can do without – and so I persevered, intent on reopening the thorny subject of takeovers. 'Surely your flair and initiative extends not only to your charity work, but to business as well,' I burbled. 'Futures must rely on your qualities a great deal – I mean, a person who can dream up Survival of the Fittest must exercise similar creativity and commitment in her day-to-day work.'

'Where exactly are you leading, Anna?'

'Well, I was wondering if that creativity might extend to expanding Futures' empire.'

'We're constantly expanding our range of rides and shopping opportunities.'

'I meant, perhaps, opening new sites in other areas. Or taking over existing parks and developing them in the Futures mould.'

'We've been over this ground before, Anna,' she said testily, 'and it seems to me you're seeking an answer that would overstep the bounds of commercial confidentiality. Now, I really must have a word with a few more of our guests, if you'll excuse me. Charley, come with Mummy, darling.'

As they departed Shelley gave me a knowing smirk, and Marianne chuckled, 'That put you in your place, Miss Reporter.'

'I should know better than to try to wheedle round a professional like her.'

'Why, exactly, were you wheedling?'

'Oh goodness, Marianne, it's too complicated to go into. Let's just say I don't think I'll try again. I know when I'm beaten.'

Shelley spoke up: 'I think I'll just step outside for a bit of a walk, Ma. I feel slightly smothered after all that hot air.'

'Oh, that sounds a good idea,' said Marianne, patting her ample middle. 'I ate too much and it's making me uncomfortable. Shall we three take a stroll?'

We wandered outside, round the back of the house, where the remains of an old orchard still stood, gnarled branches winter-bare. Striding between the trees, an observation struck me. 'You seem much more at ease, Marianne. Has anything happened at home?'

'Yes, my dear, I wanted to tell you, but not where all those cronies of Liza could overhear.'

'Oh, do tell. Has Barnaby come back for good?'

She wavered, and then laughed: 'Let's say partly. I'll explain. Things weren't getting any better. Barnaby was still unhappy, and his lady-friend was unhappy because he was unhappy, and of course I was unhappy too. Anyway, the long and short of it is that she came to visit me, and we had a lengthy heart-to-heart. You know, I really quite like her, she's a spirited girl, something of a beauty, and she complimented me most charmingly. Well, she put a proposal to me, and the more I thought about it, the more it seemed the only solution. We've agreed to share custody of Barnaby.'

'What!' Shelley and I chorused.

She laughed aloud, 'It's true, he stays with her half the week and me the rest, and I hope it jolly well works, for if it doesn't we're all finished.'

'But how? I mean what – ?'

'Look, I know it sounds far-fetched, but she can give him the bedroom pleasure he seems to need, and I can give him the comfort and companionship we've built up over the years. She doesn't want him full-time, she's told me as much, she feels stifled, she needs her freedom. I must admit I too enjoy being free to please myself for a few days, and I appreciate Barnaby all the more when he comes home. He himself is much calmer, and his work's no longer suffering.'

'Marianne,' I gasped, 'I've said this before, and I'll say it again, you're a marvel.'

'Nonsense, Anna, I'm just a coper, as most women have to be.'

A twig cracked in the orchard, and Robert emerged from behind a tree a few yards away. He strode back towards the farmhouse, ignoring our presence. 'Do you think he heard?' I asked.

Marianne shrugged: 'I don't suppose it matters if he did. Robert's the least likely person to gossip that I can think of. He's so concerned about his own privacy I can't see him prattling about anyone else's.'

'Come on,' said Shelley, 'let's go back inside and get a drink. I feel a toast coming on: to Marianne and her *ménage à trois*: may we wish you a long and happy partnership.'

Nineteen

A s soon as the CID sergeant opened his log-book, I knew there was something familiar about the registration number of the stolen car. He was running through the previous day's burglaries and thefts for me, a regular routine for our Crimewatch column, and this number flashed out at me like a beacon.

'Don't tell me,' I said, pointing to the number. 'It's a yellow E-type Jaguar.'

'You're right,' he replied. 'Know anything about it?'

'It's just that it belongs to a friend of mine.'

'Correction: it did. It's over the hills and far away by now, I shouldn't wonder.'

'D'you think it's that ramraider gang from Merseyside?'

He shook his head: 'I doubt it. They go for big bulky cars that can smash armoured windows, not sports models. This is a collector's car, Anna, and I don't think it was a simple opportunist theft. Too professional. It's been targeted, and I wouldn't be surprised if it's changing hands for a considerable sum right now.'

'But surely they can't just—'

'Can't they just? Forged documents, changed registration number, there's a market for these things.'

I left the police station and tried to ring Guy at his office. His secretary said he hadn't come in yet, he was still at home. When I rang there, his answering machine was on. I left a message and went back to work.

By lunchtime he hadn't returned my call, and he still wasn't at work. Beginning to get worried, I refused the charms of the office canteen and used my lunch hour to shoot round to Guy's house.

It was a starkly-styled 1930s detached house bought for its clean lines and functionality more than anything else. The night I'd driven him home he'd invited me in for coffee while I waited for a taxi, and had taken a tipsy delight in showing off his energy conservation system and ergonomically designed kitchen. It was efficient, hygienic and utterly bereft of clutter or cosiness. I felt as though I'd have to wear sterile overshoes and a surgical gown to cook in there.

The curtains were still drawn, milk was on the doorstep and a paper protruded from the letterbox. With mounting foreboding I rang the bell. No answer. I rang again. Still no reply.

I moved round the side of the house, peering in through windows, registering only darkness. I looked through the window of the double garage: a blank space where the E-type once stood in splendour, but his other car, a Cavalier, was still there.

At the back of the house was a patio, and my footsteps rang on the stone. I could see the kitchen was as pristine and empty as the day it was installed. I turned to the curtained french windows and rapped on the shutters. Surely he must have heard me now – if he could. I stood back to gaze up at the bedroom windows. Their blinds were motionless. I listened for any trace of movement, but there was only an ominous silence.

There was nothing else for it – break the silence with a rock, and force an entry through the french windows. I picked up a prime specimen of millstone grit from the edge of the patio, turned my head in case of flying glass, and hurled it through the pane nearest the handle.

I reached in to turn the key, which was still in the lock, and flung myself back in sudden fright. Someone had touched my hand. In an instant the curtains were thrown back and a gaunt Guy Madden confronted me. 'What the hell d'you think you're playing at?' he demanded, blinking in the sudden flood of light. 'Oh, it's you. Anna, isn't it enough my nerves are completely shattered without you shattering my house as well?' Still in his dressing-gown, despite the hour, he looked very definitely ill.

'I'm sorry, Guy. I heard about your car being stolen and I thought you'd be upset. I came round to see how you were, and when the house was all in darkness I thought something might have happened to you.'

'And so you broke a window in fear of finding a corpse?' He gave a hollow laugh. 'It's nice to know someone cares.'

'Look, you've got bare feet – you'll cut yourself if you're not careful. Let me sweep up the glass. I'll pay for the window, of course.'

'That's what I like, a tidy and remorseful house-breaker. Pity my car thief wasn't more like you. Well, you'd better come in and make yourself useful now you're here.' He slid back two bolts and I stepped inside while he went upstairs. I found a dustpan and brush in the immaculate cupboard under his immaculate sink, and set to work, finishing it off with a blast from a vacuum cleaner so powerful it sucked everything in its maw like a wind tunnel. Then I rang a glass merchant, who said he'd call round and fix the damage that afternoon.

By the time my task was complete, Guy had reappeared, freshly showered and dressed in a baseball shirt and tracksuit trousers. 'Coffee?' he asked. 'It's still breakfast time for me, I'm afraid. I didn't get a hell of a lot of sleep last night. Then I took a pill and zonked out till you came a-calling.'

'Let me make you something. You look like death warmed up.'

'Really? I thought I was putting on a pretty good show of rude health and good manners in the circumstances, but since you are so brutally honest, I'll stop the pretence.' His face was ashen, and his tone became tense. 'I look lousy, I feel worse, I hate myself for letting my car be stolen, I hate the bastard who took it, and I hate the bloody world for getting on my back.' He gripped the edge of the kitchen worktop with suppressed rage.

'Just go and sit down in the living room, Guy. I'll bring you some coffee and toast and we can talk.'

He shut his eyes and nodded, moving off stiffly.

The coffee was fragrantly brewing, the toast warm, the cups laid neatly on the tray and everything done perfectly – in keeping with the master's lifestyle – when I heard a stream of expletives issuing from the master himself.

I rushed through to the living room to find him pacing like a caged tiger, and when he saw me he shuddered to a halt.

'Guy – for God's sake! What's the matter with you?'

'Everything!' he howled back. 'Everyone's out to get at me. This bloody letter arrived this morning. And now I discover I've been burgled.'

He held up a crumpled sheet of headed notepaper, but was quivering so much I could not read a word – all I saw was the logo of the military aircraft plant. I reached out to take it, but he snatched it away.

'No – I was putting it away in my desk, trying to be calm and collected about the whole thing – and that's when I realised the desk's been gone through.'

'Gone through?'

'Somebody's been looking at my papers, somebody's sneaked in here and sneaked out again, and blasted well pawed my private files with his dirty sneaky fingers.'

'How do you know?'

'Because the lock's been forced. And because ever since Llew's house was broken into I've left tiny traces, hairs over drawers, bits of thread between sheets of paper. So I'd know if they were disturbed. And I know. God help me, I know they've been in here.'

'But surely you have a burglar alarm.'

'I do, but it's not on when I'm in the house. Not when I'm zonked out upstairs from too much booze or sleeping pills. These people know what they're up to, Anna. I have window locks all round but I've just found a neat hole in the glass in the downstairs loo. They're not like you coming blasting in with a rock to wake up the dead.'

'If these people are as professional as you say, who d'you think it was?'

He looked at me as though I was simple: 'Futures of course. Creatures from Futures, looking for "intelligence",' he parodied, wagging his head. 'Haven't they got enough? What do they want out of me?'

'Well, have they stolen anything?'

He turned to the desk drawers that were hanging forlorn and violated: 'I don't know. I just know they've been in here. I haven't had time to look.'

'Come into the kitchen, away from here. Drink some coffee, calm down, and then we'll come back and look, all right?'

Calming good-looking men when they're in trouble might be good for the ego, but it certainly eats into a lunch hour. I was going to have to ring Ellis and tell him I'd be late. Considerably late, if Guy's present demeanour was anything to go by. He was breathing heavily, but he allowed himself to be pulled kitchenwards and sat down, coffee at his elbow. I explained I'd have to ring the office. He assented without a word.

When I came back, still smarting from Ellis's observation that I'd better get some copy out of this because he wasn't paying me for an afternoon's nooky, Guy had not moved.

I noticed that the crumpled letter was still in his fist.

'What's in the letter, Guy? What upset you in the first place?'

'Don't you know?' he snapped. 'Everyone else seems to know my business. Aren't journalists supposed to poke their noses into other people's affairs? Just like company spooks? Don't give me the innocent look – you know, you know what this is all about.'

'I presume it's about your being fired from the aircraft plant.'

He narrowed his eyes at me: 'I suppose it's the subject of gossip all over the resort now, is it? Who told you?'

'Guy, you know I can't say. But don't worry, you're not being gossiped about, not that I've heard.'

'You can't say? What kind of can't is that?'

'A journalist must protect her sources. It wouldn't be fair—'

'Fair?' he loomed over me, poking a finger toward my face. 'What's fair in being talked about behind your back? What's fair in being spied on and having your car stolen and—'

'Look, you're upset, it's understandable. Perhaps it'd be better if I left now. We'll talk about this later, when you've calmed down.'

I picked up my bag and went for the door, but he got there before me and blocked my path.

'You're not leaving this house, Anna, not till I know who's been spreading malicious rumours about me.'

'Guy, it was no scandal-monger, but you can stand there till you expire of machismo. I won't tell you who it was.'

He stood, immovable, his hands gripping the doorposts. Well, I'm nothing if not resourceful. I simply left him standing there to make my exit via the french windows.

I was fiddling with the lock when a heavy hand

gripped my shoulder, a foot rammed into the back of my knees, and I fell to the floor with Guy Madden's heaving force mounted on my chest.

He pinned my hands to the Axminster and I looked up into his bloodshot eyes. This was not quite the missionary position I had fondly imagined.

'Tell me who's been shooting their mouths off, making me look like a fool,' he hissed in my face.

'Nobody made you look like a fool, Guy. Only one person mentioned it to me, and that only in passing. Nobody's been spreading this stuff around. Listen to me. Has one word of this appeared in the paper?'

'No.'

'D'you think it wouldn't have done if I could make it stand up? I had to do my job, Guy, I had to ask questions about it – it's what a journalist's supposed to do. I've asked the press office for corroboration, I've asked company executives I know and trust. Nobody, but nobody, would confirm it at all. End of story. I don't print stories based on hearsay from one solitary person who might have an axe to grind, Guy. I'm not that kind of reporter.'

I felt the tension in his thighs relax slightly. 'No, I don't suppose you are,' he said tiredly.

'Is it true? Is that why you're so upset?' I asked, trying to understand this hulking man on my chest. 'I'm not being a journalist now, Guy, I'm asking as a friend.'

He gave a heavy sigh, and leaned down to kiss my eyelids: 'This is how I treat my friends, I give them hell and throw them on the floor. What kind of a jerk am I?'

'One who's been under a great deal of strain, and is only human.'

He rolled off me, and helped me up. 'Can we start again?' he said. 'Let's go back to where I was drinking coffee, and you were telling me to calm down.'

I walked towards the kitchen, only to feel his hand again on my shoulder, much more gently now. I turned round, and he buried his face in my neck: 'I'm sorry, Anna,' he whispered. And then he was kissing me, long and softly, on the mouth. All things come to those who wait, even if they have to suffer hulks on the chest while they're waiting.

I pass quietly over this moment of bliss, and will only say that by the time we did return to the kitchen I needed a glass of cold water to cool my ardour. He was, after all, still vulnerable, and in any case, ardour is all the better for being kept in suspense.

'Anna, if I tell you this,' he said, 'I want it to go no further. I only tell you to demonstrate exactly how much strain I've been under.'

'My lips are sealed.'

'I was fired.'

I registered suitable disbelief.

'It happened,' he went on, 'after I bailed out of an aircraft. The newest design in the air. I was practising for a show – you know, aerobatics, the show-off stuff – and let's just say something went wrong. I had to press the ejector button and come down the hard way. The plane crashed.

'Near the perimeter fence,' I added. Of course I knew of the incident. It had been all over our paper.

'Right, not only that, but near the caravan site, and it burst into flames. It was only by a miracle the wind was in the wrong direction and it didn't blow up a propane gas store on the site.'

'But the miracle did happen. I mean, no one was hurt.'

'No, but they could have been. The local worthies kicked up a stink, of course – the MP, councillors – they wanted something done about it.'

'And you turned out to be the something that was done.'

'Yes. The company fired me. Said there was nothing wrong with the plane and I had been acting in a dangerous and reckless manner. They said I could go quietly, and they would simply tell the local worthies in confidence what had happened, and assure them it was an isolated incident that had been satisfactorily dealt with.'

'And had you acted in a dangerous and reckless manner?' I asked, thinking of his current track record.

'No, I bloody well hadn't. I'm a good pilot, I know my stuff, I'm not some hare-brained rookie. In simple terms there was something wrong with the plane's design that caused it to stall, the avionics couldn't cope, and the company daren't admit that because it's pinning its hopes on this plane for export sales. So they used me as a scapegoat while they secretly redesigned it. Pilot error.'

'Surely you could seek some kind of redress?'

He sighed: 'I took legal advice and claimed unfair dismissal because there was nothing wrong with the way I carried out my job. I thought they'd acknowledge the truth and settle out of court to keep the whole thing out of the papers. But the letter that arrived today informed me that they've decided if I want a fight they're going to make it a public one to defend their plane. It must mean they've ironed out the gremlin and they'll never admit it even existed. They want to go to an industrial tribunal. Their big guns against my solitary pistol. What chance do I stand?'

I shrugged diplomatically: 'What about your former colleagues, the other pilots. Wouldn't they back you up?'

He gave a hollow laugh. 'I'm all right, Jack, that's their motto. They're not rocking the boat because they know they'd be rolled overboard like me.'

To me that raised doubts – after all, their lives would have been in danger if Guy's story was true. But this was not the time to play doubting Thomas. I stroked his hand; a thin comfort but it was all I could think of.

'All I want is a clean sheet, Anna. It's not that I want my job back, not now Llew's been killed and I've taken on the park. I just want to get on with my life without this slur on my name. You can understand that, can't you?'

'Of course,' I soothed him. 'Come on, let's see what your phantom burglar's stolen, if anything. Let's do something practical about this whole thing, rather than brooding and getting worked up.'

He took my hand and squeezed it, and I guessed he was saying thanks.

Three items were missing from his files: a projection of Mad Mad World's operations over the next five years, a detailed report on his version of the aircraft accident, and the papers and log-book for his E-type Jaguar.

The combination sent him into the stratosphere. When the shouting stopped I ferried Scotch from the drinks cupboard to his shaking hand, and stroked his arm. Then I called the police and sat by him when they came to take the details. The window-man had also arrived, and I saw to him. By the time everyone had gone night had darkened the sky.

We had a quiet meal and went to bed. It was worth waiting for.

Twenty

The pleasures of the bedroom don't last long. Or at least, they didn't with Guy. Naive old Anna, thinking a roll between the sheets could tame the animal that raged in his head. Oh, he enjoyed our intimate interlude just as much as I did, but he left it behind as soon as he woke, raring to get out and take on the world again. After a few repetitions of this I began to wonder whether I was just a healthier substitute for a sleeping pill.

The crux of it was he felt provoked beyond endurance. The break-in at his house and the theft of his car affected him much as my car thief had me – deeply. He felt violated, at the mercy of malevolent forces, and he did not know where they would strike next. Added to this, his continuing phobia about Futures, and his feud with the aircraft company, and you can imagine, he was madder than a bull tangled in bunting.

The principal symptom of this madness was that he threw himself into activity. Unlike a woman, who might withdraw under siege, cocooning herself in self-pity and refusing – quite sensibly – to come out until the coast was clear, Guy was intent on clearing the coast himself. He sped from solicitor to police to car dealers to Mad Mad World, berating them all for failing to keep up with his manic demands, and he even went back to Futures, covertly tracking the moves of the top directors, convincing himself that he would catch them at some skulduggery if only he was assiduous enough.

I tried to keep this frenetic agitation in check, but it was like urging moderation on a religious zealot fired up to wipe out the infidel and conquer the world.

I was fond of him, and I'll admit his physical attentions were at first as luscious as cream cakes to a weight-watcher, but even cream cakes can pall – especially when you're sharing them with a human whisk. So I quietly let him go his unsweet way, hoping that he would eventually wear himself out and see sense. All he needed to do was sit tight, let other people do their jobs, and manage Mad Mad World to the best of his abilities instead of fighting dragons in the shadows.

One dark, sleety night when I came home from work Matt Whittaker was waiting in his car outside my flat. I didn't see him until he loomed up behind me as I put the key in the door, and I was so astonished that I was sharp with him.

'Matt, what are you doing here?'

'I'll go away again if you feel like that. I just had some news I thought you might want to hear from a friend, rather than the police.'

I glanced at him when he said 'friend' and he looked worried and uncertain.

'Oh gosh, I'm sorry Matt. I didn't mean to be so rude. It was just that you startled me. Come in, please, come inside out of this dreadful weather.'

He came in and we shook the sleet from our clothes. I hung up his coat and parked my dripping umbrella, and when we were both somewhat drier and more composed, he said, 'Guy's had an accident.'

'What kind of accident?'

'Car.'

'Is he all right?'

'Cuts and bruises to his ego, but I believe he'll live.'

'Where is he?'

'Hospital, being checked over and cleaned up, but they're not expecting to keep him in overnight.'

'I must go to him, he'll need someone to—'

'Wait.' Matt caught my sleeve. 'Just wait a minute, Anna.'

His expression was so serious I sank on to the couch. A latent fear was on my lips before I knew it: 'There was someone else in the crash wasn't there? And it was his fault. He's killed someone.'

'Why d'you say that?'

'Because he's been so crazy lately, driving around like a whirling dervish.'

'There was someone else involved, more seriously injured than Guy, but it wasn't fatal.'

'Who?'

'Liza Boyd-Adams.'

'Oh no . . .' My voice trailed off into a silence filled by a lash of sleet against the window pane. It sounded so cold and vindictive, I involuntarily flinched.

Matt eased his bulk on to the couch beside me and took my hand.

'What was he doing, Matt? What on earth did he think he was doing?'

'Look, I know what he's been like lately. It must have driven you crazy. I don't think he's good for you, Anna, not good at all.'

'Good or not, I got myself involved with him and I can't just walk away when the going gets tough.'

He looked stung. I tried to soften my words: 'Matt, you're right, it hasn't been easy dealing with Guy. But I should have seen something like this coming. I should have stuck in there and stopped him before he damaged himself or anyone else. I did walk away. I'm blaming myself, you see?'

'Then you shouldn't,' came the curt reply. 'He's the only one to blame for his behaviour, Anna.'

'How badly is she injured, do you know?'

'I know a little. Guy rang the office, I took the call. She had to be cut out of the wreckage, apparently. She was unconscious but she came round in the ambulance. Leg injuries. They suspected fractures. That's all he could say. They'll know more by the morning.'

'What exactly happened?'

'Guy Madden thought he was the star turn in a gangster movie, that's what happened, and he ought to grow up.'

'I don't need the commentary, Matt, just give me the facts.'

'He rammed her car into a concrete lamp-post.'

'Deliberately?'

'Either that or he was driving down an open road singing Zip-a-dee-doo-da with his eyes closed. I wouldn't put it past him.'

I sighed: 'He's been following Futures people all round the area. Liza especially. He found your company profile on her computer. He thinks they've stolen information. He thinks they want to take over Mad Mad World.'

'I may look like Dumbo, Anna, but believe me, I know what's been going on.'

'You're not Dumbo,' I couldn't help but smile.

'I think I am, sometimes. Like when I turned all hurt and resentful because you turned down the PR job. That was the dumbest thing I've done in a long time.'

'I was sorry too.'

'I was too wrapped up in myself to read the fine print beneath the headlines. You said you didn't want my job, I read you didn't want me. And then I had to stand by when you hooked up with boy racer Madden.'

My jaw tensed. Guy was in hospital, or at least on his way home from one, and Matt had come round to kick him while he was down. On the other hand, Matt had never stalked me in the street, he'd never hurt me with preposterous accusations, he'd never used brute force to throw me to the floor, and he'd never been so brittle and intense that I hardly dared move. Matt had been kind and considerate and funny. Even in bed, he'd made me laugh. Such men are worth their weight in gold, and Matt's weight was considerable.

I kissed him lightly on the forehead. 'So, Matt, what do you think should be done about Guy?'

'He needs treatment – no, I'm serious, Anna. The man's off the wall, or in today's case, off the lamp-post. He's a danger to himself and everyone else in this state. Not least you. And I'd never forgive him if he hurt you.'

'Did you meet him before all this blew up? I mean, what was he like before? I don't know him normal, I only know him wound up like a record playing at triple speed.'

'To be honest, he's been trouble from Day One. Ever since he started coming in to advise on that virtual reality stuff – Llew brought him in as a consultant.'

'But that would be just after he lost his job at the aircraft plant. He was bound to be upset.'

'There's upset and downright ornery. He was rude to the staff, rude to his father – and he had stand-up rows with Llew. Rows that were so bad, I wouldn't be surprised if he lost control and—'

His words hung in the air like a poised knife. Was he going to say Guy thrust the blade into his own brother's heart?

'And what, Matt?'

'Nothing. No. I shouldn't have said that.'

'You didn't.'

'No, I didn't.'

But he could have; the words were waiting on his tongue, ready for expression. I could see why he would think such a thing. But Matt wasn't Guy. Matt knew when he was going too far.

Whether he said the words or not, their seed had been planted, and they grew like a poison-weed in my head.

A proud man who'd been fired from his job, reduced to consultancy work in the family firm, taking orders from his brother. Did it all become too much and end in violence? He wasn't taking orders any more, he was for all practical purposes head of the family firm. Is that what he'd wanted, had Llew simply been in the way?

I shook my head: 'No, no, I can't believe it, Matt.'

'Can't believe what?'

'That . . .' I daren't say it either. 'That he'd deliberately cause a crash to hurt Liza Boyd-Adams.'

'With her car crawling up a lamp-post and his nose up its exhaust? Get real, Anna, the man's dangerous. He has a certain charm, I grant you, but so did Hannibal Lecter. He is certifiably insane, and we've all made allowances for too long.'

'How can you say that?' I was appalled. 'He's not a murderer.'

'He tried to kill someone today.'

'No, Matt. I won't hear this.' I cramped up into a ball with my hands over my ears, and I was shuddering. 'You'd better go.'

Instead of doing that he put his arms round me, and began to rock me like a child.

'Quiet now,' he said. 'I'm sorry, I went over the top. I shouldn't have said those things. It just makes me angry. He acts like the only person that matters in the world is Guy Madden – he's a maverick pilot on his own strike mission and God help anyone who gets in his way.'

He was right. I felt so miserable, he felt so warm and comforting that when he kissed me I kissed him back, unheeding of the conscience whispering faintly in my brain, 'Fickle, fickle, fickle.'

'Guy?'

The apparition who opened the door to me later that night looked drained of all energy, rake-thin, his skin almost translucent except for an angry bruise on his forehead. He wore a neck-brace and a dressing-gown and that was it.

'Come in, Anna,' he said tiredly. He led me into the living room and slumped on the sofa, as stricken as the poet Chatterton gracefully dying in his attic.

'How are you feeling?' I asked.

'I'm not worth your kind enquiries, Anna. Better leave me alone so I can quietly fade into obscurity and do no harm to anyone else.'

The thought of Guy quietly fading into anything was so incongruous I almost smiled. Instead, I asked, 'Have you been given a sedative?' thinking this could be the only reason he was immobile.

'I was, but I didn't take it. Just aspirin for the head. Your eyes don't deceive you, Anna, this is the real Mad-Dog Madden, whipped into submission by the scourge of his own conscience. I nearly killed a woman today. I could have killed myself too. That wouldn't have been any loss, but the woman would.'

He looked at me wanly, and then drank from a glass of water at his side, moistening his dry lips.

'Shall I tell you what I thought I was doing?' he said. 'Just to show how crazy I've become? I was following Liza Boyd-Adams to a stockbroker's. It's a regular journey, I've followed her before. This time I resolved to get there before her, and confront her on the steps. I had no clear idea of what I was going to say – scream at her about Jolyon Burchill's tax affair, howl that they were targeting my company, accuse them of wiping out my brother . . . It had all been building up inside me until I could bear it no longer. All I knew was I couldn't keep these people at arm's length any more, I had to shout in her face instead of skulking in the shadows. And so, as soon as she took this route I realised where she was going, and I went faster to try and pass her, and she went faster because she thought I was chasing her, and she tried to turn out of my path and misjudged the corner because she was too busy staring at this madman in her rear-view mirror, and she hit the lamp-post. I was so insane, I drove straight after her. I didn't know what I was doing. My sanity had completely broken. I couldn't have turned the wheel to save myself.'

'You must have been paralysed when you saw what was going to happen. You must have been in shock.'

'Shock?' he echoed cynically. 'The shock of the crash was nothing compared to the shock of realising exactly what I'd done. All I had in my mind was that I'd killed Liza Boyd-Adams. I got out, and raced to her. She was deathly still, I couldn't open the door. The passenger door had flung open on impact. I went to that side, and her briefcase had flown out. Banknotes were blowing out of it, everywhere, and I trod on all this money and scrambled over the crumpled seat praying she was still alive. She was breathing, but her leg was horribly bent under the dashboard. I had to get out. To be sick. People came, ambulances, hospital. I thanked whatever god I have that she'd survived, and I wished myself dead. I've caused enough pain to last a lifetime.'

'I suppose you'll face a court case for dangerous driving,' I said as gently as I could.

He nodded, 'It's no more than I deserve.'

'Did you tell the police what was behind it all?'

'How could I? How could I tell them I suspected Futures of all kinds of dirty tricks, including Llew's death, and ended up wrapping one of their executives round a lamp-post? I'd've been charged with attempted murder, never mind dangerous driving.'

He gave a deep sigh of self-disgust. He looked very, very tired, and had lost weight since I last saw him. He mustn't have been eating as the mania consumed his energies and sucked him dry. I made him a hot, milky drink, then I helped him up the stairs, and laid him down on the bed. I held his hand until his breathing became long and deep, and he slipped into the oblivion of sleep. Then I left a cheering note by his bedside, and slipped away myself, back to my solitary bed.

Except I didn't sleep. I couldn't. I turned one way and wanted Guy, I turned the other and was drawn back to Matt and, when eventually I fell into restless dreams, I saw myself being torn in two.

Twenty one

'Anna, is that Anna Knight?'

The woman's voice on the phone was faint, and Ellis Clancy was cackling with laughter so much I could hardly hear. 'What? Yes it is Anna. Who's this?'

An inaudible reply.

'Just hang on a minute – Ellis, pipe down for goodness sake. This is a bad line, and I can't hear myself, never mind my caller.'

'Oh, temper, temper,' he chaffed. 'Someone got out of the wrong bed this morning.' Nevertheless, he did quieten down and I turned back to the phone.

'Sorry about that. Hello – hello? Are you still there?'

The line was still open, I could hear a child's cry in the background, but my caller seemed absent. I was just about to put the phone back in its cradle when she spoke.

'Anna, it's Penny Worthington.'

My turn to be dumbstruck. She took my silence for forgetfulness: 'You remember, you came to see me at Janette's house?'

'Of course, of course I remember. For goodness sakes, Penny, where've you been, where are you? Janette's been worried sick, the police have been scouring the country for you.'

I must have sounded angry. 'Don't think badly of me, Anna,' she said. 'I did it for the best. I had no choice. I only rang because – I know it's a bit long ago now – but I saw the story in the paper, about you and Janette, when the bloke made off with your car. It's been preying on my mind. I'm sorry you and Janette have had this trouble, because of me.'

'Just come back and go to the police and end the trouble, then, Penny, it's in your hands.'

'I – how's Janette?'

'Janette's a survivor. She's coping. But she's had to stop working, she's short of cash and she's at the end of her tether worrying about you.'

'Tell her I'm OK. For now, I'm OK. Tell her I'll – I'll get some money to her, to make up for all this. I'll be in touch with her when I can, but I daren't . . . the police wouldn't believe me. I'm scared.'

'What are you scared of, Penny?'

Silence. 'Are you listening to me, Penny? Please, just tell me where you are.'

'I can't.' I noticed that when she raised her voice the words echoed, as though she were standing in an uncarpeted room, or a hall in a large old-fashioned house. Faintly I heard the child cry once more, footsteps on a stair, and another woman calling, 'Linda, Linda.'

'I have to go,' said Penny. 'Please, just pass my message on to Janette. I'm all right, and I'll make contact when I can.'

'Penny, don't go – where can I get hold of you? Give me a number.'

'No, it's best you don't know.'

'Have you got a job?'

'I – I'm all right.'

The pips went. She was using a pay-phone, and didn't have any more coins to feed it. 'I have to go,' she repeated. 'I'm sorry you've been dragged into this – ' And then the line went dead.

The call troubled me deeply. I left the frantic newsroom and went to the Ladies, just to stand against the cool tiles and think. I tried to put together all the clues that I'd heard in the background of her phone call. The echoing stair, the child, the other woman. They fell apart like jigsaw pieces, refusing to fit. And then I tried to put myself in her place. Where would I go if I was running away, if I had to leave home and find a safe haven, leaving no trace of where I'd gone? It must be local for her to have seen the story in the paper. I suddenly had a hunch I knew where she was, and the pieces fell into shape.

It was a quiet road, in a quiet part of town, chosen precisely for that reason. It was a road going nowhere, a cul-de-sac, and the house stood at the end of it, shielded by trees, surrounded by a moat of a garden. The gate was childproof. This household was constructed to keep its inmates safe inside, and the rest of the world out. It was, in fact, a hostel for battered women.

I only knew of its location because I had written an article when it first opened, two years before. I had interviewed the organisers and publicised its facilities – all on the strict understanding that I tell no one where it was. Some battering husbands have an annoying habit of trying to find their wives, and some beaten wives have an annoying habit of riling their husbands just for the drama of it. The least help they are given to get together, the better.

I reached the front door and pressed the buzzer. A box on the door frame barked into life, asking who I was. I said my name and said I was alone. An eye appeared in the peep-hole to confirm my story. Then the door opened and shut behind me.

'Come in, come in, Anna,' said a frayed-looking woman, plump from too much cheap, filling food, wiping an inky hand on her skirt. 'Just had an accident with a felt-tip pen, I won't shake your hand. What brings you to our home sweet home?'

'I'm looking for someone, Tricia. I don't even know if I'm in the right place, but I've been looking for some time, and I just had a feeling she might have come your way.'

'Name?'

'Penny Worthington.'

Tricia rubbed her chin, smearing it unwittingly with red ink: 'Penny? Penny who?' I repeated the name. 'No, no I can't say we've had anyone answering to that. Mind you,' she said, trying to be helpful, 'we don't always get the truth, you know, when people come here. I don't ask them to swear on the Bible.'

At that moment an upper door opened, and a woman with dark frizzy hair came out of it, carrying a baby. As she came down the stairs, Tricia looked up at her: 'Linda, you've not heard of a Penny Worthington – Linda?'

Linda had seen me, and had fled up the stairs again, but not before I'd caught a glimpse of her face.

'Penny!' I shouted. The door slammed. 'Tricia, it's her, I know it.'

I was about to leap up the stairs but Tricia stopped me, her hand on my sleeve: 'Whether it is or not, Anna, it doesn't look as though she wants to see you. She came here in quite a state, but she's been trying to get over it, looking after the children for the other mums. I have to protect her. Come into my office and tell me what this is all about.'

So, over a cup of weak, powdery coffee, in an office overflowing with papers, files and paraphernalia like the aftermath of an earthquake, I told her Penny's story as I knew it. I rounded off with the recommendation that the best course for Penny was to go straight to the police, and tell them the truth instead of cowering away getting distraught.

'From what you say, I couldn't agree with you more,' said Tricia. 'I'll see if I can coax her down to talk.'

She went out, and I heard her exclaim, 'Linda – where are you going?'

I shot out into the hallway – Penny was halfway down the stairs with a heavy bag. She'd had her rust-red hair cut off, dyed dark and permed like Janette's, but she could not change her face.

'Penny, please,' I beseeched her, standing rock solid at the foot of the stairs so that she could not pass. 'Tell me what you're afraid of. I only want to help you.'

A toddler, bumping down the steps behind her, grabbed her skirt, and she looked down at it, suddenly filled with anger: 'Get off me, all of you. Leave me alone!' And then she sank down as tears welled up, dropping her bag, clothes tumbling from her hasty packing.

'Linda . . . Penny,' soothed Tricia, rushing to scoop up the chastened child. 'Look, just talk to Anna a little while, she won't bite, and it might do you good, love, you've been getting more and more nervy lately. I'll let you use my office, away from the kids, eh?'

Penny shook her head: 'No . . . no . . . I can't. I have to meet someone.'

'I know,' said Tricia, 'but you said that wasn't till half-past. There's time for a little chat.'

Tricia's reasonableness was difficult to resist. Penny allowed herself to be guided into the office, and I shut the door behind us.

'I've been looking for you a long time, Penny,' I said. 'I'm not going to tell anyone where you are if you don't want me to.'

'How did you find me?'

'I've been here before, and it's a refuge for women who want to escape – I made an educated guess. I had to see if you were all right.'

'I told you I was, on the phone.'

'I know, but . . . you sounded to be in a state. I only want to help.'

'I rang to say I was sorry. Anna, it wasn't a cry for help. I'm not worth helping. Just keep away, I'm bad news.'

'Janette doesn't think so. Janette thinks a lot of you,

Penny, and she's had a raw deal out of all this. Don't you at least owe her an explanation?'

She bit her lip, I'd touched a nerve. I pushed on: 'I saw your car one day, chased it all over Northport, finally tracked down the garage you'd sold it to. It was you who sold it, wasn't it?' She nodded. 'The garage man didn't recognise the photo I showed him. Course, I can see your hair's different, but he said you had a fatter face.'

'I had an accident when I left Janette's, I was so upset I drove into a bollard. I hadn't fastened the seat-belt, I hit my head on the windscreen. Nobody saw, but my face was all bruised and swollen. I covered it in make-up and dyed my hair, sold the car, and came here, said I'd been battered by my boyfriend.'

'Ah yes, the boyfriend. He must be a hell of a guy for you to sacrifice your freedom, your friend, your home – even your identity.'

She was shaking her head in distress: 'You don't understand, we were in it together. That's why the police'd never believe me.'

'In what together, Penny? Come on, this boyfriend would have to be King Midas and Adonis rolled into one to have such a grip on you.'

She refused to answer, chewing her lip, her body shaking.

'You can't go on like this, Penny. This is no life for you, you're frightened to death. Is that what this is all about? Death? Llew Madden's?'

She let out a blast of pent-up breath: 'See – that's what the police'll think – that I did it. That's why I ran away.'

'Penny, Penny – there are other suspects for Llew's death that you don't know about. He was up to his neck in a business feud for one thing, with all sorts of shady goings-on. You're innocent until proven guilty, scream it out until you're blue in the face.'

'Innocent?' she sneered. 'I wanted him dead, remember. How innocent is that?'

A white car was drawing up in the road outside. Penny checked her watch, her face taut. 'He's early,' she said with a nervous glance at me. 'My visitor, I'll have to go. I – I'm selling my watch, you see, to raise a bit of cash. This man's come to see it.'

My shoulders slumped – an interruption, just when I thought we were getting somewhere: 'That's all right, you go. It shouldn't take long, should it? I'll wait here, we still have things to talk about.'

I saw her leave the refuge and go down the path to the parked car. She did not hesitate to get in.

A sliver of doubt entered my mind, enlarging quickly into full-scale suspicion. She would not have got straight into a stranger's car, and she would not have given the address of the refuge just to a watch-buyer. I looked round the office for a weapon that would speak louder than words, despaired over the heaps of paper-clips and broken pens, grabbed something in desperation and went out.

From the garden I could see the back of the car. They were sitting in the front seat, both their heads bent. Softly I shut the gate, bent double, and crept toward the driver' side. The window was open to let out his cigarette smoke. I heard a conversation, and it was not about watches.

'I won't do it, I've told you, I've had enough,' came Penny's voice.

'It's just the once, Penny, I swear,' he was coaxing. 'We both got screwed by Madden, we both deserve to get some money out of his rotten family business.'

'We've got the money. You've sold the E-type.'

'Correction: I've got the money. Your share's to come, but if you want it you've got to earn it.'

'For pity's sake, I did earn it, I know it didn't work out like we planned, but I kept my mouth shut.'

'It isn't enough.'

'I've helped you all I'm going to, just give me my cut,

like we agreed, and get lost. I never want to see you again, I never wanted this.'

'Too late, blossom.'

Penny was going to lose this clash of wills, and I was not going to hang around to let it happen. I rose up outside his window and he looked up, his eyes the same as when he'd up-ended me in a car park and stolen my car.

'What the bloody hell?' He threw his cigarette at me and rounded on Penny. 'You grassed, you little cow, get out of here, get out!'

He pushed her, and that seemed the last straw that broke her stubborn stone-walling. 'No,' she yelled. 'I've had enough, I'm going to turn you in,' and she clung on to his arm. He lurched across to open her door and try to shove her out, and I took the opportunity to aim my weapon through the open window. I squeezed, and a shot of quick-acting, limpet-strong superglue hit the steering wheel. He saw what I was doing and ripped himself away from Penny, who quicky escaped. The car rocked as he tried to push me off, jerking my arm, but the super-glue still squirted from the tube, smearing his clothes and hands.

He wound the window up to prevent further attack, stared at his glued palms for a second in disbelief, then tried to turn on the ignition, release the handbrake and put the car into gear. The adhesive was already coagulating, everything he touched sprouted strings of sticky mess, and when he tried to turn the steering-wheel it bonded to his hands.

Tricia had come running to the gate, and I shouted to her to call the police. The car lurched forward, but juddered to a standstill. The smell inside must by this time have been overpowering, he tried to get out but his hands were clamped, and he slumped in his seat looking ill. My own fingers were stuck to the tube, and I only hoped the combination of drying glue and dizzying fumes would keep him prisoner.

Penny rushed in front of the car as if to stand guard. 'That's right,' she addressed him through the windscreen, 'you stay where you are, murderer, I hope they put you in chains and throw away the key.'

The word seemed to rouse him: 'Murderer?' he shouted, and elbowed the door-handle, beating with his shoulder until it burst open. He stuck out a foot, but could go no further. 'You've the nerve to call me murderer? You're a liar. All I ever wanted was the bastard's car.'

'Yes, that's what you told me,' she hissed with menace.

'It's true. It was mine by rights!' he howled back, the steering-wheel shaking in his crippled claws. 'Llew ruined my life, lost all my money and left me to rot. That Jag was mine in the first place – it should've been mine when the business went down the pan. I didn't have family money to fall back on like him.'

So this was Rodney Zale, Llew's former partner, forced by grievance and poverty into breaking the law.

Penny glared poison at him, and her words poured out, half aimed at me, half at him, too long dammed to stop: 'No, you didn't have family money, but you did have me. Both of us had sob stories against Madden, both of us wanted to get our own back on him. That's why I agreed to help you get the car. I told you where he lived, what his habits were, what days he went to London – everything. Only on the day, it all went wrong, didn't it? Llew Madden came back unexpectedly, and he found you in the house trying to get the car's papers. You panicked, you killed him and got away with nothing. You think I'm stupid not to guess what really happened?'

'It's not true. I got out when I heard him coming,' he rasped. 'And where were you? You were supposed to be looking out, to warn me, but you weren't there. You were crazy, you hated the guy enough to follow him in and knife him. If any name's in the frame, it has to be Penny Worthington, and that's what I'm going to tell the cops. You aren't fitting me up for murder.'

'I ran away, I ran away!' she wailed, then turned to

me despairingly. 'You see, that's why I couldn't go to the police. I did hate Madden enough to want him dead. I was there, I fit the picture, that's what the police'll say.'

'But so does he,' I protested.

'Watch what you're saying,' spat Zale.

'He had to have done it, I knew that, but I was guilty too,' she was shaking her head, 'I was half to blame for taking him there, and he'd only done what I'd wanted to do so many times. I felt so guilty and afraid and lonely, I just wanted to hide, that's why I left Janette's.'

Zale shook his head in disgust and slumped back in his seat. Penny covered her face with her hands, I put my arm on her shoulder, trying to buoy her up: 'Why did you see him again, then, Penny? Why's he here now?'

She looked at me wearily: 'Because I needed the money. He did get his hands on the Jag in the end, and he still owed me my share, because we got in this mess together and I'd kept my mouth shut. I couldn't get a job or social security with no proper name, so I told him where I was. Then today he says he's not going to give me my money after all, unless I help him sell some secret stuff – papers he got from Guy Madden's. It's just too much, on top of everything else, Anna, I'm finished. Tell the police, get him put away, get me put away if it comes to it. Anything's better than this rat-hole kind of life.'

Tricia and another woman were peering anxiously over the gate, trying to see what was going on. I guided Penny to them and went to watch over Rodney Zale until the police came. His anger had gone now, he sat there immobile, white-faced and silent, as though sickened not just by the fumes but by his ruined life. Who says hell's in the next world?

Twenty
two

I t was not every day, nor even every decade, that a certain grizzled chief inspector nearing retirement offered to buy a reporter a thank-you drink. This reporter was still wondering whether she'd heard right when he said, 'I'll meet you in the Flying Horse in fifteen minutes,' and put the phone down.

And so, after a little jousting with Ellis over the identity of my latest urgent assignation, I arrived at the Flying Horse twenty-five minutes later. Chief Inspector Alex Anderson was checking his watch and readying himself for retreat from the bar when I tapped him on the shoulder. 'Anna,' he gave a forced smile. 'what can I get you?'

Since it was such a rare occasion, and since I was in walking distance of the office, and since, dammit, he owed me this, I said, 'A Wild Turkey on the rocks, please,' and smiled sweetly.

He paid up, picked up my drink and his own pint of best bitter and gestured to a corner table where we could talk. 'I shouldn't be doing this,' he said as we sat down, 'it's like saying thank you for going behind my back. You should've come to us when you thought you knew where Penny Worthington was, instead of charging in willy-nilly.'

'Well, you know me,' I smiled, savouring the bourbon's delicious aromatics along with the moment, 'willy-nilly's my middle name. Show me a missing woman and I'll charge after her.'

'You could've scared her off, and Zale too.'

'I think she was far more likely to have been scared off by a couple of your blue uniforms wading in with their size ten boots. She was very near breaking point. I got her to talk, I got her to the point where she turned on Zale.'

He gave an amused nod. 'I know, you win. You got a result, as we say. That's why I'm here, I owe you thanks. But next time, call us, OK?'

Umm-hmmm, I thought, one drink, one expression of gratitude, so far so good. But, chief inspector, you're not going to get off so lightly. 'How is Rodney Zale now?' I asked, as offhandedly as I could.

'Oh, the doctors've managed to unglue most of his moving parts, I'm only grateful you didn't stick his tongue down.'

'He's talking then?'

'You could say that. He's intent on fingering Penny.'

'For Llew's murder? D'you believe him?'

He sighed exasperatedly: 'What do you think?'

'I don't know, but the fact that you've only charged her with lesser offences gives a pretty solid indication of what you think.'

He nodded. 'I'm inclined to believe she's telling the truth now. Did you know Janette Jones has offered to put her house up as surety for bail? Not that I can recommend it yet, in view of Worthington's record of disappearing, but Janette must think a hell of a lot of her.'

'Female solidarity.'

'Don't tell me, you women stick together like glue.' He gave a wry look.

'Have you been targeting Zale all along?'

He nodded: 'I may as well say it, you've probably

guessed anyway. He's our prime suspect in Llew Madden's murder, and he always was.'

'He said he was just after the Jaguar.'

'Yes, that's all he's admitting to – that and house-breaking to steal the documents. With classic models you need all the documentation you can get – adds to the value. He didn't, of course, get anything at Llew Madden's – must've been too rattled – but he did eventually steal the car from Llew's brother.'

'Presumably Penny had no involvement in that?'

'No, she'd gone, he was on his own. He watched Guy Madden's movements for weeks. He even took a false identity to get a mechanic's job at Mad Mad World so he could get near the Jag. Zale's had a lot of time on his hands since the amusement park went under. He's used it to polish his thieving skills.'

'But it wasn't just the car records that were stolen from Guy.'

'No, the other stuff seems to have been sheer oppor-tunism. When he saw the five-year plan for Mad Mad World in Guy's files, he reckoned it'd be valuable to a competitor, so he lifted it. Similarly with the aircraft accident report. Zale thought he could make money out of it – a pilot saying this fancy new aircraft's a dangerous machine.'

'And he wanted Penny to help him sell them, that's what they were arguing about when I butted in with the glue.'

'He wanted her to act as go-between for the Mad Mad World stuff, yes – he used to be in the amusement park trade, don't forget, there was a risk he might be recognised. That was too much for Penny, much more than she'd bargained for, but to Zale, well, I suppose the remnants of his business mind were at work.'

'So he's admitting all this, but still trying to blame the murder on Penny?'

Anderson nodded and took a long, thoughtful drink of his beer. 'It could even be true. The motive's there –

revenge for her daughter's death – and she did follow Madden and send him poison-pen letters. She also lied to us about her involvement in all this, and she did disappear – that doesn't count in her favour. But somehow I can't see her actually carrying it off. I'm not saying it's impossible, but Madden was a sizeable fellow, she's a wisp of a woman. It just doesn't add up.'

'Unless . . .' I pondered.

'Unless what?'

'Llew had made love shortly before his death. Maybe we've got it all wrong – she inveigled her way into his bed to stick a knife in his ribs?'

'No, no. You can forget that. She provided intimate samples on request. The traces we found on Llew don't match her profile at all.'

He shifted uneasily in his seat, as if recalling his official role and mine. 'Anna, all this has to be off the record, you do realise that, don't you?'

'Oh, completely, Alex.' I felt a faint *frisson* of delight at addressing Mr Law and Order by his first name. 'I do play by the rules sometimes, you know.'

He snorted. 'When it suits you.'

But I had him at a disadvantage, and he knew it: 'Careful,' I said. 'I'm the one who caught your prime suspect, after all.'

He admitted this gracefully.

'So, Alex, you have your suspect. What about the murder weapon?' He gave a despairing shrug. 'You've not found it then?'

He shook his head: 'With Zale and Penny trying to implicate each other, they're not exactly trying to help.'

'But . . . weren't there signs of a fight in the house that you could link with Zale? Bloodstains?' He shook his head again. 'Oh dear . . . am I to understand, Alex, that at the moment all you have is circumstantial evidence, and Penny's testimony?'

A nod: 'And even she admits she did not actually see

him do the deed. So if you've any more bright ideas, I'd be interested to hear them.'

'What? You're asking help from Miss Willy Nilly?'

He laughed: 'Have another of those pricey bourbons, Superwoman, it might give you a flash of inspiration. I fancy another beer too, what the hell. This landlord knows how to keep his ale, you've got to show appreciation.'

I got the impression the chief inspector was already winding down to his retirement. He knew he had his man behind bars, it was just a question of finding the evidence to clinch Rodney Zale as a murderer beyond doubt.

Sorry to say we did not find that evidence over the pub table, but I had found a crack in the police armoury, and I was more than pleased with my liquid lunch.

Guy Madden was feeling decidedly better – so much better he was cock-a-hoop when he came round to my door that evening, minus his neck-brace, bearing a bottle of Pauillac and a grin that said: let me in and I won't take no for an answer.

'Guy – ' I have to point out that at this moment I was mortified – old towelling bathrobe, hot oil on my hair and a face pack; I'd been having an evening of solitary indulgence. 'Guy, this is . . . an unexpected pleasure.'

'Anna, we're celebrating,' he declared, and swept upstairs into the flat.

I'll give him that, he barely seemed to notice my remarkable absence of allure. Some good-looking people are like that – so totally self-possessed they don't recognise the lack of it in others. It's reassuring when caught with one's privacies exposed, as with bathrobe, facepack, etcetera, but darned annoying when one's done oneself up to the nines to no discernible effect.

I hurriedly rinsed my face, wrapped a towel round my hair, and found a presentable kimono for the occasion. By the time I emerged he had poured the wine and was standing in the living room ready to clink glasses with me. 'A toast,' he said, 'first of all to you, my own Anna, for finding my wretched car thief.' We duly drank to me: a pleasurable, if immodest, activity on my part. 'And second, to our boys in blue, for finding my beloved Jaguar safe and intact.'

'Really – where?'

'Dover I believe. All ready to be shipped across the Channel until the customs officers impounded it – yea!' his eyes flashed, 'in the very nick of time.'

'So when can you get it back?'

'It's speeding north even now, back to its rightful home.'

'That's wonderful.'

'Yes, it is.' He seemed to slow down a little after his initial excitement. 'It's such a relief. Not just the car – everything. There I was, thinking I was the victim of some nefarious conspiracy, and it was all down to one man. Nasty, evil little Rodney Zale. The police think he killed my brother, you know.'

'I know.'

'He'd destroyed one Madden, and he wouldn't rest till he destroyed us all.'

'Well, I reckon the only thing he'll be destroying for some time to come is prison food. You're safe, Guy, you can get on with your life.'

'And I owe so much to you.' He reached for me, pulling me towards him by the collar, kissing me deeply, and exploring even more deeply the folds of my kimono. This was heavy breathing time. The towel on my head fell to the carpet as I fell to the couch and we poured ourselves into each other. One has to grasp the opportune moment in this life.

Then the doorbell rang. 'Oh God,' I moaned, 'who's that?'

'Ignore it,' he said urgently, carrying on.

I tried, but it rang again. Darn it, I lost my concentration completely, and as a result, so did Guy. Desire deflating rapidly, he adjusted his clothes and I pulled my wrap together, realising how ridiculous we were, cavorting on the couch, at our age, when there was a perfectly good bed next door.

Drrr-ing, drrr-ing. This bellringer was aiming for a smack in the teeth. I went to the entryphone and snapped, 'Who is it?'

'Anna, it's me – Matt. Can I come in?'

Oh Lord. 'No. I mean, wait. Please, just a minute. I'll be with you in a few ticks.'

I retrieved my towel and tried to look as though I'd just got out of the bath. Guy had meanwhile disappeared into the bathroom.

I went downstairs to the front door. Matt stood there, looking perfectly appealing – he even had a Winnie-the-Pooh tie, a box of chocolates and a bottle of champagne. 'Oh, I'm sorry I've got you out of the bath,' he beamed, starting to come in and wobbling on the step as I stood pat. 'I saw your light on. I knew you were in, I just wanted to bring a surprise, a little treat after what you've been through.'

'Matt, that is the most wonderful thought. But . . . but as you can see you've caught me a bit off guard. Look, I'm feeling a little unwell tonight, why don't you come round tomorrow and we'll really do justice to that champagne?'

'I could just come in and rub your back, help you sleep, if you're not feeling well. A little pampering is what you need.'

'I – no, really, Matt. I'm better off being miserable on my own with my germs tonight. It's just a 24-hour bug, I'm sure.'

The entryphone speaker crackled by Matt's head, and Guy's voice came out of it: 'Anna, you OK?'

The glare in Matt's face could have scorched a cornfield. 'I see now what your 24-hour bug is. Don't worry, I'll leave you with your germ. I wouldn't want to be infected.'

And of course, he turned straight round and strode away, as if to walk out of my life.

'No, Matt,' I wailed. 'Don't go.' I slapped out into

the street in my silly mules: 'Matt, please. I'm sorry. Look, we need to talk this through.'

'Get back inside. You'll die of cold,' he said tonelessly, as though he wished this fate upon me.

And so I went back inside, watching him go, hating myself.

Back upstairs Guy was looking through the window: 'You had a gentleman caller I see. Matthew Whittaker?'

'Yes.'

He gave what I can only describe as a gloating smile, and I resented it deeply. I went to shampoo the oil out of my hair, scrubbing as though I could wash my muddied emotions clean, then I blasted it with the hairdrier on the highest heat so that my scalp stung. Why was I punishing myself? For being so weak, so fickle. How Barnaby Knatchbull coped equably with two relationships I did not know. This was simply throwing me up and down on a switchback – one minute loving Guy, the next resenting him, one minute loving Matt, the next being rejected by him, one minute feeling pretty pleased with myself, the next in the depths of self-loathing. And the trouble was I could not choose between these two men, I wanted them both, each in his own irresistible way. See what I mean? No wonder the hairdrier nearly blew a fuse and my hair curled up in a frazzle.

Perhaps Guy had detected my umbrage, for he was unusually introspective when I returned to him. I saw he'd drunk deep into the wine bottle – there was only half a glass left – and he looked melancholy. I poured myself a bourbon, Old Huckleberry – the poor woman's Wild Turkey; it does the trick when you need a kick of alcohol to rasp your throat and deaden your nerves.

'I've been thinking,' said Guy. 'If I've any real humanity in me at all I should go and apologise to Liza Boyd-Adams. What do you think?'

'It depends,' I replied. I wasn't in the mood to placate his feelings. 'It depends whether you do have any real humanity.'

He gave me a piercing look – whether of animosity or hurt I didn't know. I'd lost the fine edge on my sensitivity.

'If Zale did kill my brother, then Futures can't have had anything to do with the murder. The only reason Liza's in hospital is because I thought her firm was guilty . . . not her, her firm . . . I owe her an apology. I'll ask if there's anything I can do to make recompense. I am trying to be more considerate, Anna. It's as if I'm fighting the dragon in my virtual reality sequence. Sometimes I feel I'm winning, other times it defeats me, and I lapse back to my old ways.'

'So . . . going to see Liza Boyd-Adams would be as much for your benefit as hers.'

'Don't say it like that. Yes it would, but I try to think what Llew would have done in my place. She deserves something more than my driving conviction and an insurance cheque.'

I conceded this, but then he went on, 'I'm not going to crawl to her, though; after all, she did have our data on her computer, and it must be there for a reason. That wasn't my imagination. She's not quite without guilt.'

A glimmer of suspicion sparked in my brain, and fuelled by alcohol, it quickly burned hot and fierce. Guy was going to see Liza not just to apologise, but to lift Futures' stones and see whether the worm of takeover would wriggle out. And knowing Guy's aggressive tendencies, knowing he could flare up and leave his conscience till later, I feared what might happen.

'She's supposed to be coming out of hospital any day now,' he said. 'I have to go over that way on Tuesday to view some equipment. I'll give her a ring, see if I can call in at her house on my way back.'

I brooded over that the whole weekend, and by Sunday night I'd decided I wouldn't be in the best of health on Tuesday. Perhaps I'd try a dubious vindaloo – at any rate, I'd be in death throes from a gastric attack and too ill to work. Or so I'd tell Ellis.

Twenty three

I arrived at the converted farmhouse around lunch-time, knowing Guy would not get there till the afternoon.

I knocked on the door and heard a tap-thud, tap-thud on the floor tiles as Liza made her way to let me in. The door opened. She was leaning on crutches, slightly breathless from the effort. Charley leapt out of a side door with the energy of a puppy, froze when he saw me, and cowered back between his mother's crutches so that she nearly fell over. I grabbed her arm and shut the door.

'Anna, it's good of you to come and see me,' she said, her voice straining for a semblance of its former confidence. 'I'm glad of the company. Robert's had to go to the book-shop, and Charley's been trying my patience a little.'

A devil in me took a piquant and damnable delight in seeing her without her contact lenses – yes, those violet eyes were a plain brown in reality – and without her mask of make-up she had shadows like the rest of us. Her designer blouse was crumpled, and a full skirt could not hide the bulk of the plaster-cast. Compared with her professional persona, all polish and perfection, she was a wraith, and for the first time I felt comfortable in her presence.

I took her through to the living room where she sank thankfully onto velvet cushions. I noticed a plough had been added to the scythes and rakes on the walls.

'I've brought you this,' I announced, trying to be bright, lifting a flowering plant out of my carrier bag. It had been the largest and most brilliant in the shop, its scarlet corollas shouting 'Cheer up, you're on the mend!' But it did not seem to shout the same message to Liza.

'Oh, how kind, you really shouldn't have.' The words were what she would have used before the accident, but all strength in them had gone. She was so tired or depressed that only the outer casing of politeness held her together.

Charley pushed a colouring book and crayons at his mother, beseeching help she could not give.

'Oh Charley, not now,' pleaded Liza, disintegrating. 'I'm so tired. I have to go to Futures tonight. For Survival of the Fittest – they really can't manage it without me. We've already cancelled one event while I was in hospital and it's not fair to the charity. Charley, please . . .' The child was still waving the book around.

'Look, Liza, you go upstairs and lie down, you're worn out. I'll take care of him. I've amused plenty of kids in my time.'

'But . . . Guy Madden's supposed to be—' She broke off, stifling further words with a half-sob.

'Does Guy's visit worry you, Liza?' I asked. 'I mean, it's bound to. He's caused you a great deal of injury. I can see you're in no fit state to see him. I'll ask him to stay away, he doesn't deserve your forgiveness.'

'Forgiveness?' she repeated strangely, and then shook her head with vehemence. 'He wants to see me. I have to see him.'

'Well, only if you're sure you're up to it. Nurse Anna thinks it's more important that you rest right now. I'll let you know when he arrives.'

She needed no further encouragement. I helped her up the stairs and she hauled her plaster-encased leg on to the bed. She lay back on the pillow and I was sure she was asleeep before I closed the door.

Charley was somewhat subdued, chastened by his mother's departure, unsure of what to do about this stranger who picked up his colouring book from the living room floor and began crayoning with zeal. I encouraged him to join in, but he simply watched me at first, blinking his blue eyes, his fair hair tousled. He was mute, confused and utterly beautiful, as Guy Madden could be at times, when he said he was sorry, when I wanted to hug him. And now Guy was coming to say sorry to Liza. Knowing me, I'd fall over myself to hug him all over again.

Gradually Charley overcame his shyness and attacked the page, scribbling red zig-zags across it with a high-pitched giggle. But his powers of concentration were short – he began running back and forth to his toybox, bringing cars, model animals, trains, which he would discard after a few seconds.

I wondered if he was hungry – the kitchen did not show any signs of lunch, past or future, and his eyes brightened at the mention of food – so I set to work, jollying him along with chatter. I'd noticed rhythms seemed to calm him, so I went through the gamut of nursery rhymes while making him sandwiches and a glass of milk. I kept up the flow while he was eating, and by the time Humpty-Dumpty had taken a great fall into Miss Muffet's curds and whey I realised I was running out of inspiration. Charley laughed uproariously, spitting crumbs and spilling milk all over the kitchen floor.

In the middle of the mopping up, the door-knocker rapped. Charley looked up in alarm as I went to answer it, the wet cloth still in my hand. It was Guy.

'What are you doing here?' he asked, not without suspicion.

'I came to bring a get-well gift,' I replied, light on the truth. 'Come on through to the kitchen. I'm just giving Charley some lunch, Liza's upstairs resting. She's still weak, Guy.'

He came through, and Charley set up a great wail at the sight of this looming stranger.

I shut the door to block out the noise from Liza while I tried to reassure him. Then I heard tap-thud, tap-thud, coming down the stairs. The door burst open as she pushed it with her crutch, and she stood, wavering, half asleep, half awake.

'Charley – is he – ? I heard the noise and I—'

She broke off as she noticed Guy, standing in the shadow of a cupboard, for the first time.

'I . . . I . . .' she was blinking, as though she could not believe who she was seeing. She seemed utterly unable to form a coherent word, and then Charley, seeing the fear and confusion on his mother's face, hurled himself at her for comfort.

She fell backwards and hit her head on a hall table. I thought I heard a bone crack but it could have been her plaster hitting the tile floor. She lay motionless.

Charley did not. Charley went wild. Howling at his mother, pulling her clothes, hauling her arm, pummelling her chest. 'For God's sake, Charley.' I rushed to grab him off, but he slipped from my wet fingers.

Guy bent over Liza, shielding her, and when she opened her eyes and saw him leaning over her, his face full of concern, she seemed to implode. Curled into the foetal position she was gasping: 'Llew, Llew . . .' on and on like a banshee.

Guy was trying to reassure her: 'It's Guy, not Llew. I'm Guy,' but her eyes were screwed shut, and with Charley's crying, we could not tell if she heard.

By now Charley was hysterical, screeching, I had to get him out. I clasped him hard by the shoulders and pushed him out of the back door. 'I'm taking him in the garden,' I shouted to Guy.

'All right, if Liza's not broken her neck or anything I'll get her to hospital to be checked over,' he shouted back.

I shut the door and heard him beseeching her, 'Hush now, Liza, it's all right. I'm Guy.'

She subsided into sobs as I grabbed the child by his sweater and pulled him towards a swing dangling from a sycamore. 'Come on, Charley,' I said sharply, my patience stretched, 'let's see if we can swing some silence into you.'

Strangely, the child did not resist this rough treatment. His energy spent, he seemed content to be pushed on to the wooden seat and swung, to and fro, to and fro – the rhythms soothing me as well as him.

Liza's reaction to Guy had been strange. He did look like Llew, but why should that upset her so deeply? The living room was visible through a large picture window, and I watched Guy carry Liza in there and lay her down on the sofa. She seemed to have recovered a little, and he knelt by her head, talking the while. This must be the famed apology. For a man who found it hard to say sorry, he was doing rather a lot of if lately. Maybe he was really changing. Maybe the knight was vanquishing the dragon.

I saw her put her arms round his neck, as he put his arms under her body. Shame, shame, and double condemnation on you, Anna, for feeling jealous of a helpless woman up to her hips in plaster. He'd be scooping her up to take her out to his car, to take her to hospital. But he'd need help with the doors.

I was about to return to the house when I heard a car draw up and the front door slam. Robert walked into the living room. Good, he'd help with the doors.

They were talking, then I heard raised voices. This was more than talking – this was shouting. Robert was trying to snatch his wife from Guy's arms. Liza was beating him off, 'No, Robert, no. You don't understand. It's not like that.' But Robert was incensed, Guy put her down on the sofa just in time to repel an upper-cut to his chin.

Oh, heaven save me from men who react with their fists and leave the thinking till later. Hauling Charley behind me I ran through the kitchen to find Robert and Guy rolling on the living-room floor in a spitting, punching mass. Robert reared up and managed to straddle Guy, pinning his arms to his chest and clamping his throat in a death grip.

'My wife – ' spat Robert, 'she's my wife and I won't have her mauled by you or any other lover.'

'Robert!' I shouted. I could do little else, trying to keep the terrified Charley from adding more chaos to the fray. 'Robert, please. Liza's just fallen over, Guy was trying to help, he was taking her to hospital. He wasn't trying anything with your wife. He's with me. He's my lover, not your wife's'.

Robert froze, giving me a disbelieving stare. 'He's with you?'

Guy gave an almighty heave and rolled free, gasping air through his crushed throat.

'Robert, leave him alone now. Can't you see this is ridiculous?' shouted Liza at her husband.

'Don't call me ridiculous, whore!' was her reward. 'You'd have it off with anything in trousers. Do you think I believe a word you say?'

'Robert – please stop this insanity,' begged Liza. 'I've only ever had one lover, and I only turned to him because I couldn't stand your jealousy. You're jealous of any man that looks at me, you're jealous of my job, jealous of my success, jealous – so help me – of the attention I give to Charley. Dear God, is it any wonder that when I found a man who gave me real affection I took it like a woman starved?'

At last Robert's head dropped and he said pleadingly: 'But I love you.'

'You call this love?' she laughed.

The laughter, a mocking, belittling laughter, seemed to snap his final reserve of reason. His eyes flashed hurt and anger, and he ran wildly towards the door. The handle slipped under his clumsy fingers, and he yelled with frustration. He finally freed it, and we heard the back door slam.

Guy and I dashed to the window, and Liza hauled herself to our side. We saw her husband running through the old orchard, careless of the branches and twigs that lashed him. Suddenly he stopped, and began scrabbling on the ground under a tree like a demented dog.

Liza shook her head with a mixture of shame and revulsion, and blurted out an explanation as though she could suppress it no longer. 'He couldn't bear always being second best, you see. He felt a failure, and his jealousy made him bitter and twisted. My affair with Llew tipped him over into insanity.'

'Tell us more,' demanded Guy.

'Llew came to Futures after he'd hired a private detective to look into our affairs. He accused us of all sorts of sharp practice, especially over the studio tour. Well, it was partly true, our behaviour hadn't been entirely ethical – but it was business, it was an opportunity we'd have been crazy to pass up. I offered him a deal: I gave him the plans for the virtual reality complex in return for not going public about our doings. I – he – we fell in love. We couldn't help it . . . so much in common – so little any more with Robert. Oh, I wanted to leave Robert from the moment I realised the truth of my feelings. And Llew wanted me, he wanted me so much, he offered to make me a partner in Mad Mad World so we could live and work together.'

'You . . .' breathed Guy. 'That's why our details were on your computer. You didn't steal them at all – Llew gave them to you.'

She gave an anguished nod to her lover's brother. He looked so like Llew she had to swallow hard before pressing on, as if to seek his forgiveness.

'The day I told Robert I was leaving him, I took Charley and a few clothes and went straight to Llew's house. But Robert phoned that night. He was . . . deranged, I suppose . . . half-drunk, and he threatened to kill himself unless I went back to him. I couldn't have his suicide on my conscience, and so I came, hoping to play for time, hoping he'd come round to the idea of my leaving. But then Llew was worried about me, he thought Robert might do something stupid, attack me, and so he followed, to see if I was all right. Robert went for him in a blind rage. Llew died here, in front of me.'

Guy and I were so stunned we both stared at the carpet where she pointed, expecting blood to well up out of the threads.

'You must have been devastated,' I croaked with masterly understatement.

'It was a nightmare. I hoped I'd wake up and it would be all right, but then I knew it was real and I became hysterical. It had the opposite effect on Robert. As soon as he knew Llew was dead he became cold and clinical, he set about getting rid of the evidence like a machine. He emptied Llew's pockets to delay identification, and then he took the knife to the rubbish tip. He came back with a roll of old industrial carpet. I remember it – brown, frayed, smelling horrible. He wrapped Llew inside it and forced me to go with him to get rid of it. We buried it in the middle of Marianne's bonfire, and put all the junk back on top of it. I wanted to crawl in myself and die, perish and go up in smoke with Llew – but I couldn't. I'd left Charley here alone. I had to get back to him, I had to live, for Charley's sake. Robert drove Llew's car back to his house, and went inside to leave the keys and wallet. He was alarmed when he came back – said he disturbed a burglar – but he didn't think he'd been seen.'

Guy's voice came, cracked and hoarse: 'Why didn't you go to the police?'

'Why? They couldn't bring Llew back, could they? Anyway I was too devastated to think rationally, I was mad with grief. Charley had to be the focus of my life, and Charley had suffered enough upset for a lifetime. I had to keep up a facade of normality for him. I thought Robert had had a brainstorm, one solitary outburst of madness, and I thought I'd caused it. The strain of going to the bonfire party as I'd promised Marianne was almost too much for me to bear – the thought of reliving Llew's death, on and on, telling the police, hearing it in court, seeing it in the papers, whispers behind my back, my career blighted – well, it overwhelmed me, I thought the nightmare would never end. I wanted to block it out. But now I know it's impossible, this is more than a brainstorm, Robert's criminally insane. I've had enough. I just want to be left alone. Me and Charley, we'll pull through.'

The child had crawled towards her, and she stroked him, crooned to him. I wondered how much of this he had understood. I wondered how much I'd really understood – Lord, we enter this life naked, knowing nothing, and see what a devil's hash we can make of it before we leave.

Twenty four

I got straight through to Chief Inspector Alex Anderson. It's amazing what a bit of suspect-catching can do to oil the wheels of police–press relations. 'Ah, Alex, what do you want first, the good news or the bad?'

'If there's bad, I want to hear it,' he said huffily.

'You're barking up the wrong tree with Rodney Zale – he did not murder Llew Madden.'

'What?'

I could envisage his face, aghast at the prospect of a neat theft and murder package falling apart before his retirement.

'Now for the good news, I know who did kill him, and . . .' I glanced through the window to where Robert was still digging, '. . . he's about fifty yards away from me now.' Hurried explanations followed before I put the phone down and went out to the orchard where Guy was standing, keeping guard over Robert, watching him with a mixture of venom and bafflement.

'He keeps shifting his digs, he won't stop, he's quite demented,' Guy muttered.

The jealousy-crazed husband was clawing at the

earth with his fingers, pawing at the soil, plastering his clothes, his head, his mouth in it. Between gobbets of earth he parroted: 'I'll win, I'll win, I'll win.'

I grasped his shoulder, anxious to stop this madness. He turned his grimy face to me, and spat: 'I still have the edge, I still have it. She won't win, I won't let her. I'm cleverer. I'm cleverer.' Then he laughed, hooting through his soil-black teeth.

Guy grabbed him forcefully: 'Robert, stop doing this to yourself, come on out of there. You can say all you've got to say to the police.'

I doubted whether the police would get anything coherent out of him for a while. Robert was about as sane as a werewolf on mescalin at full moon. In a while we heard the sirens blaring. When the police came crashing through the orchard Robert was still playing bulldozers, by now emitting a toneless dirge, completely in a world of his own.

He did not stop scraping until they clamped handcuffs on him, which maddened him like a bridle on a mustang. Thrashing wildly, kicking his tormentors away, his tears making runnels in the mud and on his face, he struggled all the way to the police van.

We told the police Liza needed medical attention, so they agreed to leave the interview until later. When we got back in the house, she and Charley had disappeared. I heard movements upstairs and found her in the bedroom, struggling to change her clothes. Charley was not helping, trying to paw her sweater away as soon as she took it from the wardrobe.

I sat on the bed and held him on my lap while she finished. She moved with a fierce concentration – gone was the tired wraith and the emotional confessor – Liza was girding up for effort.

'I have to get ready,' she said, picking up one shoe, 'for Survival of the Fittest. It's not easy trying to look your best with a cast and crutches like a ball and chain.'

I was astonished. 'You surely can't be carrying on with that after what's happened?'

She stopped, midway through fastening the shoe, and stated with Iron Lady intensity: 'I have to, they need me, they can't do it without me. Besides, I've promised – I can't let them down.'

'Liza, don't be stupid.' She gave me a stubborn glare. 'Apart from all the upset, you need to be checked over at the hospital. You took a nasty fall. Then there's the police, they said they'd wait till you'd had medical attention, but they'll be wanting to interview you as soon as possible. You'll have to be available for them.'

'I don't need to go to hospital,' she snapped, 'I'm all right. As for the police, a few hours won't make much difference. I've rung my mother to tell her what's happened. She's coming to collect Charley, so I'll be available all night if they want me – but not until after Survival of the Fittest.'

'Liza I really don't think this is wise. You're not doing yourself or the charity any good if you collapse in agony midway through the Rat Race.'

But I may as well have been spouting hot air. Cashmere skirt, mohair sweater and antique pendant completed the chameleon change from distraught Liza into Ms Boyd-Adams, finance director and nobody's fool.

'No one's going to collapse,' she said patronisingly as though I were a simpleton. 'It's not as if I'm going in to work full-time.'

'You'll be going back into hospital full-time if you're not careful.'

'I've made up my mind,' she said, with finality, sitting in front of a mirror to apply her violet lenses.

Then, with equal finality, her eyes clamped shut and she cried out as if a fierce pain ripped through her skull, her spine stiffened and buckled and she blacked out on the floor.

Bumping downstairs on the ambulance stretcher brought her back to consciousness.

'Charley – where's Charley?' was her immediate thought.

I was with him in the hallway. 'I'll look after him until your mother comes, Liza, it's all right.'

'But – Survival – I have to be there.'

Dear God, did she have to play Miss Goody Two-Shoes to the limit? My patience cracked and I snapped, 'The charity will carry on without you, Liza. You're not indispensable, it's time you realised that. No one is. I'll ring Marianne – they'll manage. Marianne's the best coper in the world.'

'Liza.' Guy came forward, touching her agonised face. 'Look, I'll come with you to the hospital. The doctors'll know what's best for you. Leave it up to them.' The voice must have been so like Llew's that she paled, lying back under a sense of loss as palpable as the blanket she pulled over her.

Charley held my hand tight as he watched his mother go. My holding and rocking him seemed to have instilled a sense of trust, and he did not fuss at being left in my care.

Guy followed the ambulance in his car, fleeing the house like a man haunted.

'Come on, little fella,' I said to Charley as he watched the Jaguar disappear down the drive, 'we've got some telephoning to do.'

Marianne was horrified to hear the latest developments, particularly about Robert. 'I knew he was suffering, but don't we all from time to time? He had such an inferiority complex, poor man, and he bottled things up to such an extent, something had to blow.'

'What I can't understand is how Liza could simply brush it all under the carpet, carry on living with him as though nothing had ever happened.'

'Liza thinks she's invincible. It took this road accident to show her she wasn't. We'll carry on tonight as best we can, my dear, it's too late to cancel. It won't be easy, I'm not altogether *au fait* with her system, but tell her not to worry, Survival of the Fittest will survive without her.'

'Marianne, I . . .'

'Yes, dear?'

'How's it going? You know, you and Barnaby and . . .'

'Amanda. Fingers crossed, my hearties, we're all pulling together and keeping the ship afloat. It's just the same as an ordinary marriage, really, except there's two others to think of instead of one. Half a man is better than no man at all, believe me, I'm even inclined to think it can be better than a whole one, if you get the half you want – but don't spread that around. Not in front of the bishop, anyway.' She gave one of her uproarious laughs.

'But, Marianne, I – oh, never mind. I'm glad it's working out so well for you.'

'So am I. After all, look what happens when you can't work things out together. Llew Madden on a bonfire, Robert in jail, and Liza – well, what does Liza have left?'

'A disturbed child and her memories.'

'Exactly. People think Barnaby and Amanda and I are potty, but I know which way I'd rather be.'

I let her go to prepare for the night's event, and sat with Charley to await his grandmother's arrival.

He was restive, so I brought some toys down from his bedroom, playing with him absently while I ruminated over Marianne's economical half a man and my greed for a double portion, hoping to take my mind off what had happened. It was no use thinking I could do a Barnaby – play pig-in-the-middle – males would never be so magnanimous

'Bla-a-gh!' went Charley, and I saw him attacking a teddy bear with an Action Man while Minnie Mouse stood by.

I watched more carefully. The bear and the man tumbled and grappled while occasionally he made the mouse squeak in fright. Was he re-enacting the fight between Guy and Robert, using the toys? I let him carry on, intrigued, but also feeling that it might help the boy get his feelings out in the open.

He stopped, looking round for something, some missing prop. Out of Action Man's kit he took a tiny plastic dagger. He held the knife in Action Man's hand and plunged it into the teddy bear's side.

I realised then he must be reliving not today's fight, but an earlier struggle. This was not Guy or Robert rolling on the floor, but Llew and Robert in a struggle to the death in front of Liza.

I watched him shake his head and start all over again. This time he gave the knife not to Action Man but to Minnie Mouse. Surely he'd got it wrong? Her paw held the weapon, her paw thrust the knife, and he started to repeat the show. The teddy bear and Action Man fought, the knife was thrust – by Minnie Mouse again – and Action man stood over the prone bear.

I sat back, wary of jumping to conclusions. To Charley the mouse in a skirt could easily represent a man – he could not master meaning in the way most people can. I let him play on, but I was watchful now. If the child's replay was telling me something I did not want to miss it.

Twenty five

'Ellis, I got hold of a damn good story yesterday, and I need to be let off the leash to chase it up.' I stood by his side at the newsdesk in a gesture of pleading.

He was not impressed: 'I thought the only chasing you were doing yesterday was down the S-bend. Or was that just a damn good story? I don't appreciate being fed crap, Anna, either you're sick or you're not, don't lie.'

'I was sick,' I lied, 'but I got better quicker than I expected. I had to go see Liza Boyd-Adams yesterday afternoon, and this story dropped in my lap.'

'I'll drop something hot and smelly in your lap if this is another scam. What happened?

And so I told him, attempting to evade the hot and smellies by arguing for a background interview with Liza. Background material cannot be used until a court case is over, but I wanted to get to Liza while she was still vulnerable, in hospital, where the floodgates of confiding might be open.

'Wait a minute,' returned Ellis, still suspicious about my spurious malady, 'if she told you all this yesterday, why didn't you get it all down, there and then?'

'Ellis, at the time I could hardly whip out a notebook, and my memory's a poor substitute for her story in her words. We could get more out of this,' I pressed. 'I don't want her to clam up before we've heard about her love for Llew. How it all started, what she went through.'

Go on, call me a vulture, feeding on other people's anguish just for a story – I've heard it before. But people still go out and buy the stuff in droves. Ellis knew that. Ellis also knew I tell it straight, if people don't want to talk, I don't invent, I don't intrude, and best of all, I don't cause lawyers to ring him in a lather. That's why he let me go.

Before I left, however, I had an interesting call from Marianne, in great excitement after their success the previous evening at Survival of the Fittest.

'You managed all right then, without Liza?' I responded.

'All right? We hit the jackpot – record takings. It really is amazing, Anna. We're nearly a third up on our usual amount. I can't believe it, I'll have to count it again.'

'You must have had a bigger audience than usual.'

'Not appreciably.'

'Who were the teams?'

'They were just smallish printing companies. I wasn't expecting any great shakes, to be honest, but we passed the bucket round in the interval and the audience must have been extra-generous.'

Hmmm, I couldn't imagine smallish printing companies generating that much excited cash-giving, but I let it pass. Marianne was highly pleased and Shelley's wages would be paid, and that was all that mattered for the moment.

I got to the hospital a little after 10 a.m. and, knowing the wing Liza was in, I went straight there. A nursing sister came out of her office when she heard my enquiry. 'I'm afraid Ms Boyd-Adams checked herself out first thing this morning. It was against our advice, but then she'd have left last night if we hadn't sedated her. She's a very strong-willed lady.'

I could see the strong-willed lady in the orchard as I drove toward the farmhouse. She had discarded her crutches and was lurching about between the trees, seemingly staying upright by sheer determination. As I walked round the back of the house I saw she was actually gathering branches and twigs, many of them broken by Robert yesterday, and piling them in a heap. Her breath came in short gasps as she leaned on a shepherd's crook which had earlier adorned the living-room wall.

She was so intent on her work that she seemed not to notice my arrival. Thankful for my soft-soled shoes, I decided to take advantage of this, sliding into the shadow of the old dairy which they'd converted into a garage.

Her normal sleek bob of hair was unkempt. She wore a holey, dirty old sweater which looked as though it was Robert's gardening attire, and some faded corduroy trousers, similarly Robert-sized, which covered her cast. It was like seeing Princess Diana in a potato sack: she could make potato sacks look good enough for the catwalk – but why bother? To tidy the orchard, OK – but why was that so urgent? Why was she doing it in her physical condition? Why didn't she simply pay someone else?

She had made a substantial pile by the time she stood back to rest on her crook. But she did not rest long. She picked up a carrier bag and pulled out a bottle, pouring its contents on to her handiwork. Sniffing the breeze, I detected spirit fumes.

Then, shifting her cast and using her crook, she gradually lowered herself to the ground and sat under a tree, recovering her breath. Again she did not stay still for long. I heard the clink of metal in the carrier bag, and saw her take out a trowel. She was digging, digging under one of the trees where Robert had scrabbled the day before.

I crept forward, slowly. She was half turned with her back towards me, her attention on the deepening hole in front of her. Even so I carefully kept to the soft grass hillocks, avoiding twigs, crouching low. Childhood hours misspent watching Tonto play second fiddle to the insufferable Lone Ranger had at last paid off. Tonto would have been proud of my silent tracking as I approached Liza's bent back; she never heard a thing. She gave a murmur, more of a muffled exclamation, as she reached into the hole.

I don't know what I expected her to bring out of it – a muddy white rabbit? A mole upset at being woken too early? Not a filthy plastic bag, which she delved inside like a child at Christmas.

But it was no Christmas present she brought out into the light. It was a knife, a long carving knife with black blood on the blade and dark stains on its wooden handle.

I exclaimed, my foot fell on a twig. She heard. Her head whirled round and she saw me. I had already stood up, anticipating confrontation, and tried to look as nonchalant as I could. 'Liza,' I smiled. 'You shouldn't be doing this in your condition. Let me help.'

I had wanted to see how she'd react, whether she would hold the knife up to me in triumph. But the knife had disappeared back inside the bag at the very first instant. She regathered her forces and quickly overcame her shock. 'Anna – what are you doing here? I mean, don't they have any work for you to do?'

'I am working – see?' I held up my notebook. 'Just wanted another word about Llew, if you're up to it.'

'I . . . Later perhaps. I just have to finish this clearing up operation. The orchard was such a complete mess, I couldn't bear to leave it. Look, I've nearly done it now. Why don't you go inside and make us both a cup of coffee? I'll be in shortly.'

'If you're sure?'

'I'm sure. Just help me upright again, would you?'

She leaned on my shoulder and I pulled her up, then walked away, alert as a bat's radar. I heard the bag rustle once again. I heard a match being struck, and felt the air shift as her pile of branches leapt into flame.

'No you don't, Liza!'

I swirled round and ran. Her arm was already swinging back, ready to fling the grubby bag with its weight of guilt into the blaze. I launched myself into the air and snatched it from her hand.

'Why are you doing this?' I demanded from the other side of the fire, stamping on twigs whose flames licked my feet. 'This is the knife that killed Llew, isn't it? Why didn't you tell the police where it was?'

Her eyes were lit with anger, frustration, hatred of me for being agile while she was encumbered. 'I didn't know,' hissed out between her teeth. 'I didn't know where it was until Robert came here yesterday. He wouldn't tell me where he'd hidden it.'

'But why were you trying to destroy it? You've already said Robert killed him, why destroy the evidence?'

'What do you expect me to say, Anna? You've caught me here, like a fox in a trap, I don't have to explain why.'

'But you do, Liza.' So help me I actually grasped the knife, careful to keep the bag wrapped round the handle, as I pointed the blade towards her. Would I have used it? I'd sooner have leapt into Vesuvius, but she wasn't to know that. 'Look at the knife, Liza. Bloody fingerprints have dried on the handle. I believe they're yours, not Robert's.'

She froze, the fire's heat reddening her cheeks, her breath heaving. She was about to speak when a child's shout came from the driveway, and Charley and his grandmother emerged from a newly arrived car.

'Charley!' shouted Liza, desperately, 'Come to Mummy.'

The boy came, and I cursed the untimely interruption as I lowered the knife behind my back. The grandmother waved and disappeared indoors.

'Ah, Charley Mouse,' cooed Liza, wrapping her arms round him, transferring her stress into loving emotion, 'Look at the big bonfire we've made for you.'

'What did you call him?'

'Mouse. Charley Mouse. It's been a pet name since he was a baby. He looked like a little pink mouse, didn't you my darling?' She buried her face in his hair.

'Then . . . all this cover-up was for him?'

He'd made the mouse thrust the dagger in the bear. The mouse, the child, the knife. Had Liza invented a cover-up to prevent her blighted child living with more stigma, being called a killer?

'Yes, yes, all for him.' Her voice was breaking.

Grandmother appeared at the kitchen door, calling Charley, asking if he wanted a drink. Liza's face fell as he escaped her grip, ran back to the house and the door closed behind them.

I aimed the knife again and renewed the pressure: 'We'll start again Liza. Tell me exactly what happened.'

'No, I don't have to tell you anything.'

'Tell me, Liza, or I'll tell the police you have things to hide – tax evasion, for instance – that wouldn't go down well on a finance director's CV.'

She gazed back at me, startled.

I bluffed on: 'Jolyon Burchill got more than he declared from selling his record business, didn't he? And you've been helping him shunt it into offshore trusts to evade capital gains tax.'

She breathed out, not with shock, but with relief: 'More than he declared? Nonsense: extra payments were added after negotiations that you journalists never heard about, that's all. As for tax evasion – that's ridiculous. Every penny that went into the offshore trusts is being used to invest in Jolyon's other business ventures. He's expanding, creating more jobs, not using it for his own benefit, or his family's. That makes it not liable for tax; it's a legal loop-hole, Anna.'

'Then why the secrecy?'

'Normal business confidentiality.'

'And it's legal?'

'Perfectly.'

'Then – ' I was thwarted. I ploughed on, prepared to take an even wilder chance to get at the truth. 'Then you've been siphoning money from Survival of the Fittest. Marianne told me last night's takings were a record – a third up on the usual – strange coincidence, your not being there for the first time. That's why you were so keen to get there yesterday, wasn't it? Of all the low-down tricks in the world, taking money meant for dying children to line your own pocket. Just think how that'd look in our headlines, Liza.'

'No.' She put her hand over her face as though the flames were licking too hot. 'No.'

'No? Then what about all that cash you were carrying in the car when you crashed? Banknotes flying everywhere, Guy Madden said. Where did that come from? I'd say the takings and the sponsorships at Survival of the Fittest. And where was it going if not into your stocks and shares?'

'Stop, stop – ' she was stuttering, her words indistinct, but through the sounds I detected, 'Not me – Charley.'

'Charley again? Come on Liza, you can't keep shifting the blame on to a child who isn't responsible for his own actions. If Charley killed Llew—'

'No-o-o!' she yelled, in a rage with me now, 'Charley's innocent, I killed Llew, I killed him, I killed him, I am responsible.'

I was silenced. She went on, almost in a whisper, 'Let me tell you what really happened, then you'll understand why I've acted this way. It was all a dreadful accident. Robert attacked Llew, they were fighting, I ran into the kitchen to get something to stop it. I found the knife, I just wanted to frighten Robert, but he wouldn't listen. I had to stop him. I thrust it at his shoulder, but he ducked away, and I fell forward on to Llew. I plunged the knife into my own lover's heart.'

She was ladling on the distress, her eyes darting back and forth between me and the knife, which did not waver.

'Robert had never touched it. He told me to pull it out of the body. I was so upset, and I couldn't bear to see

Llew like that, so I did pull it out. But then he used a glove to pick it up and I never saw it again. He used it as blackmail, to make me stay with him. He said he'd use it to accuse me of murder unless I stayed. I don't care about myself any more, but Charley, he needs me. Give me the knife now, please Anna.'

'No, there's got to be more, Liza. You could have gone to the police and told them this. Any jury would have listened sympathetically. But you're not exactly a sympathetic woman, are you? You're a thief, stealing children's charity money, and that's what I'll tell the police unless you convince me otherwise.'

Her eyes flashed defiance, she edged closer toward me, and I changed tack, 'Look, I'm prepared to listen to your side of the story, Liza. I can understand you've been under intolerable pressure.'

She swallowed, and brought all her remaining powers of persuasion to bear on gaining my complicity: 'I'm not a heartless swindler, Anna, believe me. Everything was so perfect – the house, my career, my family – and then it all started falling apart. We bought the house at the top of the market, the mortgage was fierce, then Robert lost his research job, the bookshop struggled and there was Charley's education to pay for. We slid into debt, I was working harder than ever, but nothing seemed to go right for us any more. I couldn't bear it, and worst of all Charley was suffering. The fees at his American school are so steep – £30,000 a year, plus the air fares – but he had such a difficult start in life, and this school was his salvation. There seemed nowhere else I could turn – and then I thought of the charity money. It was for children, after all. I know Charley wasn't dying, but that money could help him live as full a life as possible. I started taking a little here and there, and then more and more. I meant to straighten things out before anyone could discover, but the bills mounted up and I got too far embroiled.'

'Did Robert know anything about this?'

'That was it, that's why he had a such hold on me, Anna. I took care of his bookshop's finances and I'd started using its account to clear some of the charity money. He became suspicious when he checked the bank statements, he knew his bookshop hadn't taken that much, he demanded to know what was going on. I had to tell him. He knew what a fix we were in – I thought he'd support me. But he used it to threaten me when I left him for Llew, first to bring me back to him, and then to keep quiet about Llew's death, so we could go on living as if nothing had happened. He said he'd expose me if I didn't do as he wanted. All he wanted was me.'

She was keening now, and holding her hand out pleadingly for the knife: 'If you believe nothing else about me, Anna, believe these two things. I loved Llew, he represented my escape. I was making love to him the very instant Robert rang, threatening suicide, threatening to tell about the charity money, threatening everything he could to get me back to him. Believe also that I love my child more than anything else. Anna, please understand what torture I have to live with every day of my life, knowing I killed my own lover – by mistake. Isn't that punishment enough for what I've done? Don't tell the police the truth, there's no need – I'm selling the house, I'll pay back the charity and no one need know what really happened. I'm not afraid of Robert any more, he can't prove a thing about the money. I've covered my tracks, I've destroyed any evidence he could get his hands on.'

The fire was dying down, losing its cleansing, destructive power, and my implacability was dying with it.

'Anna,' she implored, 'I appeal to you as a friend – give me the knife so I can destroy that too.'

I wavered, let her see I was moved, then said half-heartedly, 'But if I do you'll have him put away for murder.'

'He would have killed Llew if I hadn't intervened – doesn't he deserve incarceration? The way he's blackmailed me? The way he's used every trick to keep me by his side? All right, I was wrong to take the money, but it was all for Charley, and Charley needs me with him, not in jail. You're a mother, you can understand that, can't you? You'd do anything for your child. I'll move away from here and you won't ever see me again. I'll go to America, to live near the school so I can be with him constantly. Can't you see it'll be for the best? So give me the knife, Anna. Anna?'

'All right,' I breathed, 'as a mother, you've convinced me, I'll help you. But the fire's too low to burn anything now, and you've used all the wood. Come with me, I'll drive you to the sea, we'll scrub the knife clean and throw it in safe and deep.'

I gave her the knife, and she looked at me as though I'd given her life back. We heard a car, and male voices. A figure appeared round the side of the house, and Liza turned on me, blazing hatred.

'Liar, liar!' she howled, and I was just in time to grab her wrist as she lunged at me, the knife still in her hand. I gritted my teeth. Her strength seemed super-human, she was desperate, driven beyond endurance. I knew she wasn't seeing me any more, but all the enemies intent on destroying her life, all the enemies she wanted to destroy. My fingers bit her wrist like grappling irons, the knife-blade scythed between us, still black with Llew's blood. The knife-point sheared up toward my face, and stopped short as a pair of other hands came between us.

'Chief Inspector Anderson, thank heavens,' I sighed, as Liza was restrained by his assistant. 'I was just about to bring her to you, but you've saved me the bother.'

'I've saved you a lot more than that, by the looks of things, Anna. I came to interview Ms Boyd-Adams, but once again you got here before me. Will you never learn?'

Twenty six

I
t was nine months later, the end of a hot, steamy summer. Shelley and I were at Mad Mad World for the launch of a new rollercoaster – bigger, higher, longer, steeper than anything Futures currently offered.

As Guy Madden waved us forward to join the inaugural ride he looked like a man who had achieved a bigger, higher, longer, steeper success than any rival could challenge. He kissed my hand as he helped me aboard, if only because he would have looked odd kissing his own. He had singlemindedly propelled this project forward, built it in record time, with the latest equipment and safeguards. Fast, modern, unbeatable, an embodiment of his ambition. He had excelled himself, and that excellence swelled from his glistening pores.

I was glad for him, glad that he was free to concentrate on his business, now that the court case was over. I was also glad for myself, having garnered a harvest of cash selling my story to the nationals as soon as it could be printed, and it was satisfyingly splashed across the centre pages of that day's papers.

Shelley had just been reading it, crumpling the paper

in her bag as she climbed in beside me. 'Amazing how the defence counsel put so much stress on Liza's maternal instinct,' she said, 'as if it excused the fact that she was prepared to lie and swindle.'

'Kids hold much sway over their mothers, my child. For example: a great deal of this mother's hard-earned corn will be going to feed your open beak over the next couple of years.'

'I appreciate it, Ma,' she laughed, as the carriage juddered into life and started moving up the slope, 'You're willing to help me through drama college, and I'm willing to go, if only to fulfil your dreams.'

We reached the top. I couldn't look down without feeling dizzy, I couldn't look forward without wanting to scream. We started turning, slowly, approaching the first depth charge of a downslope that would send us whiplashing round the park in a tumult of highs and lows.

'Listen, Shelley, my dreams are my own affair, just you make sure you fulfil you-o-o-ours – aagghhhhh!'

No more words could be said. We were on our way down at breakneck speed, and nothing short of catastrophe could stop us. Shelley gripped my arm with one hand, the guardrail with the other. I loved that girl, and I knew she'd stick by me – we couldn't do much about life's ups and downs, but we wouldn't go off the rails as long as we held tight together.

We swung round another bend. I desperately tried to take my mind off the next drop, thinking of Liza and Robert and Llew. They'd rocked their carriage clean off the rails – Liza leaping from one compartment to the other, cheating to give her child an advantage. Crash – Llew dead, Liza dragged under the wheels of justice, jailed for manslaughter and embezzlement, while Robert still clung to the scaffold of insanity, too ill to plead. Only Charley had been thrown clear, safe in the care of his grandmother.

Whoo-aaah, oufff – down again – I shut my eyes, convinced we would smash into oblivion, but we skimmed the bottom, and whooshed up the other side in a merciless repeat. Marianne now, she'd learnt how to handle her switchback marriage: three on board – unconventional, true – but as long as everyone kept their balance, they'd stay on track. That was a more cheering prospect. I began to relish the next rush to the head as we teetered, swooped, then soared upwards in an ecstasy of exhilaration.

The climbs began to lessen, the plunges diminish – we were slowing down for the home run. It brought Penny to mind, regaining stability at last after all her upheavals. She had admitted conspiring in Zale's attempt to steal the car, and was on probation, living with Janette and her children, rebuilding her life. Zale himself had acquired an eloquent lawyer to plead the sense of grievance that led him into crime, and was under a suspended sentence to keep on the straight and narrow.

Ah, sweet bliss, we were smoothing to a halt. A large figure disengaged himself from the crowd, and Shelley leapt out to greet him. She was breathless, shining-eyed and invigorated with the thrill of the ride. How could Bulwark resist such temptation? He wrapped her in his earth-mover arms, and I watched them walk away – fast, physical – heading for Mad Mad World's high-tech globe of virtual reality and robotics in which they both revelled.

Shelley turned, beckoning me to come with them, but I shook my head: 'No thank you. I've had enough excitement for the moment – you go ahead.'

And so I was on my own again, watching Guy launch his next cargo of switchback-riders. He looked jubilant, he looked successful. He was turning Mad Mad World around, and that was all he needed. We certainly didn't need each other any more. The remaining affection between us was summed up in his wink and my returning smile as the carriages moved away.

As for Matt, he'd moved as far from Guy as possible, all the way to California to take a new job with the Disney empire which thoroughly enthralled him. He had invited me out there, but Disney exerted no similar draw for me and, at this distance, neither did Matt.

I suddenly felt wondrously at peace after the hurly-burly, and left Mad Mad World to walk on the beach, beholden to no one, pleasing only myself, kicking off my shoes to feel the warm sand under my bare feet. See, ricocheting between Guy and Matt had made me appreciate the distinct advantages attached to the solitary state. I can be pretty dense at times.